Sam looked around Abby's office. It was neat and well organized with an extensive collection of books and tastefully displayed awards. He even marveled at how comfortable her guest chairs were. *For someone who is supposed to love putting people in the hot seat, these are cushy chairs.* Just as he swiveled around to face the door, he noticed a woman heading his way. *This can't be her,* he thought in disbelief.

"Abby, if you have a minute, I need you to look at this," Leo said.

"Sure."

The woman went over to his desk.

Oh, my God, that is her!

Sam stared at the way her dress hugged her curves.

Reggie didn't tell me she was hot. How am I supposed to concentrate on what she says? Sam felt his heart skip a beat. *The woman's a brick house!*

He took a deep breath and reminded himself that he was engaged to be married.

❧

I Take This Woman

Chamein Canton

Genesis Press, Inc.

INDIGO LOVE SPECTRUM

An imprint of Genesis Press, Inc.
Publishing Company

Genesis Press, Inc.
P.O. Box 101
Columbus, MS 39703

Copyright © 2011 Chamein Canton

ISBN: 13 DIGIT : 978-1-58571-435-3
ISBN: 10 DIGIT : 1-58571-435-6
Manufactured in the United States of America

First Edition

Visit us at www.genesis-press.com
or call at 1-888-Indigo-1-4-0

Dedication

This book is for all the women who have given up on looking for love. Sometimes love doesn't look like you expect it to and many times it's often hiding right underneath your nose. So slow down, take a breath, and take in the sweet scent of love.

Acknowledgements

In times of hardship romance writers have a special mission to take our readers on a blissful journey. It's not all hot love scenes and sexy leading men. It's about the endless possibilities life offers when you open your heart. I wouldn't feel this way if I didn't have friends and family in my corner, cheering all the way. I am a born romantic and for that I thank my father, Leonard F. Canton, Jr., who always lets me know that I can spread my wings and fly as far as my heart desires. My mother, Mary Wallace, with her Southern sense of humor and frank sayings about relationships keeps me firmly grounded. Then there's my sister Natalie and my brother-in-law Donell, who continue to show each other love every day. Through challenges large and small, they always have each other's back. Then there is my brother in spirit, Joel Woodward, who always reminds me that big girls are beautiful and Mrs. Frances Watkins who taught me the importance of loving myself for the woman I am. I am most grateful to the loves of my life, my twin sons Sean and Scott who have grown to be wonderful, respectful young men. My twin uncles, Calvin and Cecil Canton, who make me feel like a cherished niece even now. I want to thank the man I love, Michael Bressler, for being a wonderful, devoted father to his daughters and for treating me like a cherished treasure. I only hope that other women can feel that way about the man in their lives.

Then I also want to thank those I've lost but carry in my heart every day: Grandma Salley and Grandma Canton; my great-grandmother Dorothy Donadelle; my great-uncle, Ernest, "Unc", Donadelle; my Auntie Ruth, Uncle Willis, and Aunt Edna. Thanks to my friends, near and far: James Weil, Eric Smith, Pearl Alston, and my favorite high school English teacher, Edward Kemnitzer. Thank you all for being in my life.

Finally, thanks to the wonderful folks at Genesis Press: Deborah, Valerie, Diane and Sidney. You are a terrific team and I thank you from the bottom of my heart.

Chapter 1

Born the oldest of four children, forty-one-year-old Abigail Carey was responsible, organized and a perfectionist. An overachiever, she was her high school's first African-American valedictorian and graduated summa cum laude from the University of Pennsylvania. Her parents, both college professors, ingrained into their children a belief in hard work and discipline.

In spite of her busy career, Abby preferred to clean her apartment herself. Her mother had managed to keep a neat home with a career, four children and a husband. Abby felt it was the least she could do with one child and no husband.

A curvy girl all of her life, at one time Abby's style was conservative with understated skirts and pant suits. That had changed ten years earlier after her divorce from NBA Hall of Fame-bound player J.J. Stokes, a second-round draft pick for the New York Knicks. J.J. was part of the team during the glory days of the nineties, topping their leader boards with the most rebounds, assists and triple doubles. Unbeknownst to Abby, for a long time he also led the leader boards in road girlfriends. When one of his girlfriends, Beebe Hudson, decided she wanted to upgrade her status, she tipped off photographers so as to bring their relationship out in the open proudly in black and white. J.J. and Abby had been married for ten years when she divorced him and dropped his name.

Abby checked her side view in the mirror. "Heck, I wonder if I can nominate the Spanx inventor for sainthood."

Abby walked into the kitchen, where she poured her first cup of the day and went to stare at the city she loved. She was energized and ready to take on the world.

Abby sat down to a stack of papers.

Abby made notes in red on the letter: *Let this be the marginal note. It's got to be short and sweet.* She continued making notes in the margins, Thinking it was Candy. The opening paragraph has to be dynamite to make an editor want to read further. It's a good thing for Candy she wasn't an editor anymore.

A former senior editor for Stillwater Publishing, Abby had been known as a dragon lady because she had wielded her red pen with samurai precision. Her authors had to be prepared to work hard and accept very blunt critiques. Those who didn't buckle under the pressure often made the bestseller lists. She knew how to make a good writer great and how to make a great writer phenomenal. While she was there Stillwater became an award-winning independent publisher and home to a number of talented, bestselling authors.

As things changed in the publishing industry, Still-water's management began to sign celebrities, reality show refugees and wannabe starlets that parlayed their sex tapes into branded cottage industries. After years of being the publishing company that cared about the story, Stillwater became focused on fluffing up its bottom line any way it could. Abby decided she'd had enough and left.

At the same time her friend and fashion publicist Shana Collingsworth decided that after spending her twenties and the better part of her thirties working for a major fashion PR firm, she was ready to strike out on her own. She and Abby pooled their talents, resources and contacts to form Carey and Collingsworth Public Relations.

Seven years later they had one of the most success-ful agencies in the country, with offices in London and New York. Abby and Shana ate, slept and breathed PR on a twenty-four-hour basis since they each lived in an apartment above their New York office.

Abby jotted one last note, and opened the newspa-per. She casually thumbed through the sections until she spied a caption that caught her eye. "Beebe Stokes in talks to join *NBA Confidential.*" Abby rolled her eyes. "I knew it was only a matter of time before this would happen," she said. Abby set the paper aside.

The sound of the phone broke the morning si-lence. Abby glanced at the caller ID. "Way too early for this phone call without a second cup of coffee," she groaned, but unfortunately she knew that if she didn't talk to him he'd just call back in ten minutes.

"Good morning, J.J."

"Good morning, Abby. How are you?"

"I'm fine, thanks. What's going on with you?"

"Why do you think there's something going on with me? Did it ever occur to you that this might just be a social call?"

"It's occurred to me, but that's unlikely, given the time of the morning," she said.

"I can't get anything past you, can I?"

"No. Let me save you a little time. Is this about Beebe's interview in the March issue of *Today's Black Woman*?"

"How did you know? It's not on the stands yet."

"I'm in public relations, remember? I know that four different magazines were in the hunt for the first interview exclusive. You do realize that the March issue will be on the stands in a couple of days, right?"

"Great," he groaned. "Like the divorce isn't going to cost me enough."

"If you're looking for sympathy you called the wrong person. I'm your first ex-wife."

"I know. I'm not looking for sympathy."

"Speaking of ex-wives, I read in the paper that Beebe is in talks to join the cast of *NBA Confidential*."

"What?"

"Don't tell me that you didn't know?"

"I didn't know." He grunted. "This is just another ploy to get out of the prenup. She wants more money."

"You don't say?"

"Well, she's not going to get a dime more than what we agreed to."

Beebe had apparently thought retirement would change J.J.'s ways, but now she was the woman scorned following the revelation of a younger girlfriend.

"You'd rather take the chance of her joining the cast of a show with no other objective than to spill all the dirty little secrets of basketball ex-wives?"

"I don't have anything to hide."

"Sure you don't," Abby said sarcastically.

"That's enough of that. I devote enough time to Beebe's nonsense. I really called about Justin. What if he reads the magazine article?"

"I don't think you have to worry about him reading it. *Today's Black Woman* isn't on his preferred reading list. Besides, I talked to him about your divorce. How's that for irony?"

"Some might call it poetic justice."

"That's certainly another way to look at it."

"I guess I should give Justin a call. Maybe Beebe should call him, too. She was his stepmother."

Abby immediately knew that wasn't going to fly. Although she and J.J. were on somewhat friendlier terms now, it had taken some time for her to view J.J. as Justin's father and not the miserable son of a bitch who had humiliated her in public. She knew that Beebe wouldn't have any qualms about denigrating J.J. to his son.

"No. I don't think it's a good idea for Beebe to call him. She doesn't have any vested interest in making sure you don't come out looking like a jackass. I wanted to call you much worse during our divorce, but I kept in mind that you're Justin's father and I didn't want to do that to Justin."

"I'm grateful you held back. Not that I didn't deserve it."

"Well, that's a bird of another color, isn't it?"

"Yes, it is." He paused. "So is there anyone new in your life?"

Ever since their divorce, J.J. appeared to be more interested in Abby's love life than she was, and he never missed an opportunity to ask her about it. In an odd way, J.J. seemed comforted by the thought that Abby didn't have a man in her life. No man in Abby's life meant there wasn't a new man around his son. It was also J.J.'s peculiar way of continuing his tradition of having his cake and eating it, too.

"Excuse me?" Abby was annoyed. "What kind of question is that?"

"It's a fair question. We do have a son together, and I'd like to know if there's another man on the scene."

"You've got some nerve," Abby said. "It's none of your business."

"I guess the answer is no, right?"

"You forfeited the right to get an answer to that question when we got divorced and I don't have time for this nonsense. I have to head downstairs to the office. Don't forget we have parents' weekend coming up soon."

"Oh, that's right. Thanks for reminding me."

"Don't you mean 'thanks for reminding me for the umpteenth time'?" she asked. "Please be sure to mark it on your calendar and make sure you show up on time and without your usual entourage."

Despite no longer being an active player, J.J. still lived the life of an NBA player. He liked traveling with a driver, valet and security.

"I'll be on time, and I'll even leave security at home, but you know I don't go anywhere without my boy Dazz."

Despite having no previous experience, Dazz Williams had been J.J.'s personal manager for more than fifteen years. He and J.J. had grown up together in Detroit and made the move to New York together. Dazz was a great front man, but the lawyers and the accountants handled the contracts and the money. However, Dazz had one other function that J.J. valued most of all: He was the groupie wrangler and interference runner for J.J.'s affairs. To say that Abby disliked him was an understatement.

"He's not an American Express Card, J.J. You *can* leave home without him. So leave him home and come to parents' weekend like a normal parent. Let's not embarrass our son in front of his friends at Choate. Okay? Later, J.J." She hung up.

Though Abby and J.J. could easily have sent Justin to one of New York's prep schools, they sent him to an out-of-state private school in Connecticut. Life there was another world, one that didn't let too many outside influences in. Though Justin wasn't squirreled away in an ivory tower, Abby's mind was at peace knowing that he wouldn't be bombarded by his father's exploits, and this made it a little easier to deal with her early onset empty nest syndrome.

Still sleeping, Sam Best was dreaming about a stack of blueberry pancakes with warm maple syrup, crispy bacon and a fresh cup of coffee. His golden arm had led the New York Giants to five straight post seasons and two Super Bowl championships. Now thirty-six years old, he was enjoying retirement, which meant sleeping in.

Is that coffee? he wondered sleepily. *Do I have an actual shot of getting a real breakfast this morning?* He opened his eyes to see his fiancée, Maria Carrangelo, leafing through a wedding magazine while she sipped coffee from her mug.

Sam and Maria met at the University of Texas. He was instantly attracted to the tall, shapely, blue-eyed brunette. An art history major, Maria had grown up in Highland Park, an affluent neighborhood in the Park Cities area of Dallas. William 'Big Bill' and Kitty Carrangelo raised Maria and her two older sisters, Sissy and Kim, as a part of Park Cities' high society with its cotillions, equestrian shows and charity events. The Carrangelo girls were a bit of a throwback to a bygone era. When they went to college, a degree wasn't their main focus; finding a husband was. Both of Maria's older sisters graduated from college with a diploma and an engagement ring, and Maria's parents expected her to follow in their footsteps.

On the other hand, Sam's parents, Don and Sara Best, raised him and his two older brothers, J.R. and Zeke, on a small ranch a mere 150 miles outside of Dallas but a world away from Maria's life of privilege. When Sam and Maria got together the only ball Maria was interested in was the kind that involved evening gowns and white glove service. Even though she was born in a state where football was religion, her idea of eating outdoors involved properly set picnic tables in the backyard, not portable hibachis, hot dogs, brats and beer in a parking lot. However, Maria wanted Sam so, she made the pig skin a part of her life.

Yet in spite of their differences, Sam and Maria fell in love. Everyone thought of them as the perfect couple, especially her parents. Sam took time to establish his name in the NFL and build a long-term plan for their future after football, which meant that marriage had to wait. At first, Maria agreed. However it wasn't long before they fell into a make-up-and-break-up pattern until Sam reached the point where his career was on the decline and it was time to make a commitment. Although they were more than a couple of years behind schedule, Maria's parents were thrilled when Sam had finally proposed to Maria with a 5-carat diamond ring set in platinum a year earlier.

"Good morning," said Maria.

"Good morning," Sam said as he sat up and rubbed his eyes.

"I was thinking that this arrangement would look nice as a centerpiece. What do you think?" She held the magazine up.

Sam struggled to focus. "It's nice."

"It's nice? Is that all you have to say?"

"Honey, I just woke up. I'm lucky I can see you."

"Fair enough." She relented. "Maybe a cup of coffee will help."

"Great."

"I think the water's still hot, but you might want to let it boil again."

"Okay. Is there any chance I could get a hot breakfast?"

"Sure. The diner serves breakfast all day." She got up. "I have a ton of things to do with the planner today." She looked at the magazine again. "I think I'll call Momma about this arrangement and get her opinion."

"Speaking of phone calls, the Museum of Modern Art left a message for you on the machine about an opening as a volunteer docent."

Although they were volunteer positions, a docent at the famed Museum of Modern Art was a coveted position that many applied for in vain."

"I know. I called them back."

"What did you tell them?"

"I politely told them thank you but no thanks," Maria said somewhat flippantly.

"Why? I know people who'd kill to get their foot in that door."

"I have too much to do for the wedding, silly."

"It's only for a few hours a couple of days a week. You can't manage that?"

"I have a ton of things to do before the wedding."

"The wedding is still four months off."

"Four months is a blink of the eye in wedding time. I want everything to be perfect, so I have to stay on a tight schedule." Maria folded the magazine under her arm. "I'd better give Momma a call from the car to see what she thinks about this style of arrangement."

"How are you going to get her opinion if she hasn't seen the magazine?"

"We both have subscriptions to the magazine. In fact, Momma gets every bridal magazine I get."

"I see."

Maria kissed him. "I've really got to get going. I'll see you later. Love you."

"Love you, too." Sam waved as he watched her leave. "Guess I'd better put the tea kettle back on." He sighed as he got out of bed and stretched his six foot, four inch muscular frame.

After putting on his robe, Sam went into his state of the art kitchen and looked around at the little-used area. "I did say that once I retired I was going to visit more museums. I didn't realize my kitchen would be the first one."

His dreams of pancakes dashed, Sam settled for a bowl of cereal. When he looked at his picture on the box, he laughed. *I guess it is the breakfast of champions.*

When the phone rang, he checked the caller ID. It was his agent/manager, Reggie Dawes. Prior to signing with Reggie, Sam had been signed with a large sports management agency. They had assigned two agents to him who had treated him like a prize bull with an I.Q. to match, even though he'd graduated with a 3.45

GPA from the University of Texas with a degree in English. Tired of being "handled", he'd learned about Reggie from a teammate and switched.

A former college basketball player, Reggie knew what it meant to be an athlete. Unlike many other agents, he wasn't all about stats and deals. He treated Sam like a colleague and a friend.

"Good morning, Reggie."

"Hey, Sam. How's it going?"

"I can't complain. I'm just sitting here eating breakfast."

"I take that you're having cereal again" Reggie said "That brown-haired, green-eyed guy who used to be a quarterback still on the box?

"You got it." Sam laughed. "I'm still on the box, and I'm still having cereal for breakfast."

"Maybe once you put that band on her finger you'll get your hot breakfast."

"That would be nice, but Maria grew up with servants and a chef so it's more likely that she'll hire someone to cook once we're married."

"At least you'll get hot meals," Reggie said reassuringly.

"I like your spin on it, Reggie." Sam laughed. "You're calling about the manuscript, right?"

"Yes. I want to know how things are going."

"At this point it's sort of just going," he said in a dejected tone.

"That doesn't sound good. How much have you written?"

"In total I'd say about forty pages."

Reggie gasped. "You need 160 more pages by Memorial Day, and at this rate they need to be print-ready pages."

"I know. I'm cutting it close."

"Maybe I can get you some help."

"You mean a ghostwriter? I told you, Reggie, I want to write the book."

"I know you do. I'm not talking about a ghostwriter. I'm talking about someone who can help you with the writing process and give you feedback. You need an editor."

"Do you have someone in mind?"

"As a matter of fact, I do. I'll call her as soon as I hang up with you."

"Wait. Aren't you going to tell me anything about her?"

"Sure, I'll tell you about her, but it will have to wait until later. I have to catch her before her day gets started. I'll stop by your place later on. What's a good time?"

"I'm not on wedding duty today so my day is pretty open."

"All right then. I'll see you around three or three-thirty."

"Okay."

Sam hung up and continued eating, wondering whom Reggie had in mind. Given that it was not yet eight and Reggie thought that whoever she was might already be at work, Sam figured he'd be meeting a real workaholic.

Chapter 2

Like a teacher returning graded papers to her class, Abby placed all her corrected query letters, pitches, press releases and synopses on each of her associate's desks. It was a routine she had grown up with. During the school year, her college professor parents had graded her homework before her teachers did, and in the summer, while other parents planned camping trips and pool parties, Abby's parents devised a summer curriculum that included a reading list, grammar exercises, history assignments and foreign language lessons. Summers were especially long in the Carey household, but her parents had gotten results. Abby was fluent in five languages.

After she'd handed out all the corrected query letters, pitches, press releases and synopses, Abby put the coffee on, checked the fax machines and made sure the printers were on and the ink cartridges were full. As she removed the overnight transmissions from the fax machines, her Blackberry rang. She checked the caller ID, then picked up.

"Good morning to you, Mr. Dawes."

"Good morning, Abby. How's it going?"

"So far it's just going. To what do I owe this early call? I didn't think big-time sports agents had to get up this early."

"These days the world of sports is like politics, it streams twenty-four hours a day and you've got to stay on top of every development as it happens or you'll be dust."

"You're preaching to the choir." Abby began walking toward her office. "What's up, Reggie?"

"I was wondering if you're free for an early dinner at Le Bernadin tonight."

"Abby smiled as she sat down at her desk. "I'm always free for dinner at Le Bernadin."

"Great. Shall we meet at the restaurant at six?"

"Sure. I'll see you there." She looked at her watch. "It's almost time for my staff to get in. We'll catch up later."

"I'm looking forward to it."

Abby hung up, wondering what Reggie wanted. She tapped her pen on the desk. *Guess I'll find out soon enough.*

Her office was situated so that she could see everyone as soon as they walked in the door, not that she needed to.

"Good morning, Shana."

"How do you do that? You didn't even look up to see who it was."

17

"It's a gift." Abby chuckled as she glanced up at Shana. "You look nice."

"Thanks."

"Is that the Tory cinch dress by Kiyonna?"

"Yes it is." She grinned.

"I'm impressed."

"Well, you hang around with fashionistas long enough you pick up a few things."

Dressed to the nines, Shana Collingsworth stood in Abby's doorway. A curvy woman with dark wavy tresses and smooth chocolate skin, Shana always had a big smile on her face. She and Abby had met nineteen years earlier when Stillwater signed one of Shana's clients to do a book on fashion. The two hit it off instantly and became fast friends. Shana had served as bridesmaid at Abby's wedding and she was Justin's godmother.

When they initially formed Carey and Collingsworth, it had seemed odd to combine fashion and book PR. Nevertheless, it worked. Shana, with her innate ability to put clients at ease, was the front-woman. Though Abby behaved well, her directness came in most handy when dealing with unruly clients or sticky financial situations.

Shana glanced towards the desks in the office. "I see you've already handed out your blood-soaked critiques this morning."

Abby laughed. "They are not blood-soaked. I just made some corrections."

"I've seen machetes do less damage," Shana said. "Speaking of damage, have you spoken to your ex-husband yet?"

"He called this morning. I told him I already knew about Beebe's interview and had talked to Justin about it."

"What did he have to say for himself?"

"What could he say? History repeated itself. He cheated on me with Beebe and now he cheated on her."

"He cheated on her with a twenty-three-year-old. God, does he realize that this girl is only eight years older than his son?"

"It's obvious he's not thinking."

"He's forty-five years old, too old for this nonsense."

"Grey hair doesn't automatically bestow wisdom."

Shana thought for a moment. "J.J. has been sporting that clean-shaven look for years; he doesn't have any grey hair on his head."

"That wasn't the head I was referring to."

Both of them cracked up.

"Woo! Thanks, I needed that. So did he ask you about your love life again?"

Abby nodded. "He says he asks because of Justin."

"I don't buy that for a minute. J.J. is like every other alpha male who believes he's marked his territory."

"So Justin and I are marked."

"Precisely, Did you tell him it was none of his business?"

"Naturally," Abby answered.

"Good. Now all you have to do is get back out there and start dating again."

"That's easier said than done, Shana. Besides, I'm forty-one. It's not as if I haven't been on dates."

"When was the last time you went on one?"

Abby stopped to think. "Six months ago."

"Try eight months ago." Shana folded her arms. "And don't let me get started about the last time you had sex."

"Do you have some kind of Abby's-date-countdown calendar or something?" Abby asked. "Besides, I have had sex. It wasn't good sex, but it counts."

"Are you talking about that investment banker? What was his name?"

"Quincy."

"Was he really that bad?"

"It wasn't like watching paint dry. It was more like watching them make paint."

"Eww." Shana made a face. "That's pretty bad. Still, that doesn't mean you shouldn't get back out there and try again."

"I'll get back out there."

"When?"

"When the right man comes along."

"Where are you going to meet him?" Shana paused. "At the rate you're going, the right man will have to walk into your office."

"Sounds good to me."

"Oh, good grief"! You're too much." Shana said exasperatedly. She glanced at her watch "We'll pick this up later. "I have to make some accounts payable calls today."

"Let me know if you need any help."

"You know I will. I'll talk to you later."

"Okay."

Shana turned and walked out.

A short time later in came senior account executive Kelly Phillips. The petite brunette handled the agency's publishing company clients. Not far behind her was their graphic designer, Reed Daly, who, at six feet, six inches tall, looked like he belonged on a basketball court. After saying their good mornings they got situated at their desks.

"Is that coffee I smell?" Kelly asked.

"Yes. It should be ready by now." Abby went over to her printer.

"Great. Come on, Reed."

"Time to get our first morning jolt," Reed added.

"This is my second jolt," Kelly said.

"Really? Too much coffee doesn't make you jumpy?" Reed asked.

"Who said I was talking about coffee?"

Laughing, they headed for the break room.

Just then senior publicist Leo De Marco breezed into the office. Always impeccably dressed in color combinations that complemented his lean body, dark hair and olive skin, he had his briefcase in one hand and a rather odd green-colored protein shake in the other.

"Good morning, Abby." He smiled as he put his things down.

Abby walked out of her office. "Hey, Leo."

Leo was drinking the last of his shake.

Abby made a face. "I don't know how you can drink that."

"You get used to it, I guess."

"Not me. If I want protein in the morning, I'm sticking to egg whites."

"There are egg whites in the shake. It also has—"

Abby cut him off. "Please don't tell me what it has in it. I'd like to keep my breakfast down."

Leo laughed and then glanced at the marked-up papers on everyone's desk. "I see you've been busy."

"Note that most of the papers are on Candy's desk. I only made minor suggestions for the rest of you."

"Ah, that reminds me," he said as he got out his wallet. "We have to get the time pool going this morning."

Coffee mugs in hand, Kelly and Reed walked in.

"If it's time for the 'how late will Candy be today' pool, I'm in. I won last time." Kelly sat down and got out her purse.

Abby shook her head. "You guys kill me. There are only three of you in this pool."

"You could join us," Leo added.

"Thank you, but I'll pass."

"I have $100 that says she'll be here at 9:30," Reed said, waving a hundred-dollar bill.

"Okay." Leo jotted it down. "What about you, Kelly?"

"I'm sticking with 9:45. That's how I got my last pair of Christian Louboutin shoes."

"Okay." Leo wrote in the notepad. "I'm going to go out on a limb and say she'll get here at 9:25."

"You think she'll get here that early?" Kelly asked, surprised.

"There's a first time for everything," Leo answered as he collected the money from her and Reed.

"How will we know when she comes in? It's not like we're going to stare at the door," Reed noted.

"That's easy. We have our own Peter Parker in Abby. Her Spidey sense will let us know the moment Candy walks in." Leo smiled.

"You three are too much." Abby went over to the copy machine. "Oh, before I forget, I'll be leaving early today," Abby said as she pressed the copy button. She turned around to a room full of statues. "What?"

23

"You're leaving early?" Kelly seemed astounded.

"Yes. You don't have to look so shocked. I have an early business dinner."

"Shoot! I was hoping you were going on a date," Leo said as he snapped his fingers.

"Sorry, Leo, no such luck," Abby said as she picked her copies up. "Okay, folks, let's get to work. We've got authors and books to promote!" She walked back to her office.

Soon the office was filled with the sounds of publicists working the phones. It was 9:25 and should have been the perfect moment for junior publicist Candace Levy to creep in, since Abby's chair was facing the window.

"Good morning, Candy. Nice of you to join us, "Abby called out as she swiveled around in her chair.

Unlike most twenty-somethings, Candy had money, or at least her parents did. She'd gone to all the right New York City prep schools and had a B.A. in communications from Vassar. Candy didn't need to work, but the pretty blonde wanted to prove she could make it on her own. However, she was still quite green when it came to public relations and her perennial lateness proved that she didn't have a head for time in a business where time truly is money.

"Damn! There's goes the pair of Louboutins I had my eye on," Kelly said.

"I'm sorry. I got off to a late start."

"I see," Abby said as she walked out of her office to Candy's desk. "You know the PR business is all about timing. We have to be able to jump on opportunities quickly."

"I'll do better."

"I hope so. Be sure to check out the notes on your press releases and pitch letters."

She walked over to her desk and looked at the papers. "Okay."

"I also need you to make a correction on the Mayfair book launch party invitation. You wrote *y-o-u-r* cordially invited instead of using the contraction for *you are*. Please change that and get it to the printer ASAP"

"I will." Candy sat down and turned on her computer.

The phone rang and Leo picked up. "Good morning, Carey and Collingsworth Public Relations." He paused. "Hi, Shana. Yes, she's right here." He turned to Abby. "Shana is on the line for you."

"Thanks." Abby picked up the phone on Candy's desk. "What's up?"

"These collection calls are killing me."

"I'll be right down." Abby hung up. "I've got to go downstairs for a while. Buzz me if anything's up."

"We sure will." Kelly smiled.

As Abby walked away, a relieved look came over Candy's face.

"You can breathe now, Candy," Leo teased.

Candy shook her head as she looked at the stack of red-inked papers on her desk. "It doesn't look like I can do anything right." She held up a press release. "Look at all this red."

"They don't call her the dragon lady for nothing," Reed said.

Although they're housed in the same six story building, the fashion and book floors were completely different. Abby's book public relations had one floor with one conference room. Her small team essentially performed their functions via phone call or email, whereas Shana had twenty-one people working under her from account executives, fashion show producers, model casters to interns. Fashion was a more fast-paced and competitive business. Though both sides had their share of big egos, the egos in fashion go from the total professional to the completely self-obsessed. Therefore they needed more room to accompany the large heads.

As Abby walked in to Shana's office, she heard her on the phone.

"I'm sorry if you don't think we delivered what we promised but we did. You had fashion editors from every major publication at your viewing. We can't help it if some of them had negative things to say about your line. That's beyond our control."

"Put him on hold," Abby mouthed silently.

"Hans, can I put you on hold for a minute? Thanks."
She pressed the hold button. "He's driving me crazy."

"Is that Hans Müller?"

Shana nodded.

"His show went off without a hitch. What's his problem?"

"He's upset at some of the things the editors wrote about his collection. He expected glowing reviews all around."

"Then he's either in kindergarten or the wrong business. Frankly, it sounds like a little of both." She paused. "We did his show a month ago, right?"

"Yes."

"Give me the phone."

Shana handed Abby the phone.

"Hello, Hans. This is Abigail Carey. What seems to be the problem with paying your invoice?"

"The problem is I'm losing money as a result of the bad reviews I got from the show your firm produced, and I don't feel as if I should pay for that."

"You are entitled to your feelings, but you signed a contract and you have to abide by its terms. We produced the show and we had all the major fashion editors in attendance, which means we met our obligation. We can't make them love your collection. This is a democracy. If you want to make sure people fawn over your every design, invite the sycophants who work for you. I'm sure they'd be happy to kiss your ass."

"I still don't feel I have to pay. What are you going to do about it? Sue me?"

"No. However, I will post a message on our Facebook page that says designer Hans Müller doesn't pay his bills on time." Abby pulled the phone away from her ear. "How many people like us, Shana?"

"I think it's almost 120,000."

"Yes, I'll post it to our page, where the 120,000 people who like us will see it."

"Go ahead, and I will sue for defamation."

"I suggest you give your attorney a call so he or she can explain to you that you can't sue us. You see, as long as what I say is true, I've got the perfect defense. And you are thirty days late. Moreover, if you think that you can simply go to another PR firm, remember that although we're competitors, we do talk to one another. Word gets around fast when it comes to dead-beat designers."

"Wer dieses Weibchen am Telefon ist?"

"Ich bin das Weibchen, das diese Firma besitzt." Abby answered in perfect German.

Hans gasped. "You speak German?"

"Ja spreche ich Deutsches. Rufen Sie mich nicht eine Frau. Ich habe einen Namen. Verwenden Sie ihn. Are we clear on that?"

"Yes, Ms. Carey."

"Good. Now you have until the end of today to get a cashier's check to our office to pay your balance. *Haben Sie einen schönen Tag.*" She hung up.

"What did you say to him?"

"I told him to have a nice day in German so I ended on a pleasant note."

"I mean, what did you say to him before that?"

"Oh, he called me a 'female' in German."

"I take it that's another way of saying bitch."

"It is. So I simply told him not to refer to me as a female. I have a name. Use it," Abby said as she walked over to a counter and poured a glass of Pellegrino.

"Knowing and speaking five languages comes in handy."

"You can say that again. I also know the word for bitch in Japanese, Chinese, Romanian, Korean, Portuguese, Greek, Dutch and American sign language."

"Good grief, Abby."

"If they call me the dragon lady, you know bitch isn't far behind."

Shana laughed. "You know he's never going to hire us again."

"Of course he will."

"I'll give you points for confidence and having a set of brass ones, Abby."

"Thanks." She smiled. "So how are things coming along for New York Fashion Week?"

"Overall it's moving at a good pace. I do think that I'm going to need a few more interns."

"We can put a call into Parsons and F.I.T., I'm sure they'll help us out."

There was a knock on the door.

"Come in," Shana called.

Senior account executive Lauren Delaney, Shana's right hand, walked in. A fair-skinned African-American beauty with long, wavy hair and a slim build, she reminded many of Alicia Keyes.

"I'm sorry to interrupt, ladies."

"That's not a problem, Lauren. What's up?"

"I just got off the phone with Hans Müller's office. He's having a check for the balance sent over by messenger in about an hour or so."

"Well, I'll be," Shana said, astonished.

"Wait, there's more. He wants us to do produce his next viewing."

"I told you he'd hire us again." Abby grinned.

"Will wonders ever cease?"

"I just thought you should know. I'll let you get back to your meeting," Lauren said as she left the room.

"Before I forget, I'm leaving early today. Reggie invited me to an early dinner at Le Bernadin."

"Nice. What's the occasion?"

"There's no occasion. I'm pretty sure Reggie needs a favor, and it must be a doozy."

"Did he say he needed a favor? It could be that he just wants to catch up."

Abby shook her head. "I've known Reggie since we were kids, and this is about a favor. It's no different than when we were in college and he needed my help to finish a paper."

"What? He didn't just ask you for help?"

"No. He'd borrow a car to bring me a Geno's Philly cheesesteak even though it was nearly four miles from U of Penn's campus. Then he'd ask me, knowing I couldn't resist a hot Philly cheesesteak."

"Who could?"

"Right," Abby responded, smiling.

"So even though you're going to Le Bernadin, you smell a cheesesteak."

"You got it."

"Are you going to take him to task for it?"

"No, I'll wait until after I've ordered the lobster." She grinned.

⟨∂⟩

After he ordered take-out for lunch again, Sam decided it was in his best interest to work out in his home gym. In just under an hour he'd worked up quite a sweat on his Bowflex machine.

His cell rang. "Hello?" he said as he picked up a towel.

"Hello, son."

"Hi, Dad. How are you?"

"I'm good. Were you running or something? You sound out of breath."

"I was just getting a workout in."

"It's kind of late up there to be working out, isn't it?"

"Yes, but with all the take-out I've been eating lately, I grab a workout whenever I can. It's not like I'm going back to training camp."

"I never thought I'd hear the day when you missed going to training camp." His father laughed.

"I know I complained but I liked the camaraderie and it helped me stay in shape. How's Momma?"

"She's good. She went out to pick up a few more things before we leave for J.R.'s."

Sam chuckled. "In other words, she's picking up a few more outfits for Daisy."

"She raised three boys. It's her prerogative to spoil a little girl. By the way, have you spoken to your brothers?"

"I called Zeke a couple of days ago and J.R. and I exchanged a couple of texts the other day. Why? Is there anything wrong?"

"No. I just wanted to make sure you and your brothers were staying in touch, that's all. I know Maria has gotten you waist deep in this wedding."

"She'd like to have me neck deep in it, but I have a manuscript due soon."

"That's right. How's that going?"

"At the moment, not so good." He sighed heavily.

"Well, if you have to put your foot down about all this wedding hoopla, then so be it. Let Maria and her parents deal with it. They're the ones that want all this highfalutin' stuff."

"I am the groom, Dad."

"I know. But you seem like *The Man in the Iron Mask.*"

Don didn't believe in pulling punches. Though he was a loving father to all three of his sons, he spoke his mind.

"I know, Dad. I only have to deal with this for another four months and then it will be over."

"Good. So what are you going to do about this book?"

"I'm going to write it. Listen, Dad, I've got to get changed. Reggie's coming over in a little while and I'd like to get a little writing in so I have something good to report to him."

"Okay. Tell Reggie we said hello."

"I will. What time are you leaving for J.R.'s?"

"As soon as your momma gets back."

"Okay. Have a safe trip. Kiss Momma and Daisy for me."

"Will do," he said cheerfully.

"Talk to you later, Dad."

"So long, son."

Sam took a shower and sat down to work in his office. A few hours later, he seemed to be stuck right where he started. By the time Reggie showed up he was glad for the distraction.

Although the six foot, four inch, broad shouldered, muscular Reggie was used to negotiating with some of the major players in sports, he couldn't let his biggest client know that discussing salary caps with NFL owners was easier than asking Abby for this particular favor.

Sam went to the refrigerator. "Would you like anything, Reggie?"

"No, thanks. I'm good." He sat down at the kitchen table. "You look pained, Sam. What's wrong?"

"I just spent the last few hours trying to write, and my head's killing me," he said as he opened the bottle and took a few gulps.

"Hopefully I'll be able to help you with that. I'm having an early dinner with the editor I told you about."

"I wouldn't say you told me about her. All you told me was that you were contacting her. I don't even know her name."

"Her name is Abigail Carey. She was a senior editor at Stillwater Publishing."

"Abigail Carey. Where have I heard that name before?"

"It's possible you could have read about her in the Arts and Leisure or book review section of the *Times*. She's edited a number of bestsellers."

"That's impressive, but I don't think that's where I heard her name." Sam sat down at the table. "Wasn't she married to the Knicks' forward, J.J. Stokes?"

"Yes, but that was many moons ago."

"How do you know her? Did you rep her husband?"

"No." He shook his head. "Abby and I have known each other since we were kids. I lived two houses down from her. As for J.J., I didn't know him until he married Abby."

"So you were childhood sweethearts."

"No. Childhood friends. Heck, Abby was the one who introduced me to my wife."

"No kidding. So if she's such a great editor, why isn't she still working for Stillwater?"

"Two words, pop culture," Reggie answered. "Abby graduated summa cum laude from The University of Pennsylvania with a B.A. in English and she has a master's in English from NYU. When Stillwater's books became more commercial, Abby left. She's a purist when it comes to writing."

"If you were trying to make me feel better, you're not doing a great job. She sounds scary."

"Abby is no tougher than what you handled on the gridiron. Besides, you have a degree in English."

"I have a degree in English from the University of Texas, not big-time schools."

"She's not that kind of snob."

"Okay. If you say so." He still sounded unsure.

"Great. Just see what she has to say. I'm sure you won't regret this. I'll regret this is if I'm late for our dinner. She's cutting into her agency's time for me."

"Her agency's time? She's not a full-time freelance editor?"

"No. She's in public relations now."

"If she's in PR, why would she want to help me with editing?"

"Simple, because once an editor at heart, always an editor. Trust me."

"Do I have a choice?"

Reggie laughed and patted him on the back. "I've got to get going. I'll call you later."

Sam watched as Reggie left the kitchen. "What have I gotten myself into?"

Chapter 3

"That can't be the time," Abby muttered. "Leo, what time do you have?"

"It's four-fifteen."

Abby sighed. "I'd better get out of here now if I'm going to change and make it to the restaurant on time." She rose, turned her computer off. "You'll hold the fort down for me, Leo?"

"Of course I will."

"Thanks." Though Candy was trying to hide behind the copier, Abby walked over to her. "Candy, I want to see those revised promos on my desk tomorrow morning before you send them out."

"Yes, Abby," she answered sheepishly.

"Have a good night, everyone." Abby waved as she walked out.

"You, too," Kelly said.

"Okay, Candy," Reed added. "You can stop hiding behind the copier. You're safe now."

"I wasn't hiding," she insisted as she sat back down at her desk.

"Right, you weren't hiding," Reed said.

"I don't think Abby likes me."

"That's not true. She likes you."

"That's easy for you to say, Kelly. She never picks on you."

"She's not picking on you. She just wants the best out of all of us."

"Maybe so, but it seems like I get burned by the dragon lady every day."

Leo laughed. "Believe me, you're only getting singed. But I will say this: if those revisions aren't on her desk tomorrow morning, you'll know what getting scorched by the dragon lady is all about."

Abby and Shana each had an apartment on a higher floor of their office building. Once Abby got upstairs she walked back to her bedroom sanctuary with its king-size canopy bed, pearl-embroidered all white bedding and farmhouse bedside table. After a quick shower, she slipped her curvy size 14/16 body into a black Jones New York shirtdress that she complemented with black peek-a-boo pumps.

She sat down at her vanity table and mirror. "This is Reggie, not a date," she muttered, pinning her hair up.

Abby got up and walked over to her full-length mirror. *Not too shabby*, she thought.

"I know you're going to accessorize," Shana said from the doorway.

With the both of them living and working in the building, Shana and Abby often floated in and out of each other's apartments.

"I'll wear my diamond studs and the tennis bracelet Justin gave me for Mother's Day."

Shana made a beeline for Abby's jewelry box. "I think you should wear a necklace. You need something to show off that God-given cleavage of yours." She handed Abby a white gold necklace with a heart pendant.

Abby put the earrings, bracelet and necklace on. "Now I'm going to take the bracelet off," Abby said as she put it back into her jewelry box. "I put on all my accessories and now I've taken one off. Isn't that the gospel according to Coco?"

"So you have been listening."

"Yes. But you realize I'm not going on a date."

"And you realize that I'm going to ignore that. You never know who might be in the restaurant and see you across that famous crowded room."

"I love that you're such a romantic, but that only happens in the movies. I'd better get going if I want to make it to the restaurant on time."

"Okay. Let me know when you're back so you can tell me what favor Reggie asked for."

"I will." Abby grabbed her coat and purse.

"I'll go down with you. I still have some merchandising to do."

"Now who's the workaholic?" Abby chuckled.

Dressed in his finest Italian suit, Reggie ordered a drink. He checked the time. *Abby should walk through the door any minute now. She's never late.*

The waiter brought Reggie a scotch, neat. Just as he was about to take a sip he glanced at the little paunch around his middle. *Wonder how many carbs scotch has?* He took a sip. When he looked up he saw the maître d' leading Abby to the table. He stood up as the maître d' held the chair for her. "Abby, you are as beautiful as ever."

She turned to the maître d'. "Thank you."

"You're welcome, ma'am." He walked away.

"And thank you for the compliment, Reggie."

"It's the truth," Reggie said as he sat down.

"Now I'm wondering whether I should have worn hip boots as opposed to pumps for this dinner." She grinned.

"I was only stating the obvious."

"Nicely done, Reggie." She surveyed him. "You look pretty good yourself. The world of sports management agrees with you."

"Most of the time," he said bluntly. "There are some days when I wonder wh hoe y I got into the business in the first place."

"Don't we all wonder that at some point?"

Their waiter walked over. "Pardon me. May I get the lady something to drink?"

"What would you like, Abby?"

"What are you drinking?"

"Scotch, neat."

"I guess I'll have a seltzer with a twist, please."

"Very good, ma'am." The waiter walked away.

"Are you sure you want seltzer? They make a great cosmopolitan."

"You're drinking brown liquor, which tells that I need to keep my wits about me."

"Why would you say that?"

"You're usually a gin and tonic man. You only break out the scotch when you need a little extra nerve. Remember senior prom?"

"Don't remind me." He groaned.

"You were so nervous about asking Veronica Carver you got plastered." She chuckled. "You nearly threw up all over the girl when you did ask her."

"She said yes, didn't she? I couldn't have been that bad."

"Honey, when you're a teenage girl and a guy gets drunk to work up the nerve to ask you out, it's considered romantic. At seventeen it's the closest thing to *Romeo and Juliet*. However, I must admit that it works for you when it comes to women. I think you were three sheets to the wind when you proposed to Danielle and she said yes."

"I'm still surprised she understood a word I said that night." Reggie laughed.

"She didn't need to. Every woman understands once they see that pretty blue Tiffany box."

The waiter brought Abby's seltzer.

"Thank you." She took a sip. "So let's hear it."

"You don't want to order dinner first?"

"I'm too intrigued to eat. Nevertheless, it's your choice. You can bite the bullet and tell me what you want or we can make small talk. Either way I'm ordering the most expensive thing on the menu."

"How's Justin?"

"Okay, I see you're choosing small talk." She sipped her seltzer. "Justin's fine. Thanks. How are Danielle and the girls?"

"They're doing well. Danielle's been busy with a lot of fashion shoots."

"I know. I've seen her name credited in quite a few high fashion magazines. She must be thrilled."

"She is. She even takes the girls on some of the shoots."

"They must love that. A couple of teenage girls surrounded by all that glamour, exciting stuff."

"Wow, it's hard to fathom that my little girls are growing up. It seems like I just brought them home and now they're both in high school."

"They do grow up fast. Justin's a junior now and he's about to turn 16."

"You're lucky he's not in the city prep schools. Don't get me wrong, the girls are getting a great education, but the kids they go to school with aren't your average teenagers."

"You're preaching to the choir. The bluebloods at Choate are something else, too."

"Do they have basketball at Choate?"

"No. Justin's on the varsity lacrosse team and the varsity baseball team."

"How does J.J. feel about that?"

"I'm sure he'd rather have his son play basketball, but it's not up to him."

"How tall is Justin now?"

"He's almost six feet, six inches tall and weighs 164 pounds soaking wet. What kills me is that he's still growing. He's already taller than his father."

"Speaking of his father, I heard Beebe filed for divorce."

"You know what they say about karma." Abby took another sip of seltzer.

"I'll drink to that." He raised his glass and drank. "Now to why I asked you to dinner," he began.

"I'm all ears." She leaned in.

"Do you know my client Sam Best?"

"Sure, I know Sam. He's New York's football messiah. Didn't he just announce his retirement?"

"Yes. He's hung up his cleats after thirteen years in the NFL. You know he just signed a deal with…"

Abby interrupted him. "Tandem Publishing just signed him to write his story. Congratulations. That's quite a coup."

"Thanks. We're pretty excited about it. He's on a tight deadline."

"I would say so. Tandem has it listed as a late summer/early fall release to coincide with the beginning of football season."

"How did you know that?"

"I read about it in *Publishers Weekly*. It's the publishing industry's bible."

"In light of this tight deadline I think he's going to need some help getting his manuscript together."

"Oh, do you need the names of some good ghost-writers?"

"No."

"Well, I'm sure you don't need any help with PR or marketing. Sam Best is already a brand. Great sales numbers are a forgone conclusion."

"True. The thing is, he wants to write the book himself so he needs a great editor to work with him."

Abby nodded her head knowingly. "Now I know why you invited me here for dinner. You want me to work with him."

"You are the best in the business."

"Thank you, but I have laid down my weapon. No more red pens." She thought for a moment. "Well, I can't say that I've retired my red pen entirely. I just use it on pitch letters, synopses and to torture junior publicists."

"I was hoping that you'd make an exception."

"You know what happened when Stillwater wanted me to work pop culture phenoms. I couldn't take it."

"I think it was more like they couldn't take it. What did you say about that Lizzy Conway?" Reggie tapped the table. "Oh, yes, you said her sense of fiction was as interesting as a three-minute egg."

"I was right, wasn't I? Stillwater signed her to a two-book deal and then proceeded to take a financial bath when sales for both books tanked. That's what happens when you try to turn neophyte reality stars into John Steinbeck. I don't mean any offense to Sam, but when it comes to writing, most of these pop culture icons can't string a sentence together, let alone a whole book."

Reggie couldn't help snickering. "I understand."

Abby continued on her little rant. "I spent the better part of a decade playing the role of the wicked witch because I cared about the work."

"And Stillwater had the numbers and the awards to prove it. How much did they offer you to stay?"

"There were a lot of zeros on the check, but I was done."

"That was six years ago, right?"

"Seven."

"So you've had time to detox."

"I guess so." Abby shrugged. "When is his manuscript due?"

"It's due Memorial Day weekend."

Abby was floored. "It's already February, Reggie. That's only three months away. And if I'm not mistaken I believe I read somewhere that he's set to get married the first weekend in June."

"That's true."

"Reggie, I'm an editor, not a magician."

"But if anyone can work magic with an author, it's you."

"My wand is in the shop," she said dryly.

"Come on, Abby. You're the only person I know who can do this."

"I don't know, Reggie. It's a lot to take on."

"Fine. If I can't appeal to your ego, can I appeal to you as my oldest and dearest friend?" Reggie gave her his best puppy dog look.

"You're not playing fair."

"Is it working?"

Abby folded her arms and sighed. "All right, I'll meet with him."

"Thanks, Abby, you're a lifesaver."

"I wouldn't thank me just yet. I'll decide whether I'll work with him after I meet him."

"That's all I ask. You're the best, Abby."

"We'll see if you still feel that way after I order the baked lobster and the chocolate chicory for dessert." She winked.

❦

Sam thought that an evening of romance would take the edge off his day. When he and Maria first got together, they would steal away to make love whenever possible. They couldn't keep their hands off each other. Even more than that, they could talk to each other for hours. However, over the last two years they'd seemed to go off track in every way. Their lovemaking had grown more methodical and sporadic, and they didn't talk to one another as they had in the past. Once they were engaged, Sam thought it would turn around, but it didn't. Maria was singularly focused on the wedding. She obsessed over every wedding detail twenty-four hours a day.

This evening, though, Sam was determined to turn the tide. He lit candles, chilled champagne and played soft music. The night was made for pure ecstasy. Instead, it turned out to be a means to an end when they skipped foreplay and had sex.

Coitus achieved, Sam rolled over onto his back.

Maria gave him a peck on the lips. "That was great, honey." She picked up a bridal magazine from the night table.

Sam watched her, realizing that would be all the lovemaking for the night, if it could even be called lovemaking He got out of bed and put his lounge pants on.

"Where are you going?" Maria looked up from the magazine.

"I'm going to get some juice. Do you want something?"

"No. I'm good. Thanks."

Sam grabbed the champagne in the basket. *Might as well put this to good use. One large mimosa coming right up.* He headed for the kitchen.

After he mixed a large mimosa, Sam headed for the study and sat down in front of his laptop. *Seems like I get more action from my keyboard these days.*

Ten minutes later he was still staring at the blank page. It had seemed so much easier when he sighed the contract. *Might as well write something I know I can handle.* Sam reached into the desk, pulled out his checkbook and began writing checks to Tony Webster, Hall of Fame running back, and Norman Green, a Hall of Fame center. Both players were suffering from debilitating health issues since their storied days on the gridiron.

The cause of retired players had hit home for Sam when he was in the early part of his career and met Norm Green in Detroit. Always a fan, he could recite Norm's stats from his heyday. What he didn't know was since that his retirement he was receiving a paltry $843 a month from the NFL, which was clearly not enough to maintain his health care or pay his bills. He was shocked at what happened to the man who scored a touchdown for the Baltimore Colts in Super Bowl V. However, he was even more shocked to discover that his story wasn't an isolated one. It bothered him that after bringing joy to the fans and money into the organization players could be summarily put out to pasture.

From then on Sam became an anonymous benefactor for retired NFL players. He wrote monthly checks to various players to help cover their medical and living expenses.

"What are you doing?"

Startled, Sam slipped the checks into his portfolio and turned to face her. "Maria, I thought you'd be asleep by now."

"No. I was making notes for Jessica and my pen ran out."

"Oh." He reached over and got a pen. "Here you go."

She took it from him. "Thanks. What were you doing, anyway?"

"I was trying to work on this manuscript."

She glanced over at the checkbook. "Why's the checkbook out?"

"I moved it when I was looking for something in the drawer."

"Oh." She seemed satisfied with the answer. "Are you coming back to bed soon?"

"Yes. I'll be there in a minute."

"Can't you come now? I want to show you something in this magazine. Momma and Daddy saw it and they think it would be perfect."

Sam's heart sank a bit when he heard "Momma and Daddy." Every time Maria began a sentence with them, the price of the wedding went up. "What is it?"

"It's a donut bar."

"A donut bar," he repeated. "We already have a seven-tier cake by the best wedding cake artist in New York, a Viennese table, a chocolate fountain and a candy station. Don't you think we're already bordering on sending our guests into diabetic comas?"

"No. We have four hundred and fifty people coming and they are expecting to be wowed. A donut bar is the latest trend in wedding receptions."

"Why not just add cupcakes?"

"Cupcakes are so passé."

"Oh," he said. "Wait a minute. Did you say four hundred and fifty guests? It was just four hundred people a week ago."

"Daddy had a few more people he said have to be there."

William "Big Bill" Carrangelo was a successful real estate developer who had furthered his family's fortune during the real estate boom in Dallas. He was a tall, imposing man with a gregarious nature that hid his ruthlessness. No one crossed Big Bill. However, he was a soft touch when it came to his wife Kitty and their children. Maria adored her father and would never refuse a direct request.

"Your father invited fifty more people?"

"Give or take a few," she answered, smiling. "Just take a look at the donut bar. I know that once you see it you'll love it."

He knew she would stand there until he said yes. "Okay." He shut down the computer and got up.

The phone rang.

"Who could that be at this hour?" Maria asked, annoyed.

"It's probably Reggie. I've been expecting a call from him."

Maria stared at him.

"I promise this will only take a few minutes."

"Fine," she huffed before she walked away.

Sam picked up the phone. "Hello?"

"Hey, Sam, it's Reggie. I hope I didn't wake you."

"No, I'm up. What's the good word?"

"Abby agreed to meet with you tomorrow at ten."

"She's going to work with me?"

"Not exactly," he began. "She agreed to a meeting with you."

"That doesn't sound promising."

"Perk up, kid. The point is, she's meeting with you, and that's a good thing, but you're not a shoo-in. Believe me when I say that Abby doesn't have a problem using the word no."

"Okay, I'll take your word for it. Am I in for some kind of pop quiz to determine if I know the difference between a noun and a verb?"

"No. But you do know the difference, right?"

"You're funny, Reggie," he said dryly.

"I'm sorry. Just be sure to bring whatever you've written with you."

"Okay."

"You'll be fine," Reggie assured him.

"I hope you're right." Sam took a pen and pad out. "What's the address?"

"It's 2145 Thompson Street, between Broome and Prince."

"Got it." He jotted down the address.

"All right, Sam, I'm on my way home now. Give me a call if you need me."

"I will, Reggie. Have a good night."

"Thanks. You, too."

Sam sighed. "I sure hope she grades on a curve," he said aloud as he rose and turned off the lights.

Chapter 4

Finished with her morning routine, Abby was in her bedroom rummaging through her walk-in closet. *What in the world am I going to wear?* She stopped short. *What the hell am I doing? I haven't even decided if I'm going to work with this guy.* With that she pulled her dark olive Ralph Lauren Zelma jersey dress. "This will work." She walked out and got dressed.

Shortly afterwards Abby was in her office reviewing Candy's revisions and attaching Post-Its with more notes. "That should do it," she said aloud as she placed the papers on Candy's desk. It was time to continue playing her game of phone tag with Zach.

She picked up the phone on Candy's desk and punched the numbers and got the answering machine. "Hi, Zach, it's Abby. It seems like we're destined to play phone tag. Please give me a call so we can discuss Mollie West's appearance on the show. Thanks. Or, in other words, tag, you're it." She hung up the phone and went back to her office.

By nine-fifteen, Leo was heading for Abby's office.

"What can I do for you, Leo?" Abby asked without looking up from her computer.

"I will never get used to your Spidey sense."

Abby laughed. "Have a seat."

"All the book clubs have confirmed for the Return to Romance event at the Harlem Tea Room on Madison Avenue."

"That's terrific. What's the problem?"

"I haven't been able to get Tanya from Willow House to send over any review copies."

"The event is in three weeks."

"Right." He nodded.

"Is she aware that we need to provide the book clubs with at least one review copy per title before the event?"

"I thought she understood."

"There are five authors coming. So we're only talking about thirty books."

"Yes."

Abby picked up her phone and punched numbers.

"Good morning, Willow House Publishing. This is Dana. How may I direct your call?"

"Good morning, Dana. It's Abigail Carey calling. How are you?"

"I'm well, Ms. Carey. How are you?"

"I'm just peachy, thanks. Is Ted in?"

"Yes. If you hold for a moment, I'll see if he can pick up."

"Thanks."

Abby tapped her pen on the desk while she listened to the hold music.

Theodore Tinsdale was the publisher and president of Willow House. A distinguished man of fifty-six, he was a former prosecutor for De Kalb County. His late wife, Sandra Willow Tinsdale, was a beloved English teacher who instilled her love of reading in all her students. After she died of breast cancer, her memory inspired Ted to start Willow House Publishing. It had become one of the most successful independent publishing houses in the country.

"Hello, Abby. It's good to hear from you," Ted said in his usual jovial tone.

"Hi, Ted. How's it going?"

"Something tells me I'll be better equipped to answer that question after this phone call." He chuckled.

"Then I won't keep you in suspense. You know we're handling the Return to Romance author event, right?"

"Yes."

"Well, we haven't received any review copies to send out to the book clubs who have confirmed their attendance, and we are now at the three week countdown. We need only about thirty books."

"In the economy, only is a relative term."

"Okay, Ted, let's get down to brass tacks. We are talking about mass-market paperbacks, not trade paperbacks or hardcover books. It costs you pocket change to produce them and you handle your own distribution. So don't hand me the economy line, especially since you're poised to sell more than thirty copies at the event."

"You're hitting me with the loss-leaders argument."

"And you know that I'm right. So when can we expect the books?"

"I'll have Tanya send them out to you priority today."

"Thank you. Now that wasn't so hard, was it?

"Not for you." He laughed. "No one can get anything past you, can they?"

"They can try, but I've been in the publishing business for nearly twenty years."

"And it shows."

Abby laughed. "You know, Ted, I hate to twist arms and run, but I have an appointment coming in shortly."

"No problem. It was good talking to you. Take care."

"You, too." She hung up. "Okay, you're all set, Leo. Tanya's sending the books out today via priority mail."

Leo looked relieved as he stood up. "Thanks, Abby, you're the best."

"You're welcome." Abby leaned back in her chair as he left. *When he stands to make nearly $7,000 from this one event. I can't believe it.* She looked at her watch and saw she still had time to get more things done before dealing with what she was sure would be the NFL version of *Entourage*.

❧

Sam was sitting in the back of his Mercedes on the way to Abby's office. He nervously kept opening and closing his portfolio. *I need to stop this. The number of pages will not magically double no matter how hard I wish.* He closed his portfolio for what he hoped would be the last time.

His cell phone rang. It was his friend Franco Corona. Franco was a retired baseball player who, at age forty-one, now made a living as a motivational speaker. Franco had immigrated with his parents to the United States from the Dominican Republic when he was seven years old. His parents had worked hard to keep a roof over the heads of their seven children. In high school Franco was a phenomenal catcher and received a scholarship to Nebraska before joining the New York Yankees' AAA Scranton/Wilkes-Barre team. Eventually he was called up to the big leagues and subsequently became one of the Yankees' best hitting catchers.

"Hey, Franco," he said cheerfully. "How are you?"

"I'm good, buddy. How are you?"

"Okay for the most part."

"Well, that's not a ringing endorsement. What's going on?"

"I'm on my way to meet with an editor about my book and I'm a little nervous."

"Who are you meeting?"

"Abigail Carey. Have you heard of her?"

"Yes. She's a real ball-buster."

"What? How do you know her?"

"I don't know her personally, but Javier Cantu does. She worked with him on his book."

Javier Cantu was another retired baseball player who at the end of his career authored a tell-all book about the not-so-sunny side of America's pastime. Not only did he reveal his infidelity and use of performance-enhancing drugs, he named others as well. His book had become a bestseller seven years earlier, but his name was still mud in Major League Baseball.

"From everything I've heard about her so far, his book doesn't sound like one of her kind of projects."

"It wasn't. She worked for Stillwater Publishing at the time. Javier told me his nightmares still have a red hue."

"If you're trying to make me feel better, you're failing miserably. She's going to massacre me."

"No, she won't. The truth is, Javier got great reviews. Even he says that much of the credit should go to her. She took a guy who never paid attention to writing anything other than autographs and girls' phone numbers and turned him into a credible author."

"Now that sounds more reassuring."

"Wait a minute. She left Stillwater right after Javier's book was released. Is she working for Tandem now?"

"No. She's in PR."

"Then how did you get her to agree to edit your book?"

"She hasn't agreed to work with me yet. I'm meeting her this morning so we can discuss the possibility of working together."

"I see. Did Reggie set it up for you?"

"Yeah. As it turns out he and Abigail grew up together." Sam looked out the window. "It looks like I've arrived at my destination. I'd better get going. Give me a buzz later."

"Okay, pal. Take care."

Sam got out of the car, walked up to the building's entrance and pressed the buzzer.

"Carey and Collingsworth Agency, may I help you?"

"Sam Best here to see Ms. Abigail Carey. I have an appointment."

There was a long pause.

"Hello? Is anyone there?" Sam asked anxiously.

"I apologize. Did you say Sam Best, as in the former quarterback for the New York Giants?"

"Yes."

"Please come up to the second floor."

The buzzer sounded.

Sam entered and walked down the hallway to the waiting elevator. He had a funny feeling as the elevator doors closed.

When the doors opened, Sam was overwhelmed by a throng of excited women.

Startled by the level of noise, Shana walked out of her office to investigate. "What in the world is going on out here?" Shana elbowed her way through staff and models until she reached Sam.

"Excuse me, ladies, get a hold of yourselves," she said loudly.

The noise immediately died down.

She extended her hand. "Good morning, Mr. Best. I'm Shana Collingsworth. How can I help you?"

He shook her hand. "It's nice to meet you, Ms. Collingsworth. Please call me Sam. I have a ten o'clock appointment with Abigail Carey."

"Please call me Shana. Abby's office is on the fourth floor."

"Oh, I was told to come to the second floor."

"Really? I can assure you that I will get to the bottom of that." Shana shot an accusing look at her staff. "In the meantime, I'll take you upstairs to Abby's office. Please follow me."

"Thank you."

Shana pressed the button for the elevator and she and Sam stepped in. A few moments later they were walking through the book PR floor.

Kelly's mouth dropped as Sam passed her desk. "Is that who I think it is?" she whispered to Candy.

"If you think it's Sam Best, then you're right." She grinned.

Shana led Sam into Abby's office, which was uncharacteristically empty at the moment. "Please have a seat. I'm sure Abby is around here somewhere."

"That's not a problem," Sam said as he sat down.

"Can I get you anything while you're waiting? Coffee, tea or a bottle of water?"

"No, thank you. I'm fine."

"Okay, then I'd better get back downstairs. It was lovely meeting you, Sam."

"Likewise." He smiled.

After Shana left, Sam looked around Abby's office. It was neat and well organized with an extensive collection of books and tastefully displayed awards. He even marveled at how comfortable her guest chairs were. *For someone who is supposed to love putting people in the hot seat, these are cushy chairs.* Just as he swiveled around to face the door, he noticed a woman heading his way. *That can't be her,* he thought in disbelief.

"Abby, if you have a minute I need you to look at this," Leo said.

"Sure." She went over to Leo's desk.

Oh, my God, that's her. Sam stared at the way her dress hugged her curves. *Reggie didn't tell me she was hot. How am I supposed to concentrate on what she says?* He felt his heart skip a beat. *The woman's a brick house.* He took a deep breath, reminding himself that he was engaged.

A smiling Abby walked into the office. "Good morning, Mr. Best. I'm sorry if I kept you waiting." She extended her hand.

Sam stood up to shake her hand. "You didn't keep me waiting. It's a pleasure to meet you, Ms. Carey."

Abby sat down at her desk. "Please call me Abby."

He sat down. "I will, as long as you call me Sam. Mr. Best is my father."

"I hear you caused quite a commotion on the second floor." She chuckled.

"Yes, it would seem so."

"That's probably old hat to you by now."

"You would think so, but you never really get used to it."

"You have a point. Before we start, can I get you anything to drink? Or would you like to wait until the rest arrive?"

Sam looked confused. "The rest of who arrive?"

"The rest of your people," she answered matter-of-factly.

"You mean my entourage?"

"Yes."

"I don't have an entourage, but I do have a driver. I could call him upstairs to join us if you'd like."

"No." She felt a little flush. "I'm sorry. I just assumed."

"There's no need to apologize. A lot of athletes fit that profile. I'm just not one of them."

"That's nice to know. So what about something to drink?"

"Water would be nice, thank you."

She got up and went to the small fridge behind her desk. "Would you like sparkling, mineral or flat?" she said, slightly bent over.

Sam was distracted by her derriere. "Sure."

"Which would you like?" she inquired again.

"Oh, sparking water would be fine."

"Sparkling water it is." Abby grabbed a cold bottle of Pellegrino and handed it to him. "Here you go."

"Thank you." Sam quickly gulped down half the bottle's contents.

"First let me congratulate you on your deal with Tandem and your upcoming wedding," she said as she sat down.

"Thanks."

Abby leaned back in her chair. "So what are you writing about?"

"Oh, I thought Reggie would have filled you in."

"Reggie's not writing the book. You are."

Suddenly the cushy seat didn't feel so comfortable. "Well, it's about my life, football, being in the NFL and the lessons I've learned along the way."

Before Abby could respond, Sam's text tone went off on his cell phone. "I'm sorry. I thought I set the silent mode." Sam's face flushed with embarrassment as he checked the message.

"That's all right. Do you need a minute?"

"No. It's just my fiancée texting me about something for the wedding, that's all."

"Are you sure you don't want to respond to her now? It could be important. I can wait."

"No, that's okay."

"Okay. Reggie told me the manuscript is due by Memorial Day weekend. How much have you written so far?"

"Forty pages," he said somewhat sheepishly.

"You signed the contract with Tandem in August, right?"

Just as he opened his mouth to answer, Sam's text tones went off again. "Excuse me, this will only take a second." Sam put his phone on vibrate. "Yes. I signed the contract in August."

"Then you played an entire season, announcing your retirement in January."

"I don't know what I was thinking. It seemed doable at the time."

"It always does." Abby smiled. "Did you bring what you have so far?"

"Yes." As he took his portfolio out and placed the contents on Abby's desk he felt his phone vibrating. He quickly hit ignore and sent it to voice mail.

Abby quickly leafed through the pages. "How long is the manuscript supposed to be? I mean, did they give you a word or page count?"

"I think the contract says 220 pages." His cell phone vibrated again. "I'm so sorry. Maria knows I have this appointment."

"It's not a problem. Take the call. I can leave if you need privacy."

"Please don't leave. This will only take a minute."

"All right." She nodded. *I doubt it will take only a minute.* She figured that a defensive tackle didn't have a thing on a woman with a wedding to plan. Given the tenacity his future wife had shown in the last ten minutes, she felt impressed that he'd managed to write forty pages.

Sam turned around in the chair and hit the talk button. "Yes, Maria?"

"Why haven't you answered my texts or calls? Where are you?" she demanded.

"I'm in the editor's office. She and I were talking about my manuscript."

"You're in her office now?"

"Don't start, Maria. What's so important?"

"Our planner just informed me that the linen supply may not have the tablecloths in our color. I need to know how you feel about peach."

"I don't feel anything about peach. Is that the reason you called?" he asked, incredulous.

"Yes. This is *our* wedding and I wanted your input."

"I don't know why this is an issue. The wedding is four months away." He stopped himself. "If you're fine with the color change, then I'm fine with it."

"That's not very helpful."

"Why isn't it? I just gave you carte blanche."

"That's just another way of saying you really don't want to make any decisions about the biggest day of our lives. You're more interested in getting me off the phone."

"Maria, the manuscript is due before the wedding and I'm trying to make sure that I make the deadline so I'll be free to focus on the wedding and us."

"Since you put it that way, I'll make the call. Just don't be upset when you don't see the original color we chose that day."

"I won't. I'll talk to you later."

"Okay. I love you."

"I love you, too," he muttered quickly and hung up. He turned around to face Abby. "Again, I beg your pardon for the interruption."

"There's no need to apologize. Is everything okay?"

"Yes. The crisis has been averted," he said jokingly.

Abby laughed and then picked his forty pages up. "Okay, I'm going to give this a read and we can get together sometime tomorrow. Will that work for you?"

"Does this mean you'll work with me?"

"Maybe," she said slyly. "I'll know more once I've read it." Abby opened the appointment scheduler on her computer. "Does the morning or the afternoon work better for you?"

"Neither. I'm on wedding duty all day tomorrow."

"What time is your first appointment?"

"Ten forty-five."

"How about we make it an early breakfast meeting between seven and seven-thirty. Is that too early for you?"

"No."

"Good. I'll be in the office by then, so I can buzz you into the building. Remember to bring your outline, notebook and a list of any facts we might need to research, okay?"

"Okay."

"Don't you want to write this down? The first rule of working with an editor is to take notes."

"Oh yeah. " He searched his jacket, took out his memo pad and pen and jotted her instructions down.

"All right, then, I think we're good," Abby said as she stood up.

"I'm looking forward to your thoughts," Sam said, coming to his feet.

"Good." She walked him to the door. "I can have one of my publicists escort you downstairs just in case there are any stray models lurking about."

"I think I can handle it." He laughed. "I'll see you tomorrow."

They shook hands.

"You have a good day." She grinned.

"Thanks. You, too," he said as he walked away.

Abby watched him walk away. *Cute but engaged. Besides, I learned my lesson with J. J. No more professional athletes. My psyche can't take it.*

"Hey, Abby, are we working the PR for Sam Best's book?" Leo asked.

"No. He doesn't need us to help him sell books. He could sell sand at the beach and people would line up."

"That's true. So can I ask why he was here?"

"Sure, you can ask." Abby smiled, and then went back into her office.

⋘∞⋙

Before Sam could settle in for the ride home, his cell phone rang. He knew who it was without looking.

"Hi, Reggie," he answered pleasantly.

"Hi. How did it go with Abby?"

"What? No how are you?"

"Don't be a wise guy."

Sam laughed. "I think it went pretty well. We have a breakfast meeting tomorrow to go over my forty pages."

"Great."

"You know, I have a bone to pick with you."

"You have a bone to pick with me? What did I do?"

"It's what you didn't do. You didn't tell me how pretty Abby Carey is."

"Pardon me?"

"I think you heard me. I was expecting a librarian with glasses or something. I wasn't prepared."

"To be honest, Sam, it never dawned on me to mention her looks. You're getting married in four months."

"I know, but I'm not dead. You could have warned me."

"There are millions of pretty women in New York City. If I had to warn you every time one was about to cross your path, I'd have to give up my day job."

"You're right. Forget I said anything. Besides, she seems to be a bit of a pill."

"Abby's ways can be hard to swallow."

"Hard to swallow is an understatement. She gave me homework."

"That sounds like my Abby." Reggie laughed.

"What did you get me into, Reggie?"

"Stop your kvetching. It's nothing you can't handle."

"Speaking of handling things, I'm on my way home to see if indeed the latest wedding crisis has been averted."

"I'm not going to ask."

"You're a smart man."

"I'm going to be busy with meetings all the rest of the day. Let me know what happens with Abby tomorrow."

"I will."

"Talk to you later, buddy."

"See you later, Reggie."

Sam stared out of the window, unable to get the image of Abby out of his head. Then he snapped back to reality. *I better pull it together before I get home. This is work and nothing more.* Anxious to get his head on straight he picked up his phone and keyed in numbers.

"Come on, Dad, pick up," he said aloud.

It went to voice mail. He hung up and tried another number.

"Hello?"

"Hey, J.R.," he said.

"Hello, little brother. What's going on?"

J.R. was the oldest of the Best brothers, and named after their father. Everyone called him J.R. Tall and broad shouldered with dark brown hair and piercing blue eyes, he was the spitting image of Don Best. J.R. had played minor league baseball for the farm teams of several major clubs. However, after a little more than a decade, baseball lost its appeal and he became an insurance agent. Within two years he was able to open his own successful agency.

"I'm on my way home to deal with more wedding stuff."

"What else can you do for this wedding? Even the circus stops at three rings." J.R. laughed.

"You are too funny," Sam said facetiously.

"I'm sorry, Sam. I know you're under a lot of pressure these days."

"I take it you've talked to Dad."

"Yes. He told me about the book and all the wedding details."

"By the way, where are Dad and Momma? I tried calling his cell earlier and it went to voice mail."

"They took Daisy out for breakfast in town. I think he left his phone in the kitchen."

"Oh, I bet they're in heaven."

"All three of them are. Daisy loves when Gramps and Grandma come to visit."

"Was Tammy able to make any more room in the closet?"

"Just barely." He laughed. "Momma bought enough outfits for Daisy to change clothes three times a day. I keep telling her that she's seven years old now and she's growing like a weed. But you know Momma."

"She's going to do what she wants."

"Exactly," he agreed.

"Well, I'm nearly home now. Can you tell Dad that I called?"

"Sure."

"Thanks. Give Tammy my love."

"I will."

"I'll talk to you later, big brother."

"You take it easy, Sam."

He hung up. "Bryan?"

"Yes, sir?"

"Do me a favor. Let's swing over to the florist."

"Sure."

Sam pondered what lay ahead. Maria had seemed okay about the linen stuff, but he'd play it safe by bringing her flowers.

Chapter 5

After a brief staff meeting in the conference room, Abby went back to her office. Just as she was about to leave, a caption on the front page of *The Post* caught her eye. *What's this?* She picked the paper up. *The Estranged Wife of J.J. Stokes Raises the Stakes in Their Divorce.* She sighed heavily. *Looks like Beebe is pulling out all the stops to get out of the prenup.* Abby shook her head. *Guess she didn't realize that J.J.'s attorneys made sure the prenup was bulletproof.* Almost feeling sorry for her, Abby tossed the paper onto her desk and walked out.

"I'm taking lunch downstairs if anyone needs me," she announced.

"No problem, Abby," Reed answered.

Abby grabbed a salad from the break room and headed downstairs to Shana's office.

"Hey, Shana, what's up?"

"Hi," Shana answered as she stared at Polaroids on the corkboard.

"Wow, that's a lot of models." Abby leaned against Shana's desk.

Shana shook her head. "I know. I don't know how we're going to narrow it down to twelve girls. They're all so pretty."

"It's going to come down to how they walk and if they're available for the show."

"You're right about that. Cedi will be here tomorrow and then we'll have the final decision."

"I'm excited that he's debuting the first plus-size line at Fashion Week. We've come a long way, baby."

"I hear that. Speaking of excitement, why didn't you tell me that you were meeting Sam Best today?"

"Because I didn't know I was meeting him until dinner with Reggie."

"Oh, was he the reason Reggie invited you to Le Bernadin?"

"Yes. He's one of Reggie's clients. Reggie asked me to edit his book."

"I'm sorry. Did you say *edit*?"

"Yes. And before you say anything, I haven't decided if I'll work with him yet."

"Of course you're working with him. You could have said no last night. Admit it, you're intrigued."

"I guess I am, even though I swore off working with athletes a long time ago."

"He's cute."

"Yes, he is," she said off-handedly.

"Come on, Abby, don't pretend you didn't notice the man was drop-dead gorgeous. I mean, he nearly caused a stampede down here."

"And here I thought that fashion people didn't care about sports."

"They don't have to care about sports to get excited. They can smell a good-looking man with money a mile away."

Abby cracked up.

"So when you say edit his book, are you going to write it, too?"

"No. I'm not a ghostwriter. I'm going to help him flesh his story out. He has to deliver two hundred and twenty pages by the end of May and he's only written forty so far."

"Woo, that's a tall order."

"I know. That's why we're meeting tomorrow morning to get started."

"He doesn't know what he's in for." Shana chuckled. "Football training camp in the dead of summer is going to seem like a walk in the park on a cool autumn day."

"It can't be helped. I don't have a lot of time to play with him. He's got a deadline and he's getting married in four months."

"The red dragon lady rides again."

After making up for the peach linen incident with a dozen roses in the same color, Sam got a reprieve from wedding duty to hang out with his best friend and best man, Bo Clemson.

Sam and Bo had roomed together in college. Sam was the star athlete on campus, and, at five feet, nine inches, with a slight frame, Bo was his studious sidekick. However, what Bo lacked in physical stature he made up for with personality and an impeccable knowledge of sports, which he used to get a job in sports broadcasting at ESPN just before the network exploded into America's mind and vocabulary. Working as a sports analyst made for a comfortable family life in a 2,700-square-foot luxury home on Long Island's north shore. He even had a man cave complete with a big screen plasma television, wet bar and two Lazy Boy recliners.

"Thanks for having me over," Sam said as he got comfortable in a recliner.

"No problem." Bo poured two cold beers at the wet bar. "Here you go." He handed Sam a cold, frosty glass.

"That looks good. Thanks." Sam took big gulps. "Ah, I needed that,"

Bo sat down. "I guess you did. You nearly finished the glass in two gulps."

The two men laughed.

"I'm solo until tomorrow afternoon when Amy gets back with the kids. You want to order a pizza?"

"No, I'm good. You go ahead if you want."

Bo looked down at his little beer belly. "I think I'll pass, too. I can't metabolize pizza and beer like I used to. I can't do a lot of things like I used to." He drank his beer. "Not to mention the fact that the camera adds ten pounds. That's why this is light beer."

"It tastes good to me."

"Good. So how are things? How are the wedding plans coming along?"

"It's all systems go in that department. Maria is in overdrive these days. She's already blown through two wedding planners. We're on our third. I just hope she can go the distance."

"There's something that happens to some women the moment the engagement ring is on their finger. It's like they're on a mission."

"I know. Maria wants everything to be perfect, and no detail is too small to overlook. Seriously, I think she's making Eisenhower's plans for D-Day look like something he scribbled on a bar napkin."

Bo laughed. "How's the guest list?"

"Her father invited fifty more people. Now we're up to four hundred and fifty guests."

"I hate to say it, but what did you expect? Her father is a big shot in Dallas and she grew up in Highland Park. They may not be in New York's social registry,

77

but they're at the top of the one in Dallas. And Maria's the baby, to boot. You've got your hands full."

"Don't I know it?"

"I feel for you, buddy. Have you told your family?"

"No. You know how my family is, strictly low key and down to earth. All of this pomp and circumstance just isn't their cup of tea." He shook his head. "They thought the guest list was too much at two hundred people. How am I going to tell them we're up to four hundred and fifty guests?"

"I know what you're saying, buddy. Still, you should tell them before the wedding. You don't want them to be surprised."

"You're right. I will."

"So let's change the subject. How's the book coming along?"

"It's been slow going, but hopefully that will change by tomorrow if Abby takes me on."

"Who?"

"Abigail Carey. Do you know her?"

"I don't know her personally, but I know she used to be the senior editor for Stillwater Publishing."

"I gave her what I've written so far to review."

"You're feeling nervous about it, huh?"

"Yes. What if she thinks I'm a total idiot who's beyond help?"

"She won't."

"From your lips to God's ears." Sam finished his beer. "I feel like I'm in grade school again waiting for my teacher to hand my paper back to me. Only I never had a hot teacher in elementary school." The minute the word 'hot' escaped his lips, Sam knew he was in trouble.

"Is that right?" Bo grinned.

"Don't look at me like that. All I said was that she's attractive."

"No, you said she was hot."

"Same difference," Sam quipped.

"No, it isn't. Helen Mirren is attractive. Beyoncé is hot. Do you smell what I'm cooking?"

"Yes, but it's a moot point. I'm engaged, remember?"

"Who can forget with Maria calling and texting you every two minutes when you're not in her sight?" Bo said jokingly.

"She hasn't done either this evening."

"That's because you're in the suburbs. She knows I'm married with children. What are you going to get into with me?"

"Not much. No offense."

"None taken," Bo answered quickly. "I like being a boring married man." He grinned. "But what's going to happen when you start working with this hot, I mean attractive, editor?"

"I have to get this manuscript completed. Maria will have to deal with it. End of story."

"Famous last words," Bo said as he raised his glass. "More power to you."

❧

Her day over, Abby kicked back with a glass of Riesling in front of her laptop as she completed her Skype call to her son Justin. Her face lit up when she saw Justin's curly brown hair, light brown eyes and smile on the screen.

"Hey, Mom."

"Hey, gorgeous. You are a sight for sore eyes. How are you?"

"Good. How are you, Mom?"

"I'm fine, but you look a little tired. Are you sure you're all right?"

"Yes. I just got back from lacrosse practice."

Abby shook her head. "You know, I still don't understand this winter lacrosse thing. When I was a kid they only played in the spring and early fall. Now it's practically all year 'round."

"Things are different now, Mom. I'm having fun."

"You say that now, but baseball season will be here before you know it."

"I'll have fun with that, too."

"I'm glad you're having fun, but—" she began.

"Don't worry, Mom, I'm making good grades."

"Good. I know that you're aware of your dad's divorce, but there have been things in the news lately that might bother you."

"Are you talking about *NBA Confidential?*"

"Yes. How did you know?"

"I read it in one of those magazines in the pharmacy a few days back."

"Why didn't you say anything?"

"What was there to say? If Beebe wants to join the cast, I don't think Dad can stop her. Can he?"

"No."

"There you have it." He shrugged.

"That's a very grown-up answer, but are you sure you're okay?"

"I'm fine, Mom. It's not like this is something new with Dad, anyway."

In the year leading up to the divorce, J.J. had made no secret of his and Beebe's separation. Even as Beebe held out hope, he was photographed with a plethora of young women at nightclubs, sporting events, boating and out on the town. The last straw came when his latest paramour showed off her 'friendship' ring from Jason of Beverly Hills, jeweler to Hollywood stars and athletes alike. Beebe filed for divorce the same day.

"I know, but still," she started.

"Seriously, Mom, I'm okay."

"Okay, if you say so." She nodded.

"I do." He leaned in closer to the camera. "Mom, are you still in the office?"

"No, I'm in the apartment." She turned the camera so he could get a full view and then turned it back. "See?"

"Why are you still wearing your hair pulled back at home?"

"Oh, I didn't even realize I still had it pinned." She removed the pins and let her hair fall. "Is that better now?"

"Yes. No offense, Mom, but you look like a hard-nosed school teacher when your hair's pulled back like that."

"Then maybe I'll get a pair of glasses and a ruler to complete the look." She smiled.

Justin laughed. "Seriously, Mom, I'm just glad that you're not still in the office. That's progress."

"Thank you. That's high praise coming from you. I do have a little work to do here but all I'm doing is reading Sam Best's work."

"Did you say Sam Best? As in the one who played for the Giants?" he asked, incredulous.

"Yes. Your Uncle Reggie asked me to help him with the book he's writing."

"In that case do you think you can get an autograph for me before you rip his writing to shreds?"

"What makes you think I'm going to do that?"

"Experience, Mom. I've seen you correct greeting cards."

"I've done nothing of the sort. Stop exaggerating."

"Maybe I am a little, but you *are* tough."

"He's a big boy. I'm sure he can take a little constructive criticism."

"Hey, Mom, they're getting ready to close the cafeteria and I want to get something to eat before I have to get back to the dorms."

"Okay, honey. Same time tomorrow?"

"Okay."

"Love you."

"Aw, Mom," he groaned.

"All right, Justin. Peace out."

"Peace out, Mom." Just before he ended the call he held up a piece of paper that said *Love you too, Mom*.

Though some parents would have relished the peace of not having a teenager in residence, Abby missed the sounds of video games, television wrestling and ESPN. A quiet house meant she would have time to listen to her thoughts and wonder whether she was truly happy as a single woman. However, this evening was a little different. She had Sam Best's words and a glass of wine to help her keep those thoughts at bay, at least for the night.

Abby made herself comfortable in the little reading area she'd set up in her bedroom near the window. As she opened the portfolio, two pieces of paper fell onto the floor.

"What's this?" she said as she picked the papers up. "Two checks for $40,000 each?" Her eyes popped open wide. She imagined they had something to do with the wedding. Tom Webster and Norman Green sounded a little familiar. She couldn't remember where she'd heard the names before. No matter, she'd think about it later. She turned to the first page. "I'd better read and find out if this is indeed Mr. Best's Opus."

Chapter 6

When Sam got back from Bo's, Maria was busy looking at table embellishments sent over from the florist. By the time he showered and got ready for bed, she was busily making notes in her wedding planner.

"Did you have a good time at Bo's?" She looked up.

"Yeah, it was nice. We watched a few games."

"That's nice."

Sam slipped into bed. "Oh, I don't think I mentioned this before, but I have an early meeting with my editor tomorrow."

"What do you mean? How early? You know we have appointments, and you promised."

"Yes, I know, and I'm going to keep my promise. The meeting is at seven-thirty, and I shouldn't be any more than an hour and a half at the most."

"What kind of editor sets a meeting for that early in the morning?"

"The kind of editor that knows I have a tight deadline and need all the help I can get to clear the decks before the wedding."

"Are you sure? This is a female editor. How do I know that she doesn't have designs on you? She could be an undercover sports groupie who wants to steal you away."

Sam laughed. "I doubt it. She was married to J.J. Stokes."

"Oh, wait a minute. Was she his first wife? What's her name?"

"Abigail Carey."

"Yes. I remember now. He cheated on her with his second wife. You know, I think I read somewhere that the second wife is divorcing him for the same reason." She shook her head. "I'm telling you, karma's a bitch."

"True. Now are you a little less worried?"

"Fine. Just be sure you're back here in time."

"I will." He kissed her, then turned off his light and went to sleep.

❧

The next morning Abby finished her routine a little earlier than usual so she could bake for the breakfast meeting and take her mind off her edits. Though very few people could tell from Abby's steely demeanor, editing made her nervous. In truth, she agonized over every red pen mark she made much in the same way the author did over every word he or she wrote. Her slash and bleed approach was really the equivalent of a skilled surgeon's scalpel, and, like a surgeon, she wanted the best possible outcome. "That should do it," she said aloud as she finished putting the breakfast treats on a platter.

The phone rang.

She didn't bother looking at the caller ID, as she was pretty sure she knew who it was. She took off the apron that had protected her black DKNYC fitted sheath dress from flour. "Hello, J.J."

"Hello. I won't ask you how you knew it was me. I know you have caller ID."

"I didn't have to check the caller ID. You are the only one who would call me at this hour."

"It's nice to know I still stand out," he said smugly.

Abby rolled her eyes. "Get to the point of this call, J.J. I know you have one."

"I wanted to know if Choate is going to have more than one parents' weekend this semester."

J.J. had grown up with a distant father who didn't know how to express his love for his children. He was there to provide for J.J. and his older brother but he was stingy with his love and praise. The pattern continued with J.J. and Justin. Though there was no doubt that J.J. loved his son, he didn't really know how to spend time with him. At first Abby blamed it on his NBA schedule, but once his career was over, he still wasn't there for PTA meetings, band concerts and even school sports events. He would try to make up for it by buying Justin things. It began with the latest toy and progressed to video game systems, video games and high tech televisions. While Abby was bothered by the idea that J.J. seemed comfortable buying his son's affection, she was really worried about the day when Justin became comfortable with it, too.

Abby immediately started to fume. "Oh, you'd better be kidding me. You are not trying to get out of this parents' weekend. You've had plenty of notice to get your schedule together."

"Well, Dazz…" he started.

"It figures that he would have something to do with this."

"You know he isn't all bad. If he didn't set up my appearances we wouldn't be able to keep Justin in that fancy private school."

"That's a lot of baloney and you know it. You have plenty of money. This is about your ego and having people fawn all over you. Well, I have news for you. When you have children it isn't about you anymore. You missed the last event for parents at the school. You'd better make this one, or so help me God I'll—" she started.

"What are you going to do?"

"I'll return Beebe's attorney's call. I've been blowing him off for weeks. Maybe next time I'll make myself available."

"I can't believe you'd resort to blackmail."

"I don't want you to disappoint your son again. So yes, I have no problem blackmailing you."

"Fine," he huffed. "I'll tell Dazz to reschedule."

"Good." She thought for a moment. "Oh, there is something I want to ask you."

"First you blackmail me and now you need something from me?"

"Yes. Besides, it's just a question."

"Shoot."

"Do the names Tom Webster and Norman Green sound familiar to you?"

"Yeah, if you're talking about the two football Hall of Famers. Why?"

"No reason. I heard someone mention their names the other day and I couldn't remember who they were at the time."

"Now am I off the hook?"

"You're off the hook for the question, not parents' weekend."

"Fine. I'd better call Dazz now."

"Tell Dazz I said hello," she said facetiously. "Talk to you later, J.J."

When it comes to that man some things never change, Abby thought as she shook her head. She couldn't help wondering about the two large checks. She knew both Webster and Green had charitable organizations, but the checks were made out to them, not the organization. Sam Best was more intriguing that she'd thought he'd be.

Abby went downstairs and set up breakfast in the conference room for the session with Sam. Then she put the balance of the breakfast treats in the break room and made two pots of coffee.

The intercom buzzed.

"Oh, is it seven-thirty already?" She looked at the clock. "It's only seven-fifteen. He's early." She smiled.

Abby went to the intercom. "Yes?"

"Hi, Abby, it's Sam."

"Come on up, Sam." She pressed the buzzer.

Abby quickly pulled out her compact and checked her makeup and hair. *What am I doing? This is business.* She put her compact back.

Abby waited for Sam by the elevator door. A few moments later the doors opened and Sam stepped out.

"Good morning."

"Good morning, Abby. I know I'm a little early."

"That's not a problem. I rather like that you're early. It tells me that you're serious and anxious to get to work."

He smiled, and then took a whiff. "What's that I smell?"

"Oh, it's nothing really, just some muffins and things I made for the meeting."

"You made them?"

"Yes."

"You really didn't have to go to all that trouble."

"It was no trouble. Let's just say that you have your game day rituals and I have mine." She smiled. "So if you'll follow me…" She turned to lead him to the conference room.

Sam's eyes widened when he entered the conference room. There a table was set for breakfast with coffee and juice.

"I did say this was a breakfast meeting."

"Wow." He was speechless.

"Have a seat." She motioned to a chair. "Please feel free to help yourself." She pointed to the tray set in the middle of the table.

"This is better than the cereal I usually eat."

"And here I thought Wheaties was the breakfast of champions." She smiled.

"I won't tell if you don't."

Abby laughed. "You've got yourself a deal." She picked up the coffee carafe. "Would you like some coffee?"

"Yes, thank you."

Sam watched as she poured. He bit into one of the two muffins he had on his plate. *Smart, gorgeous and can cook. This could be trouble for you, old boy.*

Abby couldn't help chuckling.

"I'm sorry if I'm making a pig of myself. This is so good."

"Thanks." Abby took one of the small banana nut muffins.

"Is that all you're having?"

"I'm fine with this. So please enjoy."

"It's been ages since I had muffins like these."

"Thank you, but you've probably had better at a hotel."

"No hotel could match these," he said as he held up the muffin.

"Don't you live with your fiancée?" she asked, puzzled.

"Yes, but Maria's better at making reservations."

"I see. I hate to break this up, but do you have your assignment?"

Sam stopped and handed her his memo pad. "Here you go."

Sam watched in suspense as Abby read his work.

"Please continue eating. I'm just reading for now." Abby flipped a page over.

"Okay," he said hesitantly and continued to eat.

"Is your fiancée from Texas, too?" Abby asked without looking up.

"Yes. She grew up in Highland Park just outside of Dallas. Have you ever heard of it?"

"As a matter of fact, I have. Wasn't there a big murder case there some years back?"

"Yes. It was quite a scandal. Before that I think the worst thing that ever happened was someone wearing white after Labor Day."

Good sense of humor. That's promising, Abby thought, laughing. "So your fiancée comes from money."

"She comes from a lot of money. Maria is the youngest of three and she grew up with equestrian lessons, housekeepers, cooks and chauffeurs."

"That sounds nice. What about you?"

"I grew up on a small farm about 150 miles outside of Dallas. Both of my parents worked. My father was a physical education teacher and my mother worked part time in the town library but she made breakfast for my brothers and me every morning." He sipped his coffee.

Abby surveyed the table. "If anything, I'd say it's a continental breakfast."

Sam let her statement pass unanswered. "What about you? You don't strike me as someone who grew up in a small town."

"No." She laughed. "I'm a native New Yorker. I grew up in Baldwin, which is about six or seven train stops from Penn Station on the Long Island Railroad."

"Oh, okay. Now I see. You grew up with continental breakfasts."

"I had three brothers and now I'm the mother of a teenage boy. Though I love to cook, a quick continental breakfast gets the job done in the least amount of time."

"I bet."

"So you're the youngest, right?"

"Yes."

"Did your brothers play sports?"

"Yes. My oldest brother J.R. played baseball in high school and college and spent some time in the minor leagues. Zeke played basketball in high school and college."

"That must have made your father happy."

"It did but I think he wanted all three to us to play football like him. He was All American in high school and went to college on a football scholarship." He shook his head.

"What position did he play?"

"Quarterback," he answered. "He was on track to be drafted by the NFL."

"What happened?"

"Even though his scholarship gave him a full ride, he went back to my grandparents' farm to work during the breaks." He took a deep breath. "There was an accident. He fell off a tractor and it ran over his arm."

"Oh my." Abby winced.

"The doctors managed to patch him up, but his throwing arm was never the same."

"That must have been hard for him."

"It was, but he finished college, married my mother and became a physical education teacher. He's never really far from the field."

"How old were you when he first put a football in your hand?"

"I can't honestly say that I remember. It seems like I've always had a football in my hands. But I think I started pee wee football when I was five years old."

"Five years old?" Abby said, surprised. "That's kind of young even for the pee wee league."

"I know. My father got a special waiver so I could play."

"He saw something special in you."

"I guess so. It seems like all my childhood memories are pigskin-colored. My father spent hours with me in the backyard practicing throws, teaching me how to stay in the pocket and how to throw when there's no protection."

"Would you say great football players are born or made?" She sipped her coffee.

"I think it's a little bit of both. My father didn't force me to pick up a football. I naturally migrated to it and he just built on that."

"Okay." She nodded. "Now you have what you need to redo your outline."

"What?"

"I want you to add what we just talked about into your outline."

"I didn't do an outline."

"That explains a lot," she said matter-of-factly.

"I thought it would be better to free write it."

"If you were doing fiction, I'd say that was fine. However, this is an autobiography. You need an outline to anchor your story."

"Okay."

Abby reached over and grabbed his portfolio that was on the chair next to her. "I read your first draft last night." She picked a red pen up. "Overall, your grammar and structure were solid. However, you're all over the place. It might make sense to you, but, as a reader, I don't live in your head, so I don't have any idea where you're going. An outline will help you establish a natural progression for your story."

"You're saying it wasn't good." He sounded dejected.

"I'm not saying that per se. What I am saying is that you don't seem connected to your own story. There are points where you seem like a biographer writing about someone else."

"Ouch," he said half jokingly.

"I'm sorry to be so blunt, but given your success, you strike me as someone who believes in pursuing excellence both on the field and off. I'm going to help you create a book that people will read for what you put into it, not just because your name is on the cover." She opened the folder.

Sam's eyes bulged when he saw how marked up the first page was.

"I made notes in the margins to help you and I typed out some guidelines for you."

Sam took the folder. "Whoa." He was in shock.

"What can I say? Red is my signature color."

He laughed. "Can I tell you something?"

"Sure."

"With the exception of all the red ink, this has been less painful than I thought it would be."

"Did you think I was going to draw actual blood?"

"Well, yes."

Abby laughed. "It's nice to know my reputation as the dragon lady is still intact."

"I was expecting you to be a real b—" He stopped short.

"Ah, don't say it yet. I'm not finished. You might change your mind." She reached for her Blackberry. "It's the second week of February, so it's time to get you on the stick." She checked her calendar. "Three days from now is Saturday. Can you have the changes plus another chapter by Saturday?"

"Do I have a choice?"

"Not if you want to make your deadline. But if it's too much, I know a lot of really terrific ghostwriters who could bang this out in no time. All I have to do is pick up the phone. It's up to you."

"No. I want to write my story."

"Okay. Oh, wait, Saturday is usually the day couples meet with vendors. We could meet on Monday."

"No. Like you said, if I'm going to make my dead-line, I have to get cracking. I'm sure Maria and Jess can handle things without me."

"All right then, how about 10 a.m.?"

"Done," he answered emphatically.

Abby entered it into her Blackberry. "Okay."

Sam reached across the table and put his hand over Abby's. "Thank you for taking me on."

Abby was unnerved by the surge that rushed through her body. "You're welcome," she said as she quickly moved her hand away. She looked at the table. "It looks like we did a pretty good job of making the food disappear."

"Who are you kidding? I made it disappear." He chuckled.

"Glad you enjoyed it. I've got to get to my work and you need to get back to your fiancée."

"Yes."

"Oh, before I forget." She took out an envelope and handed it to him. "This fell out of your portfolio."

Sam looked in the envelope. "Thank you."

"No problem." Abby stood up.

Sam picked up his portfolio and stood up.

As Abby walked him to the elevator, Sam noticed the offices were still empty.

"What time does your staff get in?" He looked around.

"They usually start arriving at eight-thirty or so."

Sam smiled and nodded.

At the elevator, Abby pressed the call button. "Are we clear on your directive?"

Sam couldn't help chuckling.

"What's so funny?"

"I don't know." He shrugged. "I guess the word *directive* tickled my funny bone. It sounds so proper and official."

"I'm glad it tickles you, but make sure it's done when you get here. We've got a lot to do in a very short period of time."

The elevator doors opened.

"Okay, Sam, until Saturday." She extended her hand.

"I think we're past handshakes," he said as he kissed her on the cheek. "See you Saturday." He stepped onto the elevator.

Abby waved as the doors closed.

What was that about? Am I losing my edge? She stopped for a minute. *We'll see how his funny bone feels on Saturday.*

⤜∾

As his driver held the door, Sam climbed into the back of his Mercedes.

"Where to, Sam?" Bryan asked as he got in and started the car.

He looked at his watch. "Let's head back to the apartment and pick Maria up."

Sam opened his portfolio and stared at all the red ink. *My God, do I even know how to write? Look at this.* He skimmed through the whole thing. *There is not one page left untouched. I'm really going to have to push it if I want my re-writes to pass her test.* He let out a deep breath then suddenly remembered that she'd seen the checks but had not asked about them. Almost everyone else he knew would have. *Wow, she's got some kind of focus if she didn't blink in the presence of two $40,000 checks.* He didn't feel comfortable being in the middle of two women with laser-like focus. He wondered if it was too early for a drink.

Chapter 7

Later on that same day, Abby reviewed the spring book tour schedule in her office. Missing from the list was Book Hampton. She searched through the pages carefully.

"Leo?" she called.

He appeared in her door. "Yes, Abby?"

"Who's handling Cecilia Peterson's book tour?"

"Candy," he answered.

"Thank you. Would you have her come to my office, please?"

"Sure." He turned around. "Candy?"

"Yes?"

"Abby needs to see you." He went back to his desk as Candy slowly got up and went to Abby's door.

"Yes, Abby? You wanted to see me?"

"Yes. I don't see Book Hampton on the list for Cecilia's spring book tour. She is a Long Islander and they are supposed to be very friendly to local authors."

"I called them and they told me that I needed to send an email, which I did."

"Did they respond?"

"Yes. They told me that since Cecilia was a neighbor and not a resident of the Hamptons that they couldn't have her signing there."

"So they blew you off."

"Yes, I guess they did."

"Here's what you're going to do. You're going to call the store and speak to the manager. Tell her that Cecilia is a bestselling author with HC Publishing and that we know for a fact that they've already scheduled several HC authors who aren't residents of the Hamptons. Then let me know what happens."

"I'll get right on it."

"Good." Abby went back to leafing through the schedule. "Hey, stranger, I haven't seen you in a couple of days."

"Oh, that's as creepy as always." Shana answered as she walked in and sat down. "So how's it going?"

"It's getting crazier by the minute as Fashion Week closes in on us. Even with the extra interns it's still hectic. But I came up here to see how your meeting went with Sam Best."

"I'd say pretty well. We had our first editing session this morning."

"So that's why everyone has been coming up here this morning. You baked."

"It was a breakfast meeting."

"True, but you could have just as easily ordered food instead of making everything yourself."

"Okay, Shana, the horse is already dead. We don't need to beat it into suede."

"Fine. When's his redo due?"

"Am I that predictable?"

"Yes."

"We're meeting again on Saturday."

"You're meeting on a Saturday? That sounds like more like a date than an editing session."

"Please, I'm trying to work around his wedding duties." Abby chuckled.

"His wedding duties?"

"Yes. His fiancée either called or texted him nearly a dozen times in the short time we met yesterday. Thank God she didn't do it this morning, otherwise he'd still be sitting here."

"She sounds like one of those Bridezillas."

"She's probably worse because she's got an unlimited budget."

"Must be nice." Shana sighed.

"Now that depends on who you ask."

"You've got a point."

Candy knocked on the door. "Excuse me, Abby?"

"What happened with Book Hampton?"

"It turns out that they had a couple of dates available. I called Cecilia and we just confirmed a date in April."

"Nice work, Candy."

"Thanks." She grinned as she walked away.

"I guess that made her day," Abby said.

"No, that made her year. She's been dying to please you."

"I'm not that hard on her."

"I'm sorry, you do realize that we've met, right?" Shana said jokingly.

"So I'm a little tough on her. She has to build a thick skin for this business."

"Yes, but you might consider shedding a layer or two. You don't always have to be so hard." Shana got up. "I'd better head back to the trenches with the troops. I'll see you later."

"Okay."

Abby watched as Shana left, wondering if Shana was right. She looked over at Sam's folder. *No. If I want things to get done I've got to be tough on everyone.*

❧

Surrounded by floral arrangements in every size and shape, Sam's head spun. He and Maria were in the presence of Preston, an event designer whose list of clients read like a who's who in Hollywood, Beverly Hills, and the social registries of New York, Rhode Island and Connecticut.

It was obvious that Maria was in her glory. She oohed and aahed over everything she saw while Sam was conspicuously distracted even when the man himself walked into the room. He was a lean, elegant man with gorgeous dark skin and a bright smile.

"Hello and welcome to my design studio," Preston said as he kissed Maria's hand.

"Thank you." She giggled and then turned to Sam. "This is my fiancé, Sam Best."

"It's a pleasure to meet you, Mr. Best." He extended his hand.

Sam was still distracted.

Maria pinched him. "Ow." He winced.

"Preston is speaking to you."

"Oh, I'm sorry." He shook his hand. "I apologize. I'm a little preoccupied. I had a meeting with my editor this morning and I've got a lot of work to do."

"No need to apologize. I've written a few books, too. I know where you're coming from."

"Well, I'm sure he's going to put it out of his mind and concentrate on all the wonderful ideas you have for us."

Just then a young woman came out and tapped Preston on the shoulder.

"If you'll excuse me for a moment I have to take care of something. I'll only be a couple of minutes."

"No problem." Maria smiled.

"Take your time," Sam added.

He followed his assistant to the office.

"What do you mean, take your time?" Maria was a little hot.

"It's obvious that it's something important; otherwise he wouldn't have excused himself."

"This is important, too. In case you've forgotten, this is our wedding."

"I haven't forgotten." He tried to defuse her anger with a kiss.

Unmoved, Maria turned her face and avoided his kiss. "You could have fooled me. I thought that you met with the editor early so your day would be clear."

"That's right."

"It looks to me like you might as well still be in her office since that's where your head is."

"I'm just a little overwhelmed, Maria," he said, frustrated.

"I don't know why you signed that contract in the first place. It's not like you need the darn money for the wedding. Daddy said—" she began.

He quickly interrupted her. "That's neither here nor there now. I just have to get the book done."

"Then do me a favor and make like Scarlett O'Hara and think about it tomorrow."

Preston returned and Sam did his best to be interested in vase heights and goblets, but his mind kept drifting back to his book and, more importantly, his editor. Abby was that famous enigma wrapped in a mystery, and he was more than a little intrigued.

By the time he and Maria got back, she was positively giddy with excitement.

"I'm telling you, that man is a genius." Maria grinned as she placed the sample arrangement he'd made them on the dining room table.

"Yes, he was good."

"Is that all you can say? He was good? Look at this."

"Okay, he was fantastic." Sam sat down.

"Are you still obsessing about your book?" she asked with her hands on her hips.

"I can't help it. There's a lot to think about."

"There's a lot to think about for this wedding, too." Her cell phone rang. She looked at the display. "It's my mother. I emailed her the pictures I took with my phone." She hit the talk button. "Hello, Momma? Aren't the flowers spectacular?" She walked away.

Sam got up and headed for his office.

He sighed as he sat down and picked up his manuscript. "Red everywhere." He leafed through the pages again. Panicked, he picked up the phone.

"Hello? Abigail Carey speaking."

"Hello, Abby. It's Sam."

"Hi, Sam."

"I hope I'm not disturbing you."

"No. What's up?"

"I was just sitting here going over your notes and I wondered if you'd clarify something for me."

"Sure."

"Do I have any business writing in the first place?"

"Yes."

"It doesn't feel like it."

"Have you finished your wedding errands for the day?"

"Yes."

"If you'd like I could come by and go over a few things with you."

"That would be great." He sounded relieved. "Do you know where I live?"

"Yes. You live in The Trump World Tower."

"How did you know?"

"You're kidding me, right? You're a celebrity and you live in one of 'The Donald's' properties."

"I see your point. I'm in apartment 59-B."

"Okay. I'll see you in a little while."

"Thanks." He hung up.

Maria walked in. "Who was that?"

"It was my editor, Abby. I asked her to come by. Is that all right with you?"

"If it will get your head out of the ground, I'm all for it. My mother gave me a few suggestions for Preston. I'm going to call him. I'll be in the bedroom. Let me know when she gets here. I'd like to meet her."

"Okay."

She walked out.

Though Maria wasn't the typical jealous type, she was keenly aware of a beautiful woman's presence around her fiancé and tended to stay in the vicinity to keep an eye on things. Sam could only hope she'd stay calm when she met Abby. He took out a piece of paper and quickly dashed off an outline to make it look like he'd done some of his assignment.

❧

Coat on and ready to go, Abby stopped by Shana's office. "I'm heading out for a little while."

Shana looked up. "Is everything all right?"

"Everything's fine." She smiled. "I'm just heading over to Trump World Tower to see Sam. He's having an attack of red anxiety."

"An attack of red anxiety," Shana repeated, perplexed.

"It's the natural aversion writers have to editors when they are faced with corrections or notes."

"So basically they get freaked out."

"Exactly. I know how he feels. The same thing used to happen to me when my parents would mark my papers."

"I still can't believe your parents graded your homework."

"They believed that as teaching professionals they had to make sure their children were held to the same standards as their students. I will admit it was like having two Zorros in the house." She made the mark of Zorro in the air.

Shana laughed. "Wait a second. I didn't know that you made editorial house calls. This sounds like Sam is getting special treatment."

"It is special treatment. I'm not an editor anymore. I'm doing Reggie a favor."

"Going over to his place to hold his hand sounds like you're going above and beyond the call of duty."

"It's not a big deal. I left Leo in charge upstairs."

"Okay. I'm sure he'll hold the fort."

"I'll see you later." Abby walked out.

⁂

Overlooking the United Nations, The Trump World Tower stood majestically over the skyline of Manhattan and the East River. Once Abby's car dropped her off, she looked up at the sumptuous building before entering the lobby.

After the bellman announced her, she took the elevator to the fifty-ninth floor.

When she rang the bell, Sam opened the door. "Hi. Come on in, Abby." He motioned.

She looked around the apartment with its oversized floor-to-ceiling windows and views of the river and city.

"You have a beautiful place here."

"Thanks. Can I take your coat?"

"Yes, thank you." Abby took it off and handed it to him. "I half expected a maid to answer the door."

"The maid is off today, you have to settle for me," he said as he hung up her coat in the hall closet.

Abby smiled. "Oh, my goodness. Is that the Empire State Building and Chrysler Building I see?"

"Yes."

"It's very nice."

"Hello." Maria entered the room with her hand extended. "I'm Sam's fiancée, Maria Carrangelo."

The two women shook hands.

"It's nice to meet you, Maria. I'm Abigail Carey."

"So you're the woman who is going to whip Sam's book into shape."

"Something like that." Abby grinned.

"I'll let you get to it then. I have some phone calls to make in the bedroom. It was a pleasure to meet you."

"Likewise," Abby said.

Maria walked back to the bedroom.

"She's very beautiful, Sam. You're a lucky man."

"So they tell me. Would you like a tour of the place?"

"I'm tempted, but I think we should get to work."

"Okay. Please follow me." He led her to the office. Abby took a seat.

"So what's troubling you, Sam?" She crossed her legs.

Sam tried not to notice her shapely legs as he picked the manuscript up.

"You don't have to show me. I know what I wrote. Besides, I get the sense this isn't about a dangling participle or run-on sentences, is it?"

"Every time I sit down to write, I worry about what the reviewers are going to say and how people are going to receive it."

"That's your first mistake," she said bluntly. "Book reviewers and readers don't want you to write for them. They want to open a book and discover the man behind the blue jersey in his words."

"I don't know."

"Is this a little too much self-awareness for you?"

"I know it sounds stupid coming from someone who has his face on cereal boxes and sports drink ads, but—"

"You're uncomfortable turning inward."

"Yes."

"Where's your outline?"

"It's right here." He reluctantly put it in front of her.

He majored in English, right? she thought as she glanced over it. "You only have two things listed here."

"I know." He looked down, embarrassed.

Abby took a pen out of her purse. "Divide it into three main categories: your early years, college and the NFL. Then all you have to do is add the subcategories," she said as she finished writing. "Okay?"

"Okay."

"You're making this harder than you need to. I think you've gotten too close to it. You need to step back a bit."

"Don't I need to be close to re-examine my life?"

"No."

Sam looked confused.

"Have you ever pressed your face against a mirror?"

"Sure. Who hasn't?"

"What do you see when you open your eyes?"

"I see myself."

"But you have to step back to get a clear view of your reflection, right?"

"I never thought about it like that before."

"No one really does. What else is troubling you?"

"I know you told me to start at the beginning, but I haven't really figured out how to do that."

"You're a Nike spokesperson. Just do it. We'll figure it out as we get further along in this process. Trust me. You'll have a finished book on time."

Excited by the confidence in her voice, Sam pulled his chair closer to hers and put his hand on her knee. "Thanks."

An unexpected tingle rushed through Abby's body and she moved her leg. "You're welcome. Okay. I'd better get going." She quickly stood up.

"Do you have to leave so soon?" He stood up.

"Yes. I really should be getting back to my office. I want to give you a chance to write before our next meeting on Saturday."

"Okay. I'll get your coat."

Sam and Abby walked out into the living room and he retrieved her coat.

"Here you go."

"Thanks." Just as Abby tried to take it he stopped her.

"Allow me," Sam said as he slowly helped her into her coat.

"Okay then. I'll see you soon." Abby hurriedly opened the door and left.

The sound of the door closing brought Maria out of the bedroom.

"Did Abby leave?"

"Yes. She had to get back to her office."

"Oh. Do you feel better now?"

"Yes. You know, I was a little surprised that you didn't stick your head in the office."

"Why?"

"I know how you usually get when there are women around."

"I didn't have anything to worry about. Abigail is a pretty woman, but—"

"But what?" he asked.

"She's a little thicker, that's all."

"What do you mean, *thicker*?" Sam took offense.

"All I meant is that she's voluptuous." She folded her hands. "Why are you getting so worked up over a simple adjective?"

"I'm not getting worked up. I just wanted to know what you meant."

Her cell phone rang. "It's my mother. She called Preston." She picked up. "Hi, Momma. What did he say?" she asked as she walked to the kitchen.

I never thought I'd see the day when I'd say this, but I owe Kitty one, he thought.

Though she was still flustered by Sam, Abby threw herself back into work when she got back to her office. *I can't think about this.* She logged back onto her computer.

"Where was the fire?" Shana asked as she entered Abby's office.

"What makes you think there's a fire?"

"You practically flew right by me downstairs."

"Oh, I'm sorry. I just have a lot on my mind."

"I guess you heard."

"Heard about what?"

"Beebe was on *The View* today."

"Oh, good grief." Abby rolled her eyes. "Don't tell me. I've heard it all before."

"I won't. Are you okay? You look a little pale."

"I'm fine." Abby picked up the phone. "But I think I'm going to reconfirm my appointment with the headmaster at Choate on the fourteenth. With all of this stuff going on, I want to hear what he and Justin's teachers have to say."

"Good idea." She looked at her watch. "I'll let you make your call in peace. I'll see you later."

"Okay."

Her phone call over, Abby got up and went to the window. *Why in the world did Sam touch my leg like that with his fiancée in the next room?* She scratched her head. *That's what I get for making an exception.* When Abby closed her eyes she relived the sensation. *I have to stop this. It's bad enough that Justin has one parent who's ruled by impulse,* she thought as she went back to her desk.

Later on that night with the workday behind her, a restless Abby attempted to settle in with a book but was unable to relax. She flipped on the television and channel surfed until she landed on the NFL Network.

She was about to change the channel when she suddenly stopped and turned the volume up.

It was a rebroadcast of the National Football Players Association Board of Former Players' press conference about former players' health care. As the camera panned through the audience, it stopped to note Norm Green and Tom Webster, both of whom were in wheelchairs.

"Oh, my God." She reached over to get her laptop to Google their names.

Abby's eyes widened as she came up with thousands of topics and articles about them. She spent the next couple of hours reading about former players who could barely afford to keep up with their living expenses, including Norm Green and Tom Webster, who were at the forefront of the battle to increase former players' pensions so they could live their lives with dignity.

She was stunned to hear that The NFL Players' Association got an estimated $80 million annually from their third-party agreements, but retired players only got $10,000 a year or less. Then she realized what the checks she'd seen meant: Sam Best must be helping retired players.

Abby did a search for Sam Best and charities and found that he publicly supported a lot of charities, but there was nothing about helping indigent players. She nodded to herself, impressed. Here was a guy who put his money where his mouth was and didn't shout it from the mountain, unlike most celebrities.

Abby got up and went to her office. When she got to her desk she picked up Sam's folder and opened it to the writing exercises she'd planned to give him and ripped up the pages. He didn't deserve to wade through the exercises. He needed something outside of the box. She tapped her desk. "I'll sleep on it. Something will come to me by morning. It better come to me by then or we're both screwed."

Chapter 8

Early Friday evening Abby watched her staff as they packed up for the weekend.

Her cell phone rang.

"Abby Carey," she said.

"Hi, Abby. It's Karen Miller."

Karen Miller was the host of *Authors on Authors*, a popular primetime East Coast radio program that featured authors talking about their work and the work of the authors that inspired them. Since the show was one of the few remaining independent programs, the list to be a guest on the show was quite long.

"Hi, Karen. How are you?"

"I'm a little confused at the moment. I thought Pasqual Roman was going to do tonight's show."

"He is."

"Well the show's about to start and he hasn't called in yet."

"How long have we got until you go on the air?"

"About four minutes."

"Don't worry I'll handle it." Abby quickly hung up and called Pasqual.

"Hello?"

"Pasqual?"

"Oh, hello, Abby," he said jovially.

"Hi. Do you know that you're supposed to be on the radio with *Authors on Authors* in three minutes?"

"No. I thought the interview was at eight."

"It's at eight Eastern Standard Time."

"Oh, my goodness, I didn't realize that. I'll call in right now."

"Thank you. Have a good show."

Once she hung up, Abby took a deep breath and called Karen.

"Hi, Karen. He should be on the line any minute."

"My producer just told me he's on the line. Thanks."

"No problem." Abby got up and walked out of her office. "Who's working with Pasqual?"

Candy raised her hand. "I am."

"Can you tell me why he thought the *Authors on Authors* interview was at five Pacific Time?"

"No. I made sure I noted the time zone in his confirmation email."

Everyone in the office got quiet. A noted literary author and poet, Pasqual Roman was seventy-three years old and, though he had access to email, he rarely used it, making it necessary to call him for all his appearances.

"We're talking about Pasqual. You're his publicist. You should know he hates email." Abby scratched her head. "This has been on the calendar for months. You could have mailed him a confirmation. He will open actual mail."

"I'm sorry, Abby. I'll fix it right now."

"Forget about it. I already handled it. He's on the radio now."

"I'll be sure to call and apologize to him and Karen."

"Good, and make sure you double-check next time. Okay, ladies and gentlemen, I'm heading downstairs. Enjoy your weekend."

"Thanks, Abby. You, too," Kelly said as she collected her things.

"Thanks." Abby disappeared into the hallway.

Candy was frozen.

"What's wrong with you?" Leo asked.

"That was it? Just double-check it next time? I thought for sure she was going to tear me a new one."

"Candy, have you ever heard the saying 'Don't look a gift horse in the mouth'?" Reed asked.

"Yes."

"Then do yourself a favor. Pack up your stuff and take your old one out of here before she changes her mind," Leo laughed.

A few moments later, Abby was dodging the obstacle course of clothing racks, publicists and interns to get to Shana's office.

"Knock, knock," Abby said as she entered her office. "I see we're in full swing down here. I came to see if you need any help."

"At the moment I think we're good."

"Terrific." She sat down. "Have you heard from Raymond?"

Security expert Raymond Hanson and Shana had met three years earlier. African-American with a creamy complexion, broad shoulders and tall physique made the usually stalwart Shana weak in the knees. Though their relationship was complicated by the demands of their respective careers, they did make the effort to see each other as regularly as possible. Luckily, many of Raymond's clients were regular attendees at New York and London Fashion Week, which gave Shana something to look forward to.

"Yes. He'll be here by next Sunday."

"Great."

"I'm telling you I can't wait to see my tall drink of water. Lord knows, I'm thirsty."

Abby laughed. "Oh, don't forget I'm working with Sam tomorrow."

"How could I forget? You haven't been with a man on a Saturday in some time."

"Very funny," she said drolly. "We're working, remember?"

"A girl can dream, can't she?" Shana joked.

"You're a hopeless romantic."

"Knowing that Raymond will be here I'd say that I am a hopeful romantic. And I believe there's still hope for you."

"Okay." Abby got up. "I'll let you keep hope alive."

⟡

The floor of Sam's office looked more like the Stock Exchange at the end of the day. There was crumpled paper everywhere and the usually sharp-looking Sam had begun to resemble the paper.

Maria walked in. "Look at this mess."

"I'll clean it up later. I'm still working on the rewrites, and I haven't even begun the additional chapter."

"Why aren't you using the computer?"

"I'm still trying to figure out what I'm going to write. Once I have that done, then I will use the computer."

"I still don't know why you can't come tomorrow. We have a lot to do for the wedding. Momma asked me if I wanted her to fly up and I told her no because I thought you'd be with me."

"I'm sorry, Maria, but it seems like we have a lot to do for the wedding every single day. So what's the problem if I miss one day? We are talking about place settings, for goodness sake. I know you and Jessica can handle place settings without me."

"That's not the point," she huffed.

"Maria, I know you're not happy about this, but I signed a contract and I have to live up to my end of the deal."

"If this is about the money, I told you that my father would be happy to foot the bill for the wedding."

Her proclivity towards bringing up her parents' money was an issue for Sam. Like his father, he was a self-made and self-reliant man. The idea of taking money from her father, even though it was traditional for the bride's family to pay for the wedding, didn't fly.

"And I told you that I've always paid my own bills, and that includes this wedding."

"Fine," she sighed. "It's getting late. Are you coming to bed?"

"I'll be there in a little while."

"Okay." She left the office.

After a few minutes, Sam picked up the phone.

"Hello?"

"Hi, Reggie. I hope I didn't wake you."

"No. I was up going over some reports. What's up?"

"I'm sitting here at my desk trying to work on the rewrites Abby gave me."

"And you're feeling a little stuck?"

"A little stuck isn't the way I'd describe it."

"I'm not going to ask you if Abby gave you notes. I know she did. But the notes aren't helping you?"

"It's not the notes. I just can't seem to get it to click."

"It sounds like you have an old fashioned case of writer's block."

"If this is writer's block, I can see why Hemingway killed himself."

"Don't even kid about that. Hemingway killed himself because he was depressed."

"Okay. It's still an awful feeling."

"Maybe what you need to do is take a break for a while and come back to it later."

"I've taken enough breaks. I'm meeting with Abby tomorrow and I'm supposed to have something to show her. I have a lot riding on this book."

"I know. All I can say is do your best. Who knows? Maybe something will come to you."

"I hope so." He looked at the clock. "Listen, it's getting late and I'd hate to keep one of us from getting some sleep."

"Okay, but call me if you need anything."

"I will. Good night, Reggie."

"Good night."

As Sam was about to disconnect, he saw another call come in. It was his mother.

"Momma, is everything all right?" he asked anxiously

"Everything is fine, don't worry."

"Good." He breathed a sigh of relief. "How are you?"

"I'm well, son. I just got a message from Kitty Carrangelo."

Sam's stomach filled with lead. "Okay."

"She told me that there's going to be four hundred and fifty guests. She wanted to know if your father and I had anyone else we wanted to add to the guest list."

"Yes. Big Bill invited some business colleagues."

"It sounds like he's attempting to invite the whole Park Cities population."

"He is connected, Momma."

"I know, but this is ridiculous. It must take me two weeks to drive past that number of people on the street."

Sam laughed.

"I haven't said a word to your father. He and your future father-in-law are already oil and water."

Don Best didn't like the airs Big Bill put on. Though educated, Don spoke plainly while Big Bill made a show out of everything and was a bit of a blowhard.

"Believe me, Momma, I know."

"I'll wait a while before I tell him about it."

"Thanks, Momma," he said, relieved. "Are you enjoying yourself at J.R. and Tammy's?"

"Yes. We're having such a good time. Tammy's parents came by today and we took Daisy to the park."

"I hope you took a lot of pictures."

"We did. I just figured out how to use my email so I'll ask J.R. to send the pictures to you on the computer."

"Great. Well, Momma, I'd love to talk some more but I've got some work to do tonight."

"You're talking about your book, right?"

"Yes. I have to have something to show my editor when I see her tomorrow."

"All right," she said softly. "Don't stay up too late. You want to be as fresh as our little Daisy is tomorrow."

"I won't stay up too late, Momma." He chuckled.

"Good night, son."

"Good night, Momma."

He hung up and stared at Abby's notes, remembering that she'd said to begin at the beginning with his early football years. He sighed, still unable to figure how to do it. Knowing that the proceeds from the book were to go to people like Tom and Norm made it even tougher. A lot was riding on the book.

Early Saturday morning, Abby watched *Sports Center* while she worked up a sweat on the treadmill. A very tired Shana walked in. Tired or not, she was still dressed to the nines.

"Good morning, Shana. What are you doing up so early on a Saturday?"

"I have a breakfast meeting, if you can imagine that."

"I didn't think fashion people did breakfast."

"They don't." She yawned. "This was the only time Cedi had available to go over the show's logistics."

Abby nodded.

Shana looked at the television. "You're watching *Sports Center*?"

"Yes. It's the only station not running something about J.J.'s divorce."

"That's funny. You'd think they would cover it, considering he was a professional athlete."

"Come on, Shana. Does water roll off a duck's back? J.J. was in the NBA. The fact that he played around with a lot of women is par for the course. If J.J. fenced or played golf, he'd probably be the lead story. No one expects this kind of behavior from those guys. At least they didn't until Tiger made the news."

"True," she nodded.

Abby turned off the treadmill and stepped off. "What time are you meeting him?" Abby wiped her face with a towel.

"Seven forty-five."

"You know it's almost ten after now, right?"

"Oh, my God," Shana exclaimed. "I've got to run. I'll talk to you later." She turned and dashed out.

"See you later." Abby chuckled.

Then she realized she needed to get a move on, too. Sam would be there shortly and she had a plan to help him break through his block.

∽

When Sam arrived at Abby's, he was surprised to see her standing outside. "I wonder what's going on," he muttered as the car pulled up to the curb. *Hope she's not upset about the other day in my office. I can't afford to lose her.*

"Do you want me to wait?" Bryan asked.

"Yes, just until I figure out what's going on," he answered as he got out. He nervously walked toward Abby. She smiled at him warmly. And he breathed a sigh of relief.

"Good morning."

"Good morning. Did I get my days fouled up? I thought we were working today."

"We are working today. You can tell your driver to go. I've got you covered."

"Okay," he said hesitantly.

Bryan rolled down the window as Sam walked over. "You can leave."

"Okay. What time do you want me to pick you up?"

"She says she's got me covered. So don't worry about it. I'll see you later."

"Have a good one, boss." He smiled as he rolled the window back up.

129

Sam walked back over to Abby.

"So we're all set. Follow me. "

Sam followed Abby into the parking garage. When they came to a black Land Rover, Abby disarmed the alarm. "Hop in."

Once they were both in and buckled up, they were on their way.

"I don't understand what we're doing."

"Don't worry. You will." Abby grinned.

Sam remained quiet as Abby drove through Manhattan and over the bridge, heading east for Long Island.

He looked out the window. "I thought the only people with driver's licenses in New York were MTA bus drivers and cabbies."

Abby laughed. "I know it certainly seems that way, but I grew up on Long Island where every kid spent their sixteenth birthday at the DMV getting their learner's permit. I used to wonder why the DMV didn't rent out space for sweet sixteen parties. They could have made a killing. It certainly would have shored up the state budget."

Sam laughed. "In Texas, most everyone can drive by the time they're twelve. How old were you when you got your license?"

"I've had my license since I was seventeen."

He glanced over at her odometer. "It doesn't look like you've put many miles on the car."

"I only use it when I have to go out of town. I'd be crazy to try to drive myself around Manhattan every day. It's easier to let the cabbies do it for you."

"I can understand that. Can I ask you a question?"

"Sure, but I'm pretty sure the answer will be to just sit tight and see."

"All right, that answers my question." He smiled. "Then I guess I'd better just enjoy the ride."

"Now that sounds like a good plan."

Within fifty-five minutes, Abby pulled into the parking lot of a park in Massapequa.

"Here we are," she said. "Welcome to John J. Burns Park."

"Great. Why are we here?"

"We're here to help you reconnect with football."

"I was in the NFL for fourteen years. I'm already connected to football."

"I'm talking about football when you were a kid. Let's go. If memory serves me, there should be more than a few kids on the field."

"But it's not football season anymore."

"Did that stop you when you were a kid?"

"No. Okay, let's go."

They got out of the car and headed toward the football field, where a group of boys were playing in spite of the cold.

"How did you know?"

"I told you I have three brothers. My father used to drive them here on Saturdays for pick-up games. I think you've been spotted."

Within seconds a group of ten- and eleven-year-olds surrounded Sam, clamoring for his attention. Sam whistled to bring the group to order. "How about you guys let me toss the ball with you for a while?"

The question was met with a loud cheer.

For the next two hours, Abby watched Sam and the kids from the sidelines as he showed them different football throwing techniques. He even ran through some drills with them before getting in a couple of games. Finally worn out, he signed autographs and took a gaggle of cell phone pictures.

Sam had a great big smile on his face as he walked back over to Abby.

"Looks like you had a good time."

"Yeah." He let out a deep breath. "It was fun. And you came out here with your brothers every Saturday? I had no idea you were such a football fan."

"I have a confession to make. I usually brought a book with me. The real reason I came happened after the games."

"What was that?"

Twenty minutes later they were in Marjorie R. Post's parking lot with three bags of fast food from All American, a greasy spoon that was famous for its burgers. There was only one All American in the whole country, and people came from miles around to get their famous quarter-pound cheeseburger, fries, and a thick shake.

Sam was on his second cheeseburger. "Now I understand why you braved so many cold days. This is amazing."

Abby sipped her vanilla shake. "I know. It's totally worth the extra half hour on the treadmill."

"Amen to that." He smiled and then sipped his chocolate shake. "If you don't mind me asking, are your brothers older or younger?"

"Younger. Frank Jr. is forty. Wes is thirty-eight and Nick is thirty-six. "

"So you're all about two years apart."

"Yes," she said as she ate a few more fries.

Sam looked shocked. "You're over forty? I would have never guessed that."

"Thank you, but I'll be forty-two in the summer." She smiled. "It's nice to know my moisturizer works. Goodness knows it costs enough." She chuckled.

Sam finished his cheeseburger. "I'm not sure your moisturizer has anything to do with it. You're a natural beauty."

Abby was a little taken aback. "Thank you." His words made her a little nervous and she changed the subject. "You never told me where you met your fiancée."

"At the University of Texas."

"So you're college sweethearts?" She smiled.

"Yes, we were."

Abby was a little taken aback when he used the past tense, but she skipped over it. "What was her major?"

"Maria majored in art history."

"That's a great degree to have in New York City. Does she work for one of the galleries or museums?"

"She was offered a docent position at the Museum of Modern Art recently but she turned it down. She's worked at a few galleries and did a little volunteering with an art program, but otherwise she hasn't done a whole lot with her degree."

Abby sensed this was a touchy subject and changed gears. "Do you want to give me what you wrote or would you like a little more time." She pointed to the portfolio on the dashboard.

"No. I want you to know that I did the writing, but I'm not happy with what I wrote. . Now I know what you meant by begin at the beginning," he said, smiling.

"Good. By the way, you did the outline you showed me the other day on the fly. Didn't you?"

"I guess you've been through this with writers before."

"Once or twice." She laughed. "This was a bit of an unorthodox approach for me, but somehow I didn't think assigning my usual writing exercises were going to work."

"You assign writing exercises?"

"That's how I learned to write. It was a part of my parents' summer curriculum."

"Your parents gave you assignments in the summer? Like school assignments?"

"Yes. Dr. Franklin Carey and Dr. Phyllis Carey believed that education was a continuous process. I mean, it wasn't like I was in prison camp for the summer. We took vacations and went to the beach and amusement parks."

Sam laughed. "What did your parents teach?"

"My father was the engineering department chair at Hofstra and my mother was the romance languages and literatures department chair there."

"That's pretty heavy duty. I guess I got off easy with a gym teacher and a librarian's assistant."

"I'd say you did, too."

"Most parents just check homework. It must have been unnerving to have your parents actually grade your papers."

Abby shrugged. "I never thought about it." She sipped her shake. "Ultimately it paid off for them. All four of us went to good colleges and now we have great careers."

"I'd say so. You were an English major at the University of Pennsylvania. I bet you graduated with honors."

"I did, but that's neither here nor there at this point in my life. It might as well be a million years ago."

"I know what you mean." He munched on a few more fries. "What do your brothers do?"

"Franklin Jr. is a pediatrician in Maryland, Wes is a lawyer for the ACLU in Atlanta and Nicholas is a professor at MIT."

"Do you stay in touch?"

"Our careers make it hard but we try to spend the holidays, birthdays and our parents' anniversary together. In fact we were just in Florida at my parents' for the Christmas and New Year's holiday with all five grandchildren."

"Five grandchildren," he repeated.

"Yes. We had Frank's three daughters, Georgina, Francine and Ariel; Wes's son Adam; and my son Justin." She counted them off on one hand.

"How are your parents with them?"

"Terrific. They take them on different trips every summer and whatever other holiday they can talk us into."

"No summertime schooling?"

"Of course not," she said jokingly. "That was strictly for their children. They're retired now. My father plays golf every morning and my mother is exploring her artistic side through pottery making, painting, sculpture and whatever else the local community college offers."

"Wow. I guess it's true what they say about grandparents. Happiness is being a grandparent."

"Isn't that the truth?"

He looked at Abby in jeans, a sweater, hat and pea coat. "I have another question for you. Feel free not to answer if you don't want to."

"Are you going to ask how a straight-laced girl from the suburbs wound up with a player like J.J. Stokes?"

"Yes. He just doesn't seem like your type."

Abby laughed. "I know what you're saying. But the truth is, despite his player bravado, J.J. grew up in Southfield, a middle class suburb of Detroit."

"I didn't know that. Where did you meet?"

"I was fresh out of NYU grad school and I had just started as an editorial assistant at Stillwater. It was after work and I'd stopped by the bookstore to pick up a few books and get a latte in the café."

"I wouldn't have figured him for the bookstore type."

"He isn't. He just happened to come in for a magazine and a cup of coffee to go. He'd just started playing for the Knicks and I think I was the only person in the place who didn't know who he was. He walked over and struck up a conversation with me. The rest is history, thank God."

"I take it the divorce was amicable."

"Let's just say it was mutual. I have Justin and he's got cousins to keep him busy. Do you have any nieces and/or nephews?"

"I have one niece, Daisy. She's seven years old. She's my oldest brother's daughter."

"Daisy." She smiled. "What a pretty name."

"I think so, too. Of course after having boys my parents love having a little girl to spoil." Sam took his wallet out and removed a photo. "This was taken last summer." He handed Abby the photo.

Abby's eyes grew larger as she studied the little girl with light brown hair, blue eyes and mocha complexion. "She's gorgeous. Is this your brother and his wife with her?"

"Yes. Why? Are you shocked that he's married to a black woman?"

"No, interracial marriages don't shock me. Do they live in Texas?"

"Yes. Not all Texans are Confederate flag waving, right wing Republican hicks. My parents have been registered Democrats for years."

"Being a registered Democrat doesn't automatically make you a liberal," Abby quickly said.

"True. However, my parents are liberals."

"She handed the photo back. "They are a beautiful family."

"Thanks. My parents are visiting with them in Corpus Christi."

"Is your brother Zeke married?"

"Yes, but I don't think he and Jane are planning to have children. I think they like their lifestyle in Houston as-is."

"It is a matter of choice." She sipped her drink. "Do you want children?"

"Yes, I'd like to have at least one."

"How does your fiancée feel about that?"

"She's okay with it." He shrugged his shoulders.

"I bet your parents are excited about this wedding."

"I don't know if excited is the word I would use. They would prefer it if I was doing something a bit more low key."

"When did you get engaged?"

"A little over a year ago."

"And you've been together since college, right?"

"Yes."

"Now I understand." She nodded knowingly. "I'd imagine low key is definitely not a buzzword Maria's working with at this point."

"You'd be right. Neither are her parents."

"As long as you're happy, big or small doesn't matter."

"True." He nodded. "I have to tell you, though, this is the first conversation that I've had in months that hasn't focused on the wedding. It's a nice change of pace."

"I'm glad I could change it up for you." She smiled. Abby looked down at the half empty bag of fries. "Do you want to finish these?"

"No. You can have the rest."

"No, you take them. I'm going to do enough time on the treadmill for eating something I had no business eating in the first place."

"What do you mean? You have a great shape." He looked at her closely.

"Do I have hamburger in my teeth?" she asked self-consciously.

"No." He laughed. "I just noticed that you're wearing your hair down."

Abby tugged her hat. "I'm wearing a hat and a scarf but I figured I'd leave my hair down for warmth."

"Could you take your hat off?"

"No. My hair probably looks like a static fright under the hat."

"Please," he begged.

"You're going to keep at me until I do, right?"

"Yes."

"Fine." She took the hat off and immediately began to smooth her hair. She pulled down the visor to check her reflection. "You see, I'm a mess."

"No you're not. You're gorgeous," he said as he leaned in and gently pressed his lips to hers. Abby tried not to kiss him back but she succumbed to the soft urgency of his lips. Then ever so tenderly Sam parted her lips with his tongue. Abby felt a tingle rushed throughout her body.

She quickly pulled away. "This can't happen!"

"Why? I know you felt something. Is it because I'm white?"

"No. I don't care about that."

"You can't tell me you didn't feel something."

"Whether I felt something or not is neither here nor there. I'm older than you and I should know better."

"What does age have to do with anything? You're only five years older than me."

"Be that as it may, we just got caught up in the moment. You're engaged and I'm a woman who knows what it's like to be cheated on." She nodded. "I'm certainly not signing up to be a side dish."

"But Abby…" he began.

"Please don't say anything else. This never happened." Abby buckled her seatbelt, started the car and pulled out.

Abby seemed to have broken all land and speed records when she pulled in front of Sam's building in just under an hour.

"Here we are," she said.

"Yes, here we are. I don't know whether to be flattered or upset that you couldn't get away from me fast enough after just one kiss."

"You don't have to feel anything. It shouldn't have happened in the first place." She shook her head. "Maybe I'll have to work with you via email. Did I give you my card?"

"No, I don't want to work with you via email. I think I do better when we're face to face."

"Fine." She let out a deep breath. "Then consider this the first and last field trip. From now on we'll work in my office's conference room. Okay? That way we're not alone."

"That's fine with me."

She pulled her Blackberry out. "How's Tuesday at 6 p.m."

"Good. But isn't it after working hours?"

"Not for public relations. Most nights we're there until 5 or 6 p.m. Pacific Time."

Sam opened the car door. "Thank you for one of the best days I've had in a long time." He fixed his blue-green eyes on her.

"You're welcome."

After he closed the car door, Sam watched her drive away. *Abby Carey, you are quite a woman.* He sighed wistfully. When he turned around the doorman held the door for him.

"Good evening, Mr. Best."

"It certainly is, Charlie." He smiled as he walked in.

Once Sam got back to the apartment, he realized that Maria was still out. Buoyed by the day, he headed straight for his office, turned on the computer and began writing. Words flowed from his head to the keyboard so fast his fingers could barely keep up. Sam was feeling more focused and inspired than he had in a long time, and he knew he had Abby to thank for it.

Chapter 9

Abby made it from the parking garage to the elevator in record time. When the elevator doors opened, she let out a deep breath and stepped in.

"What is the matter with me? Why did I kiss him back?" She paced. "I should have slapped him." She folded her arms. "Oh, my God, I'm talking to myself aloud. I only do this when I like someone. I can't like someone who's taken. This can't be happening to me." She looked up. "Come on, Abby, pull it together."

When the doors opened to her living room she headed straight for the mirror and took her hat off. She looked the same.

"Everything looks good from where I'm sitting."

Startled, Abby turned around. "J.J., what are you doing here?"

Suddenly Dazz appeared. Though the same age as J.J., Dazz had one redeeming quality to Abby: he always dressed his age. Long and lean with a closely cropped haircut, the fair-skinned Dazz had a few flecks of grey around his temple.

"Or better yet, how did you both get in here? I know Shana didn't let you in."

"It's nice to see you too, Abby." Dazz smiled.

"We helped a couple of young ladies bring some clothes racks in and up to the third floor."

"I have to talk to Shana about posting your pictures in the break room as my version of America's least wanted."

"You always had a great sense of humor."

"Okay, J.J., what's going on? You didn't come here to tell me that I'm the next Kathy Griffin."

"No. I came by to tell you that I spoke to Justin and he's cool if I don't make it to parents' weekend."

"What? You missed the last one and you promised to make it this time. What could be more important than your son?"

"Nothing is more important than Justin. Dazz couldn't get me out of the appearance. We signed a contract."

"I really tried, Abby, but the owners wouldn't budge," Dazz piped in.

"Oh, I bet you tried really hard," Abby said caustically. "Don't tell me. It's a club opening in Miami."

"No. It's in Atlanta."

Abby shook her head, disgusted. "Okay, what did you promise to buy him?"

"I resent that you think I have to buy our son's affection."

"I don't think you have to buy it. You do." She folded her arms. "You've already gotten him every video

145

game system. So was it an iPod or maybe the latest iPhone?"

"The iPhone," he said quietly.

"Figures," she scoffed.

"Is that all you're going to say? I expected you'd have a fit."

"What would be the point? I'm not going to waste my breath." She exhaled loudly.

"Aren't you going to follow through with your threat to call Beebe's attorney?"

"No. I only said that to get you to take seeing Justin seriously."

"I do take it seriously," he said defensively.

"You can tell yourself whatever you want, J.J., I'm not the one you need to convince." She shook her head. "Now if you'll excuse me, it's been a long day, and I'm exhausted."

"For someone who's tired you look great. It's like you have a little glow or something," Dazz ventured.

"What?"

"He's right. There is something different about you."

"I don't know what you're talking about, nor do I have the inclination to find out. So if you please..." She walked over to the elevator.

J.J. got up. "I can take a hint."

"Apparently not," she quipped as she pressed the call button.

J.J. and Dazz walked over as the doors opened. They stepped in. "You know what else I want to say?" J.J. began.

"No. Good night." Abby pressed the button to close the doors, then rushed back to the mirror. *Do I look different?* She studied her reflection. She told herself that it was just a kiss, a simple moment of weakness on both their parts, nothing more.

∾

Sam was in the midst of writing, but he took a break to get something to drink.

His phone rang.

"Hello, Sam? How's it going?" Reggie asked anxiously.

"It's going great, Reggie."

"Wow, you sound like a completely changed person from the man I spoke to last night."

"I have changed. I had a breakthrough today. I've been writing like a madman ever since I got home. Abby did the trick."

"That's great news. I'm so relieved."

"That makes two of us. I don't want to cut you off, but I'd like to get back to it."

"Please do. I'll talk to you later."

"Okay." He hung up and, with his drink in hand, went back to the office.

❧

After a hot bath, Abby relaxed on her bed in front of the television.

Her phone rang. She checked the caller ID. *Oh my God, it's Reggie. Why is he calling this late?* She looked at the clock and realized it wasn't *that* late. The phone kept ringing.

Deciding she was acting like a nutcase, she picked up. "Hello, Reggie."

"Hello, Abby. How are you?"

"I'm fine."

"Great. I just called to thank you."

"Thank me for what?"

"For whatever you did to Sam."

"What do you mean?" Her heart jumped into her throat.

"When I called him he was busy writing away. He was a man on a mission, didn't even have time to speak to me. I don't know what you did, but it worked."

"I'm glad to hear it." Abby was relieved in more ways than one.

"He's struggled for months and now after just one editing session, he's prolific. You've got the magic touch."

"What?" she blurted out.

"All I said is that you haven't lost your touch. Are you okay?"

"I'm fine, just a little jumpy. J.J. and Dazz were here earlier."

"Oh, don't tell me he's going to miss parents' weekend again."

"You got it."

"I don't understand him. Doesn't he realize that he'll never get these years back?"

"I don't think so. It's funny. I can motivate a blocked writer but I can't motivate my son's father to spend time with him."

"It's not your fault."

"Thanks, but sometimes I wonder if I had made him spend more time at home when Justin was younger…"

"Don't go there. This is on J.J., not you."

"You're right." She yawned.

"You sound tired. You should get some rest."

"I will."

"Good. I'll talk to you soon."

"Okay, Reggie."

"Have a good night."

"You, too." She hung up.

After giving it some thought, Abby decided Reggie was right, She couldn't beat herself up for the past or J.J.'s lack of a relationship with Justin.

She called Justin.

"Hi, Mom," he answered.

"Hi, sweetie. How are you?"

"I'm good."

"What are you up to?" She heard noise and music in the background. "Where are you?"

"I'm in the gym. We have a dance this evening."

"That's nice. Are you having a good time?"

"It's okay. The music is kind of lame."

"It's nice to know that some things haven't changed about high school."

Justin laughed. "So, Mom, are you calling me about Dad?"

"How did you get so smart?"

"I am your son."

"That's my boy." She grinned. "Seriously, though, are you okay?"

"I'm fine, Mom. It's no big deal. I really didn't expect him to come anyway."

"He couldn't get out of a contract appearance."

"Mom, you don't have to explain or make excuses. I'm okay."

"If you say so. I heard you're getting an iPhone out of the deal."

"I didn't ask for it. Dad just said he'd get me the latest version when it comes out. I told him he didn't have to, the one I have now works fine. He insisted."

"As long as you're okay, that's all I was worried about."

"Don't worry. Oh, Mom, have you started working with Sam Best yet?"

"Yes. In fact, I worked with him today."

"Did you get his autograph first?"

"No."

"Mom," he groaned.

"Don't worry. I'll get his autograph, and bring it to you when I come next weekend. Okay?"

"Okay."

"Good. Now go back to your dance and have a good time."

"I will."

"Did you dance with any girls?"

"Mom," he groaned again.

"Okay. Forget I asked. Have a good time. You know I love you."

"Yes, Mom."

"I'll talk to you later."

"Okay." He hung up.

She was proud of her son; in spite of his father blowing him off, he seemed okay. Abby's text tone chimed. She checked the phone.

"Love you too, Mom," she read aloud. "That's my baby."

Her mind drifted back to how good Sam's lips felt against hers. She snapped out of it. She had to regain her professionalism and get an autograph for Justin.

≈

It was late by the time Maria got back from her day with the planner. When she walked into the office she was buoyed by a head full of ideas she was anxious to share with her fiancé.

"Hi, honey. I had a great day. Preston's people came up with some table settings that will look so elegant with the linens." She took her digital camera out. "I even took some pictures."

"Sounds great, honey. Whatever you want." Sam sounded oblivious.

"You're not even paying attention to me."

"Yes, I am." He continued typing. "Preston's people had great ideas. I heard you. I'm good with whatever you want to go with."

"I went to all the trouble of taking pictures and you can't stop and look at them for one minute?"

Sam stopped and turned to face her. "I'm sorry. I don't mean to be rude, but I've finally had a breakthrough with this book. I really just want to ride this wave of creativity. The juices are flowing."

Maria made a face.

"Remember, the more I write the faster I'll be done."

Maria sighed. "How many pages have you written now?"

"I'm up to seventy pages and counting."

"I thought the editor was supposed to help you," she said, hands on her hips. "That's not much more than what you had before."

"You don't understand. I rewrote the first forty pages I'd written before and I've added thirty more pages on top of that."

"Wow, I'm impressed. I take it back. Maybe this editor is working out better than I thought."

"Yeah, she's great."

"At this rate you'll be able to deliver sooner rather than later and then you can help with the wedding."

"That's the plan."

"Then get back to it." She kissed him. "I'm bushed and a little hungry. Do you want to order dinner?"

"Are you ordering from the Greek place?"

"Yes. I've got to watch those carbs if I want to get into my Vera Wang gown," she said as she playfully shimmied. "Did you eat today?"

Sam's mind flashed back to his kiss with Abby. "I had a little something earlier. I'm not really hungry."

"I'll order a gyro for you in case you change your mind."

"Thanks."

The moment Maria left the room, Sam was back at work. He was fueled and inspired by Abby in more ways than one. He might have eaten fast food, but the butterflies that filled his stomach were anything but fast food related. They were the slow butterfly flutters that thrilled his senses. However, he knew they also meant that if they stayed his life was about to get complicated.

Chapter 10

Sam found February a peculiar time in the world of sports. The hype of the Super Bowl was always over and a post-traumatic football withdrawal seemed to fall over fans and players alike. Sam was grateful for the opportunity to meet Bo for a beer at Third & Long in Murray Hill, as opposed to watching wedding Sunday on WE TV with Maria. He jumped at the chance.

Sam enjoyed the Third & Long bar because even though it was in the heart of the city it still felt like the ones back home in Texas, only a bit slicker.

Bo watched as Sam stopped to sign autographs before he came over to the table to join him.

"Hey, man," Bo said. He and Sam did the man-brace, the semi-hug with a manly pound on the back for good measure.

"I hope I didn't keep you waiting," Sam said as they sat down.

"No. Mr. Budweiser kept me company."

"Do you think he'd mind keeping me company, too?"

"Not at all. Mr. Bud's philosophy is the more the merrier." Bo motioned for the waitress to bring another beer over.

The waitress placed the bottle in front of Sam.

"Thank you, ma'am," he said in his best Texan drawl. He picked up the beer. "Glad to make your acquaintance again, Mr. Budweiser. It's been far too long," he joked and took a couple of swigs. "Ah, I needed that."

"Tough day in the wedding trenches?" Bo asked.

"No. Not today. Maria's busy watching wedding television."

"So you're off the hook."

"For the moment." He smiled. "What brings you to the city?"

"I had a little shopping to do."

"You went shopping." Sam was surprised.

"Yes. You do know what's coming up soon, don't you?"

"I thought your anniversary was in June."

"It is in June." Bo looked puzzled. "You really forgot, didn't you?"

"Forgot what?" Sam asked impatiently.

"Valentine's Day is coming up this weekend."

"It totally slipped my mind," he groaned.

"Obviously," Bo added.

"I've been so wrapped up with Abby that it just didn't dawn on me."

"Don't you mean that you've been wrapped up in your book?"

"Yes. Isn't that what I said?"

"No. You said you were wrapped up with Abby."

"It's the same difference."

"No, it isn't." Bo looked at his friend more closely. "What's going on with you? And don't try to tell me nothing. I've known you too long for that."

"Nothing. Valentine's Day just got lost in the shuffle. In fact, I'm pretty sure Maria forgot, too."

"Trust me, women are incapable of forgetting love's holiday. Amy was in labor with Josh on Valentine's Day and I'll be damned if she didn't ask me about her flowers and candy in between contractions."

Sam laughed.

"Make sure you pick up the bare minimum of a card and flowers. Unless something has changed that you want to talk about."

"Nothing has changed," Sam said dismissively.

"Samuel Hezekiah Best. You should know better than to try to piss on my leg and tell me it's raining. Something is up, and don't try to hand me that Freudian slip stuff, either. It was a Freudian slip when you referred to Abby as hot. Something else is afoot here."

Sam finished his beer. "Can I get another beer first, please?" He waved his empty bottle.

"Fine." Bo motioned for two more beers.

Sam dug into the beer nuts on the table.

"Here you go, guys." The waitress placed the beers on the table. "Let me know if you need anything else."

"Thanks." Sam picked up his beer. "Here's mud in your eye."

Bo raised his bottle and they both drank.

"Okay, that's enough stalling. Spill it."

"I went to Abby's yesterday with a mean case of writer's block in spite of all the notes she'd given me. So we went on a field trip and I played football with some kids in the park."

"Did it cure your writer's block?"

"Amazingly, it did. It took doing something physical for me to understand what she meant. I can't tell you what a relief that was for me."

"I might be in television, but I know exactly what you mean. I feel that way every time I file a report."

"I guess as a way to celebrate the un-thickening of my skull, we went to this fast food place in Massapequa called All American. Have you ever heard of it?"

"I think I saw it on a Food Network special on burger joints."

"Oh, man, the burgers are awesome. You should take the kids there, they'd love it."

"I'll have to make it a point to do that. What did you do after you got the food? Did you head back?"

"No. We went to another park to eat and we got to talking in her car. I'm telling you, Bo, everything felt so natural. We talked like we'd known each other for years." Sam said with a far off look in his eyes. "The next thing I knew I was kissing her."

"What?"

"You heard right. I can't blame it on alcohol because the strongest thing we had to drink was a couple of milkshakes."

"Did she kiss you back?"

"Yes." Sam's face lit up. "Then she freaked out and proceeded to break land and speed records getting back to the city."

He looked at Sam's expression. "It's obvious that you enjoyed it. Even thinking about it puts a smile on your face. But you *are* engaged."

"I know that's an awful way to feel, considering I'm getting married in four months."

"But," Bo said.

"There was just something about her that just pulled me to her."

"So what are you going to do about it? Are you still going to work with her?"

"Yes," he said emphatically. "She's a great editor. Do you know I wrote one hundred pages in less than a day? It took me four months to write the forty pages I'd done before."

"How are you going to handle it?"

"She wanted to start doing things via email, but I don't want that. I want to work with her in person. I think I work best with her face to face."

"What did she have to say about that?"

"She agreed to continue working with me. However, there won't be any more field trips. We're strictly working in her office."

"That sounds like a good plan, but we are talking about the heart. You sound more than a little attracted to her. I think you have to deal with that."

"I am dealing with it. I'm engaged to Maria. We've been together for years and everyone is waiting for us to have the wedding of the century and ride off into the sunset."

"You realize that doesn't sound like a ringing endorsement for your relationship with Maria? It sounds like concession."

Sam looked down at his beer. "Maybe it was just a momentary thing, like Abby said. She is a beautiful woman and it just happened."

"Listen, Sam, you've been around your share of beautiful women. Did you share any *moments* with them?"

"No."

"That proves my point."

"You don't think it was just a moment?"

"Do you think it was?"

Sam couldn't answer.

"If you were any other guy, I might write it off as one of those things. But I know you. You are a real gentleman. Even when you could be with a different woman every day of the week, you didn't bother. All

I'm saying is, be honest with yourself." He took a swig of beer. "When's your next meeting?"

"Tuesday."

"Then I suggest you get on it sooner rather than later."

❧

As Sunday afternoon wound into evening, Abby stretched out on the sofa with her laptop in the study and Abby checked her Google alerts.

"Hey, Shana," she said without looking up.

"I'm not going to ask again."

Abby chuckled as she turned to face her. "How are things going in the trenches?"

"At the moment they are going. Check with me again in five minutes. I might have a different answer." She sat down. "We're figuring out the seating charts, and you know how that goes."

"I take it the publicists are calling around the clock, as usual, to see where their clients are seated."

"Naturally. Only this year the reality show element has quadrupled. Suddenly I have publicists for people whose biggest claims to fame are bar fights, fake tans and on-camera sex escapades calling to find out whether their clients are in the first row."

"Somehow I don't think Anna Wintour would find it amusing to be seated next to someone from *Jersey Shore*."

"Tell me about it." She sighed. "Oh, well, it's the new reality and I've got to deal with it."

"You're a better woman than I am."

"I didn't see you yesterday. How did it go with Sam?"

"I think it went pretty well."

"Did you meet him somewhere? When I came upstairs, you weren't in your office or the conference room."

"I decided to switch things up a bit and take Sam on field trip."

"Now this sounds promising. You took him out?"

"It wasn't a date, Shana. He was suffering from writer's block. I thought a change of scenery would help him."

"Did it?" she asked.

"Yes. Reggie called to tell me that Sam was busy writing away."

"What did you do to him?"

"I didn't do anything." Abby hoped her face didn't betray her. "I just helped him focus." She looked at her screen. "Now this is interesting."

"What's interesting?"

"I got a Google alert about Beebe. It looks like she's going on the wronged wife talk show circuit, starting with *The Wendy Williams Show*."

"I didn't know that you had Beebe set up as a Google alert."

"I don't. I have an alert for J.J."

"That makes sense. Don't you mean she's going on the karma is a bitch circuit? I guess she doesn't like it now that the shoe is on the other foot."

"I don't know anyone who does. The issue of Today's Black Woman with her interview hits the stands tomorrow."

"You're not worried that Justin will see it, are you?"

"No. I already talked to him about it. Besides, I don't think you can find a copy of Today's Black Woman in Connecticut."

"Good point."

"Speaking of J.J., can we please post a photo of him in the break room or something so the temps don't let him in?"

"One of the temps let him in the building?"

"Yes. He and Dazz sweet-talked their way in yesterday. They were waiting for me here when I got back."

"I'll take care of it. What the hell did he want, anyway?"

"I'll give you one guess."

"He's not making it to parents' weekend again."

"You got it. He has a club opening in Atlanta he allegedly can't get out of."

"The man kills me. He's practically Houdini when it comes to getting out of family obligations but when it comes to anything else, he can't break out of a paper bag. How's Justin taking it?"

"I talked to him last night and he said he was fine."

"He's a great kid."

"I know. I can't wait to see him next weekend so I can give him a big hug."

"And see with your own eyes that he's okay."

"Exactly. Wait a minute. If you came up here yesterday, something must be up. What's going on?"

A wide smile washed over Shana's face. "Raymond is coming to town early. We're going to spend Valentine's Day together."

"Oh, my God, the fourteenth is this Friday? It totally slipped my mind. So what are you doing to celebrate?"

"I'm not sure yet. Raymond's been playing it cagey, but I'm sure he's got something up his sleeve."

"I'm sure he's got more than 'something up his sleeve' for you." Abby winked.

Shana giggled like a schoolgirl. "What about you? Maybe you should go up to see Justin on Friday. That way you can spend Valentine's Day with your favorite guy."

"That's a nice idea, but I don't think that a fifteen-year-old boy wants his mom hanging around on Valentine's Day. I'll head up Saturday morning as planned."

"You know I worry about you."

"Please don't worry. I'm fine. Besides, you should be concentrating on what you're going to wear for your Valentine's date."

"I really can't wait."

"It'll be here before you know it."

"Your turn is coming."

"I'm sure it is but in the meantime I've got big plans with a box of chocolates."

Chapter 11

After his talk with Bo, Sam stopped by Bloomingdale's and picked up a Valentine's Day gift. With Maria preoccupied with WE TV's *Platinum Weddings* marathon, he slipped by her unnoticed. With the bracelet safely hidden, he returned to his office to watch a little sports television. Whenever he came out to get a snack or head for the bathroom, he could hear Maria on the phone with her mother.

A few hours later, Sam joined Maria in the living room. She was on the phone again.

"Do you see that, Sissy? They created the event space for the wedding. Isn't that wild?" She laughed. "Oh, Sam's here. I'll call you later. Okay. Bye."

"How's Sissy?"

Sissy was Maria's oldest sister. She still lived in Texas with her husband, oncologist Dr. Jackson Dillard, and their three teenage daughters.

"She's good," she said as she turned her attention back to the program. "I just called her to see if she knew about Piazza in the Village in Colleyville since she and Jackson are in Fort Worth. I just saw this beautiful wedding there on *Platinum Weddings*."

"Nice. Did she know about it?"

"Yes. The debutante ball for the oldest of their daughters was held there. She said the place is gorgeous."

"Does that mean you want to get married there now?" Sam asked teasingly.

"Ha, very funny." Maria wasn't amused.

He asked as he sat down next to her, "*Platinum Weddings* is *still* on?"

"Yes. It's the marathon before they air two new episodes later on tonight."

"Oh." Sam's stomach rumbled. "Is there anything to eat around here?"

"There's an extra gyro in the fridge."

Sam made a face. "No, I don't want that. How about we go out for a late dinner?"

"It's after eight and I don't feel like getting dressed to go out. Can't you just order something?"

"Of course I can order something, but I thought it would be nice to go out for a change.""We go out."

"Yes. We go out for wedding stuff. When's the last time we got dressed up and went out for a meal?"

"Last month."

"That was my retirement dinner. That doesn't count."

"I've been looking forward to the new episodes tonight." She pointed to her notepad. "I've gotten a lot of great ideas I want to run by Jessica. We can go out another night."

"When?"

"Soon," she insisted. Her eyes were glued to the television.

His dinner plans thwarted, Sam switched to romance and began kissing Maria's neck.

"Now what are you doing?"

"I'm trying to take my mind off of food." He continued kissing her neck.

"Well, cut it out. I'm not in the mood," she said sternly.

Sam jumped up. "I give up."

"What's the matter with you?" Maria asked, surprised.

"When will you be in the mood? I mean *really* in the mood."

"What's that supposed to mean? When 'I'm *really* in the mood'," she demanded.

"Nothing," he said quietly.

"You're the one who opened the door so you might as well walk through. Spit it out!"

"Our sex life is sporadic at best," he began. "But when we do have sex it feels like you're phoning it in just to keep me quiet."

"I can't believe you said that." Maria was stunned.

"It's the way I feel."

"In case you haven't noticed, I've been a little busy planning our wedding, which is a little less than four months away."

"How could I forget? Every day is a wedding marathon around here. There are other things in life to do besides look at swatches." He threw his hands up. "You should have taken that position at the museum."

"I didn't want it, so why would I take it?"

"Maria, you have a degree in art history that you should put to use. Some people would kill to have an opportunity to work as a docent for MOMA."

"Then I'm sure they found someone else to take the position. I'm busy planning our wedding."

"What about our life?"

"What?"

"You're entirely focused on the wedding. What about planning for the rest of our lives together? Contrary to popular belief, a wedding is the beginning of a new life. There's a whole lot of stuff that comes after the dress is stored away. Are we planning for that?"

"You're saying all of this just because I wouldn't have sex with you one time?"

"You think this is about sex?"

"That's what you said."

"Sex is only one small part of a larger picture. It's like *we* don't exist anymore. We haven't been on a date in forever. The only time we eat out is when we're out running errands for the wedding, and even then we really don't talk about anything unless it's about the wedding."

"It's the biggest day of our lives. Can't you see that?"

"It's *one* of the biggest days of our lives, Maria."

"I think you're being ridiculous," she scoffed.

"And I think you're mostly concerned with making sure you live up to the Carrangelo tradition."

"Now what's that supposed to mean?"

"Both of your sisters got married straight out of college, which means you're the last girl standing."

"Sam, I think I've been more than patient. I stood by you for your entire NFL career, and I am going to have the wedding I've dreamed of."

Sam shook his head. "You've been using the word 'I' a whole lot lately, and the word 'we' doesn't seem to figure into your vision. So you know what? I think I need a break." Sam headed for the bedroom.

Maria was on his heels. "What do you mean? You need a break?"

Sam grabbed a duffle bag.

"What are you doing?"

"I'm packing a bag," Sam said as he threw some things in, including his laptop and flash drive. "I need a break."

"You need a break? Are you calling off the wedding?"

"No, I'm saying that I need some time to breathe." He picked up the bag and began to walk out of the bedroom.

Maria plopped onto the bed. "I can't believe you're doing this to me just because I didn't want to go out."

"After everything I've said, that's all you got out of it?" He walked out of the bedroom and went to the hall closet for his coat.

Maria ran out of the bedroom. "So you're just going to walk away?"

"At this point I think it's the best thing I can do for both of us before things are said that can't be taken back." He put his coat on and walked out of the apartment.

As he walked down the hall he heard something slam against the door. When he got to the elevator he called Reggie.

"Hello?"

"Hey, Reggie," he said in a serious tone.

"What's the matter, Sam?"

"I need a favor right now."

"Okay."

"I need you to get a room for me at the W hotel tonight."

"Right now?" Reggie asked, shocked.

"Yes. Can you do it?"

"It's kind of late, but I might be able to pull some strings."

"I can't hang my hat on might."

"I'll make the arrangements. Is the one at Union Square okay?"

"Yes. I really don't need to be in the heart of Times Square at the moment."

"Okay. Do you want to talk about it?"

"Not right now. All I'm going to do is get my car and drive over."

"I'll make sure the manager sees to it that you have a private check-in."

"Thanks. I owe you one."

"Don't sweat it." Reggie hung up.

The night doorman waved. "Can I get you a cab, Mr. Best?"

"No, thank you. I'm going to drive myself tonight."

"Very good, sir."

Sam went to the parking garage and got into his Mercedes.

When Sam arrived at the W Hotel half an hour later, the manager Walter and one concierge person whisked him up to the Extreme Wow Suite they had waiting for him.

"Is there's anything you need, Mr. Best, please let me know."

"As a matter of fact, there is one thing I need." Sam put his duffle bag down on the king size bed and took his flash drive out. "I need this messengered for tomorrow morning."

"Certainly, sir," the manager answered.

"Do you have stationary in here?"

"Yes. It's in the drawer." He pointed.

Sam went over to the drawer and took out an envelope and a couple of sheets of paper. He quickly wrote something, folded it and put it in the envelope along with the flash drive. "I need this to go to this address." He jotted it down on the other piece of paper and handed everything to Walter.

"We'll take care of this right away."

"Thanks."

"It's my pleasure. Have a good night." The manager left the room.

Sam looked around the sumptuous suite, then walked over to the window and looked at the city lights around Union Square. "I'm pretty sure you made a mess of this one, old boy," Sam sighed. He went over to the bed and fell back onto it like a kid. As the softness of the pillow enveloped him, he exhaled. *But at least I can breathe for now.*

❧

By 8 a.m. Monday morning, Abby had reviewed and corrected Candy's pitch letters and moved on to other agency business.

"Good morning, Kelly. You're in early."

"I have a breakfast meeting with the director of soccer for The Field House at Chelsea Piers Youth Soccer League this morning about setting up a few soccer clinics for Bob."

"Bob is the go-to guy for youth soccer." Abby smiled. "What time is your meeting?"

"Nine-thirty. I came here first so I could pick up a few more books."

"Okay. Let me know how it goes when you get back."

"I will." She began to walk out, but stopped short. "Oh, I ran into a messenger downstairs." Kelly handed Abby an envelope. "This is for you."

"Thanks." Abby glanced at it briefly.

"So," Kelly put her hand on her hip, "what's the scoop?"

"What are you talking about?"

"What's the scoop about Sam Best?"

"I don't know what you're talking about."

"There was a report on the radio this morning that said Sam had suddenly checked into the W Hotel last night."

"It's probably something someone made up."

"I thought so, too, but the envelope you received is from the W Hotel."

Abby looked at the embossing on the envelope. "So it is."

"That's some coincidence."

"That's all it is, a coincidence. Don't you need to be somewhere soon?"

"Yes, I'm going. It's obvious you don't want to share," she said playfully.

Abby couldn't help laughing a little. "Go on. I'll see you later."

"Okay."

Abby waited a few moments for the coast to be clear. Once she was sure Kelly had left, she opened the envelope, removed the flash drive and unfolded the letter.

Dear Abby,
Here's what I've written so far. I can't wait to hear what you think. Call me. 646-555-1026.
Sam

He really is in the hotel, Abby realized. Her mind flashed back to their kiss in the car. That can't be the reason.

Chapter 12

Sam awoke uncharacteristically late. Though he hadn't been drinking, he felt hung over. He slowly sat up and noticed his cell phone blinking on the night table. He picked it up.

His voice mail and text message box were filled to capacity. No surprise there. He got up and headed for the bathroom.

A few minutes later there was a knock on the door.

"Who is it?" he called.

"It's Reggie."

"And Bo."

"Just a minute." Sam closed and tied his robe.

"Good morning to both of you," he said as he opened the door.

Bo walked in, followed by Reggie.

"Needless to say you've had better mornings," Reggie said as he sat down.

"Humph." Sam plopped onto the bed.

"Are you all right?" Bo asked.

"I'm fine. And by the way, how is it that both of you are here this morning?"

"I'm here because of all the calls I got this morning about you. At least a dozen radio stations are reporting that you left your love nest suddenly last night and checked into a hotel. I called Reggie to find out if he knew anything."

"Since Bo is your best friend, I told him. We figured we'd both come to find out what the hell is going on with you."

"It's nothing. Maria and I had a fight. I just needed to clear my head."

Bo and Reggie looked at each other.

"What?" Sam asked.

"You expect us to believe that?" Reggie asked.

"Why wouldn't you believe it?"

"For one thing, it's horseshit," Bo said plainly. "I've had fights with my wife, and when I felt like I needed to clear my head I took a walk or went for a drive. I didn't pack a bag and check into a hotel."

"So what's going on? Did you have a fight about the wedding?"

"Did her father add more guests?" Bo asked.

"No."

"Then what set it off?" Reggie asked.

"I wanted to go out for a late dinner and she wanted to stay home and continue watching a wedding marathon. I got tired of coming in third to the wedding."

"I can understand that. Did you try to tell her how you feel?"

"Of course I did, Reggie."

"I've known you for a long time, Sam. You don't nip it in the bud. You let it fester and grow so you wind up exploding," Bo said.

"I know. It just seemed easier to keep my mouth shut."

"Until it isn't," Reggie added.

Sam got up and walked to the window.

"What's your plan now? Are you going to check out and go home today?" Bo asked.

"I don't know." Sam stared out the window.

"I think you need to think about it sooner rather than later. The press is already buzzing. It's only a matter of time before they swarm. And I need to call the PR people to get a statement ready just in case."

Sam unconsciously smiled as his mind flashed back to the day he'd spent with Abby and the kiss.

"What are you smiling about? We're twelve floors up."

"Nothing, Bo." He turned around. "I just thought about something."

Before Reggie or Bo could go further, Sam's cell phone rang. He checked the caller ID. "I have to take this." He went into the bathroom. "Hello?"

"Hello, Sam," Abby said.

"Hi. How are you?"

"I'm fine, but I'm a little surprised. I expected to get your voice mail."

"I saw it was you and I picked up."

"I got the package you sent over earlier this morning."

"Good. I'm anxious to hear what you think after you've had a chance to review it."

"That's the thing. I thought I would just open it and read a little but I wound up finishing it. I thought it was great. Good job. I think you're on your way to a really solid story."

"Thanks, that means a lot coming from you."

"Keep it up."

"I will. I was wondering if we could meet today. I could come by your office later."

"Are you sure you want to do that?" she said hesitantly.

"I take it you've heard the news reports."

"It's a little hard to avoid them, even for me."

"I'd really rather not wait until tomorrow evening. I want to work while I'm feeling enthused."

Abby was quiet for a few moments. "Fine," she said. "We'll make it the same time."

"So six o'clock in the conference room?"

"Yes. I'll see you then."

"I'm looking forward to it." He smiled and then hung up.

When he walked out of the bathroom, he looked like a different man.

"You look better," Reggie noted.

"I feel a little better now."

"Does that mean you're going home?"

"Not right now, Bo. I think I'm going to stay here. I didn't get much sleep last night."

Bo and Reggie stood up. "We'll let you get some rest, but we have to talk about what your plans are." Reggie sounded serious. "We can't let a story like this swirl around."

"I know. We can talk about it later." He yawned.

"All right, man," Bo said as he gave him a pound. "You let me know if you need anything."

"I will."

"Same here," Reggie piped in.

Sam walked over and opened the door for them. After the two men left he leaned against the door. "She thought it was good," he said aloud and smiled.

⤗⤙

Much to Abby's surprise Monday was an unusually quiet day and, by 5 p.m., her staff had cleared out. However, she was comforted to know that Shana would be downstairs.

After she set Sam's manuscript to print, Abby walked out of her office to retrieve it from the print station. Shana walked in.

"It's nice to see that someone has a quiet evening ahead of them."

"I guess it is nice." Abby shrugged as she collected her document. "What brings you up here?"

"I came up to tell you that I'm headed out."

"What's going on?"

"Six models pulled out of Cedi's show. We have two agencies sending models over this evening and Cedi asked me to help him choose who's going to walk in his show."

"He doesn't want to do that himself?"

"You know how much he has riding on this. It's the first plus-size fashion show at Fashion Week. You and I helped him wrangle some of the top names in plus modeling for the runway but they can't model every outfit."

"That's true."

"Do you want to come with me? The more eyes the merrier."

"I would love to but I have a late appointment coming."

"Okay. I've got to run. I'll catch you up on what happened later and you can tell me what you know about Sam. Inquiring minds want to know." She laughed.

"You're hysterical," Abby said drolly. "I'll see you later. Good luck."

"Thanks." Shana dashed out.

I'm a big girl. I can handle this. Abby returned to her office and gathered everything together. Just as she walked out she saw Sam.

"You're early."

"I was a little anxious. I hope you don't mind."

"Not at all. I'm just surprised you didn't cause more of a commotion downstairs."

"To tell you the truth I don't think they noticed me. Everyone seems to be moving at breakneck speed."

"It's the week before Fashion Week. There are only three speeds, fast, faster and warp speed."

He laughed and then looked at Abby's full hands. "Let me take that for you." He emptied her arms.

"Thank you."

"Not a problem."

Sam followed her to the conference room where he placed everything on the table.

"Would you like some water?"

"Sure." He sat down.

"I'll only be a minute."

As she turned to walk out, Sam focused on the way her pencil skirt hugged her rear. He cleared his throat.

Abby returned with two bottles of Pellegrino. "Here you go." She put a bottle in front of Sam.

"Thanks."

"You're welcome." She sat down. "If you don't mind, I'd like to get right down to business."

"Absolutely," he agreed.

"I have to tell you that I really enjoyed your re-writes. It felt more personal this time."

"It wasn't personal before?"

"No."

"You really took your time to answer," he said facetiously.

"What I meant is, while I got the facts in the first draft, it felt as if a biographer had written it."

"That's the disconnect you referred to before."

"Right," she began. "This time I heard your voice. I especially enjoyed the passage about throwing your first touchdown, how in spite of the roar and cheers of the crowd, you only heard your father's voice."

"It's true. I felt that way my entire career in the NFL."

"Now that's what I was talking about." She grinned. "I was an academic. Outside of P.E., I didn't play sports. I always wondered what moved athletes to excel and I felt I learned something from reading your work."

"You didn't like sports?"

"No. I liked sports. However, academia was the focus in my house for all of us kids. My parents didn't have a problem with intramural sports, but team sports were vetoed." She thought for a moment. "I wish I had gone out for a team sport. My son plays on his school's lacrosse and baseball teams and he's really turning out to be a well-balanced young man."

"That's terrific. Did you say lacrosse and baseball?"

"Yes."

"He doesn't play basketball?"

"He likes basketball but he can take it or leave it. Believe me, that didn't go over too well with his father."

"I'll bet not."

"This is what I was talking about. If you keep this up your book will give readers something to think about and it will be a conversation starter." She unconsciously leaned forward. "When you think about it, sports is more than touchdowns, goals, homeruns, baskets or aces. It represents the best and the worst in human nature."

"And here I thought it was about the joy of victory and the agony of defeat."

"It's about the continued drive for success and the joy when victory is snatched from the jaws of defeat."

Sam stared at her in amazement.

"I'm sorry if I went a little overboard there."

"No. Don't be sorry. You've gotten me fired up, and that's a good thing." He smiled. "You're amazing."

"I wouldn't go that far. I'm just an editor. This is what I do."

"Oh, you are far more than just an editor."

"Thank you." Abby quickly took a sip of her water. Then she took out her notepad. "I only noted a few minor changes." She tore off a couple of pages and handed them to him. "Outside of those changes, I'd say press on. You might even wind up with more pages than required."

"You think so? Tandem wouldn't mind if they got a longer manuscript than expected?"

"No. It's easier to edit down than it is to build it up."

"I can't thank you enough for inspiring me." He reached over and put his hand over hers.

Abby quickly pulled her hand away. "As I said, I'm just doing my job." She looked away.

Sam firmly grabbed her hand in his. "Why won't you look at me?"

"Would you please let go of my hand?"

"I can't. I have something to say to you."

Abby jerked her hand away and quickly got up. "Whatever it is, don't say it." She rubbed her forehead. "I think it's best if from here on out we work by email as I suggested before. Ask Reggie for my email address. He's got it. Good night." She practically ran out of the conference room to the private elevator.

"Come on," she pressed the button impatiently.

The doors opened. "Thank God."

She stepped in and then Sam dashed in just as the doors were about to close.

"What are you doing?"

Sam pressed the stop button and pulled Abby into a long, hot passionate kiss. Soon they were pressed up against the back of the elevator.

Sam pulled away. "I know you felt that." He panted.

"I don't understand. We don't know each other. How is this happening?"

"I can't explain it either. All I know is that something started to build the moment I first saw you." He gently caressed her cheek.

"But Sam," she started.

Abby practically melted in his arms as he pulled her into another long, lingering kiss.

He reluctantly pulled away. "I know what you're going to say but you should know that I want you and I know what I have to do." He kissed her again and then pressed the button to open the doors. "I'll see you soon."

As soon as the doors closed Abby's knees buckled wondering what he'd meant. Surely he wasn't saying to break off his engagement. That would be nuts. The whole thing was crazy. Abby pressed the button for her apartment.

⮾

Given the events of the past few days, Sam called his father once he was back in his hotel room. Though his father had been a coach and a mentor to him, he was also the person he trusted to give him the best advice.

"Hello?"

"Hi, Dad."

"Sam. What's going on?"

"What makes you think something is going on?"

"I just know. Now what's on your mind?"

Sam took a deep breath. "I'm in a bit of a situation here, Dad."

"I'm listening."

"I've been working with an editor on my book. Her name is Abby Carey and we've been spending a lot of time together…."

"And?"

"I think I've fallen for her."

"You think?"

"No, I've fallen for her, and I don't know what to do."

"Have you acted on these feelings?"

"Yes," he said hesitantly. "I haven't slept with her," he added quickly. "We've only kissed a few times. And before you ask, I was the one who initiated it."

"I take it that the report we heard about you being in a hotel is true."

"Yes. Maria and I had a fight. I didn't want to say anything that I would regret, so I left."

"Was that before or after you kissed Abby? Her name is Abby, right?"

"Yes. Actually it was before and after. Dad, when I talk to her it's like we've known each other for years. It's all so easy and natural."

"I thought you said she was a stickler."

"She is a stickler but when you get past that, she's really a lovely woman."

"A woman you want to know more about, right?"

"Yes."

"Does she want to know more about you?"

"I think so, but she—"

"She doesn't want to get involved with an engaged man."

"Correct."

"Then, son, I'm afraid you have some real thinking to do. First you have to consider whether this is a case of pre-wedding jitters. If it isn't, you have to be prepared in case Abby decides she doesn't want to pursue anything with you, and you really have to be ready for the fallout if she does."

"I feel like I'm disappointing you. I know how you feel about honoring commitments."

"You'd disappoint me more if you didn't listen to your heart and went through with a marriage out of some misguided sense of obligation. Her family aside, I like Maria. She's a lovely girl. However, there will be fallout."

"I've got a lot of thinking to do."

"Yes, I'd say you have some soul searching to do."

"I'll let you go, Dad. I know you and Momma had a long drive from Corpus Christi."

"That's one of the pleasures of being retired. We can sleep in."

"Okay, then, Dad. You have a good night."

"Good night, son."

Sam flopped onto the bed and stared at the ceiling. "It's going to be a long night."

Chapter 13

On Tuesday morning, Sam went back to the apartment empty-handed. He'd called Maria earlier to be sure that she'd be there and not gone for an appointment. They had some serious talking to do.

When Sam opened the door, he followed Maria's voice to the kitchen.

She froze for a moment. "Listen, Jessica. I have to go. We'll talk later. Thanks." She hung up. "You look like hell."

"I haven't been sleeping." He sat down at the kitchen table.

"The water's still hot. Do you want a cup of coffee?"

"No. If I have any more coffee, I'll be up for a week."

"Okay." She took a breath. "You wanted to talk. Let's talk."

"Maria, there's been so much happening with this wedding."

"I know, but it won't be like this forever. Just a few more months and we're home free."

"Are we?"

"What do you mean?"

"Right now it's convenient to blame our problems on the stress of planning a wedding. What are we going to blame when the wedding's over?"

"Is this still about sex and date night? You know that once this is over it will go back to way things were."

"And how were things?"

"Good."

"Really?" he said pointedly. "Are you sure?"

"Just because you say our sex life was sporadic doesn't mean it was. You were in the NFL. You traveled," she countered.

"You're right, but what about the other six months of the year? We barely went out together. When we did we didn't talk."

"That's not true. Why are you doing this? Are you trying to get out of the engagement?"

"I'm trying to get you to see things as they are."

Maria got up. "I'm not listening to any more of this." She rushed out of the kitchen.

Sam followed her. "Running away isn't going to change anything, Maria. We have to deal with this."

Maria ran into the bedroom and tried to close the door. Sam stopped her. "Let's be adults about this."

"Oh, you want to be adult about this? Is there someone else?"

"This isn't happening because of another woman."

"Then who is it about? Are you saying this is my fault?"

"No. We've grown apart. It happens."

"Bull," she shouted. "You're blindsiding me. Everything was going along fine. I don't understand." She shook her head in disbelief.

"I know we love each other, but I don't think we're *in* love anymore. That's why it was so much easier to focus on the aesthetics of the wedding. It kept us from having to look at what was going on underneath."

Tears streamed down Maria's face as she flopped onto the bed. "I can't believe this is happening."

Sam kneeled in front of her. "I'm sorry, Maria. I truly am. But I can't go through with this wedding. I'll always love you." As he stood up he kissed her forehead. "I'm going to stay at the W for a while. I'll have someone come and get some of my things. You can stay here as long as you like."

Sam's heart hurt as he heard Maria's sobs. Though he was upset, he knew they would both be better off in the long run. He only hoped that eventually Maria would see it that way, too.

A few minutes later Sam was inside his Mercedes. He composed himself and phoned his parents.

"Hello?" his father answered jovially.

Sam could hear the sound of a crowd in the background.

"Hi, Dad. It sounds like you're having a good time."

"Your momma and I are at the school's senior pancake breakfast."

"That sounds like fun. I wish I was there," Sam said somberly.

"What's the matter, Sam?"

"No, I don't want to bother you with my problems. I can call you later."

"You will do no such thing. Hold on for a minute." Sam stayed quiet as he listened to his parents talk.

"Okay. Are you still there?"

"Yes, Dad."

"I just told your momma that I was going outside for a minute. What's going on?"

"I did some thinking after our talk last night and I made a decision." He paused to take a breath. "I broke off the engagement."

"I know it wasn't easy for you."

"Maria might disagree with you."

"She's hurt. You have to give her time."

"Her family," he groaned. "What am I going to tell them? They're going to want an explanation."

"Well, they can want anything they'd like. It doesn't mean they deserve an explanation. This is between you and Maria. Where are you now?"

"I'm in my car, about to head back to the hotel."

"What are you going to do about the apartment?"

"I told Maria she could stay there as long as she likes. I'm going to stay in the hotel for a little while. I'll send someone to get some of my things."

"What happens after that?"

"I'm not sure, Dad. I guess I'll give it some time. I'm pretty sure Maria won't want to stay there much longer."

"Hmm," his father said.

"What are you thinking, Dad?"

"Maria is a lovely girl, but she is Big Bill's daughter. I think you'd be wise to expect the unexpected."

"You really think she'd be vindictive?"

"All I'm saying is to be prepared."

"I'll keep that in mind. Okay, Dad. I'd better get going. Traffic is going to be a bear. Give Momma my love and have a few buttermilk pancakes for me."

"I will."

As Sam pulled out into the street he thought about Maria and Big Bill. The Carrangelo family was known as one of the most powerful families in Texas. Big Bill and Kitty were friends of the Bush family. He quietly prayed for an uneventful breakup, but, as his father said, Bill Carrangelo played hardball with the big boys. Anything was possible, and this was one time when having endless possibilities wasn't a plus.

⊷∞⊷

Tuesday was an especially busy work day for Abby. After she'd handed out all the pitch letters she corrected. Shana asked her to help with Mark Botelli's in house model run through and dress rehearsal.

As one of the models walked, Botelli made a face. *"Essa una papera."*

"His translator is late." Shana turned to Abby. "What did he say?"

"Loosely translated, he said it's a duck."

"Gia is one of the top models in the country. Do you know how hard I had to work to get her?"

"I know." Abby studied her in the dress. "It's not her. I think it's the dress. I don't think it's hanging properly."

Shana got up and walked over to Gia. "Would you stand there for a minute, please?"

"Sure," Gia answered.

Shana walked around her. "I think you're right."

"Mark, E 'il vestito." Abby motioned to him. "Look for yourself."

He got up and looked more closely. "I see. I have to take it in a little more right here."

"You speak English?" Shana said surprised.

"Of course he does. Otherwise he would have used *lei* instead of *essa*. You know just enough Italian to get by, don't you Mark?"

He laughed. "Somehow Mark Botelli from Milan sounds better than Mark Botelli from Flatbush." He said with a full Brooklyn accent.

"Well I'll be damned." Shana was shocked.

"Will you keep my secret?" He asked sweetly.

"It's not up to me. You have to ask Shana." Abby said as she got up. *"Buona fortuna."* Abby playfully waved on her way out. A few moments later she was back upstairs on her floor.

"Hello, all." She said as she walked in.

"My, don't you look nice." Kelly smiled. "Is that a new outfit?"

Abby looked down at her black slacks and striped black and white shirt. "No. I've worn these pieces before. Though I don't think I've worn them together."

"Oh, but there's something different about you," Kelly pondered aloud. "I can't put my finger on it." She turned to Candy. "You see it too. Don't you, Candy?"

"Yes. It's like you have this little glow or something."

"Please," Abby scoffed. "I haven't glowed since I was pregnant. And by the way, that wasn't an announcement." She quickly added.

"You know my mother always says that women glow when they're pregnant, falling in love, or in love." Leo piped in.

"Since you're not pregnant is it love, Abby?" Kelly asked grinning.

"It isn't anything. Now while I have thoroughly enjoyed our witty repartee, we need to get back to work." She paused. "Was everything quiet up here?"

"It was business as usual." Reed answered. "Oh but Sam Best called for you a couple of times. He wants you to give him a ring back."

Abby's heart leaped into her throat for a moment. "Okay. Thanks, Reed." She said as she went to her office.

She sat behind her desk. *I guess I should call him back. If I don't call and he calls back, everyone will be suspicious.* She sighed. *This is what I get for being someone who's known for returning calls promptly.* She dialed the phone.

"Hello?"

"Hi, Sam. It's Abby. I'm returning your call."

"Thanks for calling me back. After last night I wasn't sure if you would."

"Well I did. So what's up?"

"I wanted to let you know that I broke off my engagement."

"You what?" Abby's jaw hit the floor. "Why?"

"When I really looked at it, things haven't been good for us in a while."

"Please tell me that I wasn't a factor in this."

"You didn't cause the break up, but…" he began.

"But?" she said anxiously.

"Being around you reminded me of what I wanted out of a relationship."

Abby turned her chair around and faced the window. "Now I feel like a homewrecker."

"You're not a homewrecker."

She felt her head spin. "I feel like I'm going to pass out or something. I have to talk to you later." She hung up. *I never thought I'd see the day when I was on the same level as Beebe.* Abby rubbed her eyes. "Hey, Shana."

"You are brilliant, girl. Botelli just agreed to sign with us for four years, and we're handling all his company's PR. That means all his divisions. We are golden." Shana said excitedly.

"That's great." Abby sounded less than enthusiastic.

"What's wrong with you?"

"I can't take it anymore. I have to tell someone."

"You're beginning to scare me."

"Do you have time to go upstairs?"

"No. But I'll make time. Let's go."

Abby got up and she and Shana walked out.

"Okay everyone I'll be in the residence for a little while but I'll be back. Hold down the fort, okay?"

"Sure thing, Abby," Kelly said.

Abby and Shana were in the hall headed for the elevator.

"Come on, no one can hear us now."

"I'll tell you in the elevator." Abby said as she pressed the call button.

The doors opened and they stepped in.

A few moments later the doors opened to Abby's apartment.

"Oh, my God," she brimmed with excitement. "You've been making out with Sam Best and you didn't say a word to me? I can't believe it."

Abby sat in one of her wing chairs. "I haven't been making out with Sam. It was a couple of kisses."

Shana sat in the adjoining chair. "You're calling it a couple of kisses?" She folded her arms. "Were your eyes closed?"

"Yes."

"Was there tongue involved?"

Abby paused. "Yes." She answered quietly.

"I know it's been a while Abby, but it hasn't been that long. You, my dear, were making out."

"Well I shouldn't have done it. He's engaged. At least he was engaged."

"Wait a minute. He *was* engaged?"

"Sometime between when I saw him," she started

"And played tonsil hockey with him," Shana interjected.

Abby scrunched up her face. "He called to tell me that he broke off his engagement." She shook her head. "This is not good."

"Do you think that you're the reason it happened?"

"I don't think I'm the main reason but he was a happily engaged guy a couple of weeks ago."

"Who's to say what goes on in a relationship behind closed doors? This may have been a long time coming for all you know."

"Do you suppose that's what Beebe's rationale was?"

"You're not comparing this with what she did?"

"It's awfully close to me."

"First of all, Beebe knowingly slept with a married man. There's a big difference between hitting the sheets and kissing."

"Tell that to Sam's former fiancée. I'm sure she wouldn't be able to see the difference. I know I wouldn't. Betrayal is betrayal."

"Any other time I would agree with you, but we aren't talking about the ultimate betrayal here. Nothing happened beyond kissing. Did it?"

"Of course it didn't."

"I'm just kidding. I'm trying to get you to lighten up on yourself."

Abby shrugged.

"So what happens next?"

"I don't know. I'm not going to be able to work with him anymore, that's for sure. I don't know how I'm going to tell Reggie."

"That's it?" Shana asked in disbelief.

"What do you mean? That's it? What else is there?"

"How about how you feel about Sam?"

"How I feel about Sam? I can count on one hand how many times we've been together. What feelings are there to talk about?"

"How about how you felt when you were kissing?"

"Like you said it was just a kiss. No big deal."

"Oh, my goodness," Shana said as she sat back in the chair. "You really like him."

"He's a nice guy."

"Leo's a nice guy, but you don't like him the way you do Sam. He made you feel something and you're scared to death."

"Oh don't be silly. I'm not scared of anything."

"Usually I would agree with you but I know you're scared of love. Besides if you didn't feel anything for Sam you wouldn't be so quick to say you're not working with him anymore."

Abby rubbed her forehead. "I feel a headache coming on."

"Take some Advil and get a Coca Cola later, but we're going to talk about this now. What else did Sam say when you talked to him?"

"He didn't have the chance to say anything else. I got off the phone."

"That figures." Shana nodded.

"Shana, I just can't go through it again." Abby sighed when she realized the words had left her lips.

"You're talking about what you went through with J.J., aren't you?"

When J.J.'s relationship came to light, some papers painted Abby as the wronged wife while the tabloids attacked her body. For months, Abby endured comments about her size and weight, with some rags going so far as to say that if she lost weight, J.J. wouldn't have cheated on her with Beebe in the first place. It was a dark period for the usually confident Abby, and one she felt she'd barely escaped from with her sanity.

"Yes. Maria Carrangelo is practically perfect. She's younger than me, brunette and thin. If I get involved with Sam, it will be the whole Beauty and the Beast thing all over again."

"You know that things are different now. We're doing a show for full-figured women at New York Fashion Week with Cedi. Five years ago that would have been unheard of so we're making progress."

"That's fine and well until you find your picture in the tabloids with the caption 'fat'. How many times have we seen tabloid at the supermarket checkout with celebrity fat and cellulite photos up close and personal. Things have changed, but not that much."

"Abby you can't let that keep you from taking a chance on love. Eventually the two of you are going to have to talk and you can take it from there."

"I know." Abby stood up. "But right now, I'd rather it be later than sooner." She looked at her watch. "We both have departments to run and I think we should get back to it."

Shana stood up. "I know. But can I say one more thing? Then I'm done for now."

"Go ahead."

"While I do feel sorry for Sam's former fiancée I don't think you should close the door on him. Love doesn't always come in the way we expect it to. So just keep an open mind and heart. Okay?"

"Okay."

"Don't say okay to shut me up. I want you to mean it."

"Have you ever known me to say things I don't mean?"

"You have a point there."

Satisfied with Abby's answer they headed back to the elevator.

❧

Like the Colossus of Rhodes, The Four Seasons ascended over Manhattan's Park and Madison Avenues. It beckoned both staid New Yorkers and tourists to enjoy the premier shops that flanked its elegant façade.

Sam sipped a martini as he sat in TY, The Four Seasons' elegant and intimate lounge on the west side of its East Fifty-seventh Street lobby. Though he usually preferred The Garden, he decided to opt for the comfort and privacy TY offered.

Bo entered the lounge and looked around until Sam waved him over.

"Hey, Sam," he said a little out of breath. "I came as soon as I could." He sat down.

"Thanks. Do you want a drink?"

He looked at his watch. "It's only three o'clock. Isn't this a little early for you?"

"It's five o'clock somewhere." He raised his glass and then motioned for a waiter. "What are you having?"

"I'm still working. So I guess I'll have a Coke."

The waiter walked over. "Yes, sir. What else can I get you?"

"He'll have a Coke. I'd also like the Kobe beef sliders with roasted onion mayonnaise. Do you think I could get fries, or should I say *pommes frites*, with that?"

"Yes, sir. I'll be right back with your drink." He walked away.

Bo studied his friend. "I will say that you look better today than when I saw you last."

"I'm glad I look better."

"So now you're feeling like hell instead of looking like hell."

"I'd say that sums it up." He sipped his drink.

The waiter placed Bo's drink on the table.

"Thanks." He said. "Now that you got me to come down here, are you going to tell me what's going on?"

"I broke off the engagement." He said bluntly.

"You did?" Bo was flabbergasted. "What happened? Did you have another fight?"

"No. I really had to take a hard look at our relationship. Things have been strained between us for a while now."

"Then why did you get engaged in the first place?"

"As crazy as this sounds I thought it would make things better."

"It never does. It's almost tantamount to having a baby to save a marriage. Are you sure this isn't a reaction to all the wedding stress? Planning a wedding can test the best relationships."

"Ironically planning the wedding made me realize just how much Maria and I had grown apart. I can't tell you the last real conversation we had that didn't involve the wedding or something wedding-related."

"I see your point."

"Then there's something else." He said as he put his drink down.

"It's the editor, isn't it? Did something happen between you two?"

"We kissed a few times."

"Is that all that happened?" He asked softly.

"Yes. We kissed and nothing more."

"That must have been some kiss." He sipped his Coke.

"It was more than just the kissing. It was how I felt, how I feel, when I'm around her."

"Do you know how she feels?"

"I think she feels the same way."

"Have you talked to her since you broke off the engagement?"

"Yes. I think she freaked out a little."

"Naturally she freaked out," Bo said. "The two of you kiss a few times and the next thing she knows, you're a single man again. Remember she was married to J.J. Stokes. The man had more assists getting women into bed than he ever had on the basketball court. She might be feeling a little like the other woman."

"She's not the other woman." Sam scoffed.

"That might be true, but most people are going to assume she is. Not the least of whom will be Maria and her family."

"So what's the proper waiting period?"

Bo shrugged. "I have no idea, Sam. I'm just playing devil's advocate. Frankly I think it's up to you and Abby. It's no one else's business. However there is going to be some fall out personally and professionally for you. I just want you to be aware of it."

"My father said the same thing."

"I assume your parents took the news of the broken engagement well."

"I wouldn't go as far as saying they jumped for joy. After all they like Maria."

"It's her family they could do without." Bo added.

"Right." Sam nodded. "My father said I needed to be prepared for anything."

"He's got a point. Once Big Bill hears about his little girl's broken heart, I really wouldn't put anything past him. Remember that D.A. that was dating Maria's middle sister, Kim?"

"Oh yeah," He nodded.

"He was an up-and-coming star at the courthouse. Then he and Kim broke up. The next thing you know he's in the public defender's office assigned to night court. The word around town was that Big Bill made some calls and made sure he was bussed down the ladder."

"Thanks for telling me," Sam said sarcastically.

"I'm sorry. I'm not saying he can do that to you. The fact is you're a multi-millionaire in your own right, but beware that he will be on the lookout for something to use."

"I'll keep that in mind." The thought jarred Sam.

"Do you know how Abby feels about you?"

"Yes. I'm going to have to pace things, but I know she has feelings for me."

If she needs more time than you expect, would that change your decision about Maria?"

"No."

"Then that's all I need to know. Technically you have a perfectly logical and acceptable reason to spend time with Abby. She is the editor of your book."

"I like the way you think, Bo."

"I guess I do know diddley." He laughed.

The waiter returned with Sam's food. "Here you go, sir. Can I get either of you gentlemen a refill?"

"Yes. I'll have another martini."

"Yes. And I will have what he's having." Bo grinned.

"You know they call this a shared plate."

Bo's eyes twinkled at the sight of the sumptuous burgers. "No. I don't want to share. Do you?"

"No."

"Case closed."

"I'll put your order in and I'll be back in a flash with another Coke." The waiter walked away.

Bo and Sam parted ways after their late lunch. As Sam walked down East Fifty-seventh towards Madison Avenue, he noticed all the luxury shop windows all decked out in red for Valentine's Day. He got his cell phone out and dialed.

"Hello, Cassie? It's Sam Best. How are you?"

"Hello, Sam. I'm well. Thanks. How are you?"

"Good. I called to ask you a question."

"Sure."

"Do you know of a good store for high quality pens?"

"Yes. Venture on Madison carries a big selection of high-end pens from Mont Blanc to Cartier."

"Great. Do you think you could get a special pen for me?"

"Of course I can. That's what a personal shopper is for."

"My only real requirement is that it be a red pen."

"Do you have a price range in mind?"

"No, but I don't want it to be too over the top expensive."

"No problem."

"Please have it wrapped and sent to me at the W Hotel in Union Square before Valentine's Day."

"I will. Is there anything else?"

"No. I think that covers it. I'll talk to you later. Thanks again."

"It's my pleasure. Have a good evening." She said cheerfully.

Sam hung up. He smiled to himself. *She did say that red is her signature color.* He braced himself for the cold and continued down the street.

Chapter 14

Abby settled in to read a magazine on the sofa. As she flipped through the pages the elevator doors opened and out walked Sam.

"What are you doing here?"

Without a word, Sam went over to Abby and took her into his arms. As the hands that thrilled millions on the football field caressed her body, Abby felt a thrill she hadn't felt in years. The feel of his breath on her neck as he kissed her made her weak in the knees. Her passion reawakened, she pulled Sam closer to her. He'd lit a fire in her and she was prepared to burn.

"Abby," he moaned softly as he opened her blouse and kissed her breasts.

"Abby."

Jolted, Abby opened her eyes.

"Are you all right?" Shana asked.

"I'm fine. I just dozed off."

"That must have been some dream you were having."

"Why would you say that?"

"You were smiling."

"I was?"

"Yes. You must have been dreaming about a man. Perhaps it was Sam?"

"Don't be silly." She brushed the idea off.

"Then what were you dreaming about?"

"I don't remember my dreams." She yawned. "What time is it, anyway?"

"It's ten o'clock."

"Oh, did you just finish the day?"

"No. I finished earlier. I've been on the phone with Raymond."

"I see." Abby smiled mischievously. "What did you and Mr. Hanson talk about?"

"Valentine's Day," her face lit up. "He's picking me up early Friday for a special evening."

"That sounds promising. Did he give you any hints?"

"He told me to pack a toothbrush and a smile."

She and Abby laughed.

"I still wish you were doing something for Valentine's Day."

"I'm heading up to Choate on Friday to meet with the headmaster. After that I'm going to relax so I'll be fresh when I see Justin first thing Saturday morning."

"I still don't see why you don't spend the day with Justin. I'm sure he wouldn't mind."

"Justin has a dance that night and I don't want to cramp his style. There's nothing worse than having your mother hovering over you all night like a helicopter."

"If you say so," Shana said with her arms folded.

"I do."

"Where are you staying?"

"I managed to get the Brae Cottage at the High Meadow Bed & Breakfast."

The High Meadow Bed and Breakfast was originally constructed in Branford in 1742 as the Jonathan Towner Half Way Tavern. It served as a travelers' stop halfway between New York and Boston. In the mid-seventies it was moved to High Meadows Farm. It was a charming place with several rooms, but the Brae Cottage was the most coveted to Abby. It had a large living room with cathedral ceilings, fireplace, a large bedroom, kitchen and bathroom. It was also separate from the inn and sat in an open field next to the woods and overlooked a pond.

"How did you manage that?"

"I booked it last year. I love Choate, but some of the parents are a little too amped up for me. You know what I mean?"

"I don't have children, so I know exactly what you mean. If I had a dime for every picture or story I've listened to, I'd be independently wealthy." She said half smiling.

Though Shana's life was filled with professional and personal success, she had one personal disappointment. She didn't have children. She had suffered for years with endometriosis and had undergone several surgeries in the hopes of being able to conceive one day. Until she met Raymond, she'd given up on finding a man that she wanted to be with let alone have children with.

"It will be your turn soon. You'll see. You and Raymond will get married and you'll hear the pitter-patter of little feet before you know it," Abby said reassuringly.

"We have to figure out our living situation before we can think about tying the knot."

"Washington D.C. isn't exactly the other side of the world. Besides, a lot of people have commuter marriages from New York to D.C. We could even open an office in D.C."

"I know we could open an office, but fashion is here in New York. I need to be here."

"Have you told him how you feel?"

"Yes."

"Are you sure you haven't just talked around it?"

Shana thought for a moment. "Maybe I have talked around it." She sighed. "How do you tell the man you love that you want him to move the career and business he's spent years building?"

"You tell him. He loves you."

"I wish it was that easy."

"I seem to remember a wise person told me that sometimes love doesn't come in the way we expect it to. Maybe it doesn't happen where we expect it to, either."

"Touché," Shana said.

"Seriously, Shana I'm sure things are going to work out. You need to trust that."

"I hope so." She sighed. "Okay. I'm going to head back downstairs and call it a night."

"All right," Abby said as she got up and stretched. "I think I'm going to do the same thing."

Shana pressed the elevator button. "Maybe you'll continue your dream about Sam." She winked.

"I told you. I don't remember what I was dreaming about."

"Okay, fine. You can be in denial if you want. But I know what the afterglow of a sex dream looks like." She stepped into the elevator. "Good night." She waved as the doors closed.

"Good night." Abby waited a few moments and then bolted for the window.

She opened the window. "Whew," she said as the cool air rushed over her. "I haven't had a hot sex dream in forever. *I only dreamed about kissing Sam and I've practically broken out into a flop sweat. If I go back to sleep and the dream picks up where it left off, I'm going to wake up in a pool tomorrow.*

❧

Once Sam had taken a shower and relaxed he dialed Reggie to update him on the latest development.

Not expecting Reggie to answer, he was surprised to hear his voice.

"Hello?"

"Reggie?"

"Hey, Sam."

"Hi. I wasn't expecting you to answer. I was going to leave a message. I hope I'm not disturbing you."

"I stayed up to finish up some paperwork. What's up?"

"I broke off my engagement," he blurted out.

"I knew things weren't going that well between you two, but I didn't think you would…" He stopped. "I'm sorry."

"Thanks."

"Are you all right?"

"I'm okay." He sighed. "I know there are things I need to know to handle this, but I'd rather talk about it tomorrow. If that's okay with you," he added.

"I understand."

Sam yawned. "Maybe we can meet for breakfast. I'll call you tomorrow."

"All right, Sam. Good night."

"Good night."

Sam fell back onto the bed and drifted off to sleep.

When Sam opened the door on Wednesday morning he found a gift bag next to the morning papers. *That was fast.* He thought as he picked everything up and closed the door. He tossed the newspapers on the table before he sat down on the bed and opened the bag. "Cassie didn't waste any time." He pulled a red Cartier box and opened it. "Perfect," he grinned.

⌒∽◇∽⌒

As Abby placed the last paper on Candy's desk, her Blackberry rang.

"Hello?"

"Good morning, Abby." Her mother said cheerfully.

Though Abby was her only daughter, Phyllis Carey was never the kind of mother who wanted them to dress alike. She was a pragmatic woman who was more concerned with her daughter's intellect. Growing up, Abby always looked preppy. She never wore the latest teen fashions clothes. It was a style she maintained until she met the fashion-savvy Shana and stepped up her wardrobe.

"Hi, Mom. How are you?"

"I'm good. Your dad just went to the course and I'm about to head to my pottery class. I'm going to glaze the plate I made earlier this week."

"That sounds like fun."

"I think so, too." She paused. "Although I should probably take some time to straighten this place up before I do anything. But you know I've slacked off when it comes to housekeeping."

Abby laughed to herself. When most people lived with the five-second rule, it was a thirty-minute rule in the Carey house. And despite her mother's claims of laziness, she was sure the rule had dwindled to a mere twenty-eight minutes. "So what else is going on, Mom?"

"Nothing really," she said. "I really called to see how Justin's doing."

"Justin's fine. I'm going up there for parents' weekend on Friday."

"I saw the magazine."

Abby sighed. "I talked to Justin about it before it hit the stands, Mom."

When Abby brought J.J. home, her parents were less than thrilled. NBA or not, he wasn't the man they pictured for their only daughter.

"That man… I told you athletes think with the wrong head."

"Not all athletes are like J.J."

"He certainly doesn't make a case for putting a positive spin on them."

"I know, Mom." She sighed. "What can I say? He's Justin's father."

"You're right. Anyway how is Justin taking the news? Is he okay?"

"He seemed to take it in stride. It was like it didn't faze him at all."

"That could be an act."

"I realize that, Mom. That's why I'm heading up to Choate on Friday to get a report from the headmaster and teachers about him."

"Good. They'll give you an objective look at how he's really doing." She paused. "Oh, would you look at the time. I've got to get to class soon."

"All right, Mom. You have a good time."

"I will. Be sure to give Justin our love and tell him to call us."

"Okay, Mom."

"I'll talk to you later, Abby."

"Bye, Mom."

No sooner did Abby hang up her phone, it rang again.

"Did you forget to tell me something, Mom?"

"Abby?"

A cold feeling ran down her spine. "Beebe?"

"Please don't hang up."

"What do you want, Beebe?"

"I'm actually calling to see how Justin's doing."

"You are?" Abby was shocked.

"I know it might surprise you, but I am concerned with how this is affecting him. How is he?"

"You and J.J. are airing your dirty laundry in public. How do you think he is?"

"I am sorry for that. Justin's a good kid. He doesn't deserve this."

"Then why don't you and J.J. work whatever out and get on with your lives? It's not like J.J. hasn't been through this before. Leave the publicists and lawyers on the sidelines and work through the issues. Once that's done call the lawyers and send out a press release. It's that simple."

"I wish it was that easy. J.J. is playing hardball with the prenup."

"What did you expect?"

"I thought he would be fair."

"If I recall correctly, all is fair in love and war. At least that's been my experience. Don't forget I've been on the receiving end too." Abby scoffed.

Beebe didn't utter a word.

"So do me a favor, don't ask me how my son is doing, okay? You're only interested in yourself. Bye, Beebe." Abby hung up and then sat down at her desk.

This is why I can't get involved with Sam. After everything that happened with J.J. and Beebe, I would seem like a hypocrite to Justin. He doesn't need to have two parents splashed across the gossip columns. She shook her head. *I don't want to push my luck. Sam will just have to understand my position. I'm a mother first and a woman second.*

Leo walked in. "Good morning, Abby."

"Hi, Leo. How are you?"

"Good," he said as he put his bag down. "But you don't look so good. Is anything wrong?"

"No. I was just thinking about next week's schedule."

"That's right. You're going to Fashion Week."

"I'm going to support our clients, check out the fashions and play enforcer for the front-row crashers."

In their own version of good cop/bad cop, Shana played the role of the welcoming publicist and co-producer for their client's shows. Unafraid to bark our orders or call people out, Abby checked names against the guest list and worked backstage with the production staff to make sure the show went off without a hitch.

"I still can't believe people try to steal seats."

"It's Fashion Week and everyone wants to be in the front row. So I've got to be the bouncer."

"You're far too pretty to be a bouncer."

"Thank you, Leo." She smiled. "I'll probably make up some folders with everything that needs to be done next week before I leave for Choate. I'm leaving you and Kelly in charge."

"Not a problem. We'll follow our marching orders."

"Thanks, and please be sure to stay on Candy's time. I don't want her to think that since the cat is away, the mice can walk in anytime they want."

"Don't worry." He took out his morning concoction.

"Ugh," Abby said emphatically. "I'll be in my office. I cannot bear to watch you drink that thing."

"It's better than you think, but it is an acquired taste."

"I'd rather not acquire it, thanks." She turned and went into her office.

Chapter 15

Although Maria had agreed to Sam coming over to the apartment, he was still a bit apprehensive as the elevator doors opened up.

Come on, Sam. You can do this. She sounded fine on the phone. He reminded himself as he walked down the hall. Once he was outside the door, he nervously jingled his keys.

Suddenly the door opened. "Just come in already, Sam. I thought it was Christmas with all the jingling out here." Maria said and then walked toward the living room.

Sam closed the door and followed her. Once Maria sat on the sofa, he stood there like a stranger in his own house.

"Sit down, Sam."

"Thanks for meeting me. I really wanted to—" he started.

"So who's the whore?" Maria asked, cutting him off.

"What?" Sam was taken aback.

"I found bank statements, Sam and you've had large sums of money going out on a monthly basis. Who's it for?"

Although Sam had switched to online banking on the advice of his accountant some time ago, he made a beeline for his office. Maria was hot on his heels.

"What the hell?" Sam said as he looked around his disheveled office. There were papers strewn everywhere. It was obvious a category five hurricane named Maria had blown through.

"What did you expect me to do? Did you think I was just going to pack my things and slink away? I wanted to get to the bottom of why my fiancé suddenly announced that he didn't want to get married without any explanation."

"That's not true. I told you why. In fact I came over here so we could talk like two civilized adults. I thought we owed our relationship that much."

"Oh, the old 'I love you but I'm not in love with you anymore' excuse was supposed to be your all-purpose out. Then I found these," she said holding up a small stack of papers. "This told me all I needed to know."

"Maria, I'm not supporting a mistress."

"Then where has this money been going?"

"It was my money to do with as I pleased. I don't have to render a detailed account for you."

"Well if that answer doesn't say it all."

"Maria, I didn't come here to fight with you. All I wanted to do was talk."

"We can talk. Just tell me where the money has gone," she said as she folded her arms.

Sam got annoyed. "This is useless." He threw up his hands. "Call me when you're ready to talk and to listen." Sam got up and left the apartment in a huff.

As he pressed the elevator call button his cell phone rang. "Hello?" He answered abruptly.

"Hello, Sam? It's Abby. Is this a bad time?"

Sam was actually relieved to hear Abby's voice. "No not at all, Abby. How are you?"

"I'm fine, although you don't sound so good. I can call you back."

"No. Don't be silly. I'm on the phone now. What's up?"

"I wanted to know whether you'd be available to meet for a late lunch today."

"Sure."

"Great. How about we meet at Pete's Tavern at, say, 2:30?"

"That sounds good to me."

"Terrific. I'll see you there."

"I'm looking forward to it." Sam said as he stepped into the elevator.

"Okay. So long," Abby said.

"See you later." Sam hung up the phone. *Maybe this day won't be a total bust.* He smiled as he pressed the lobby button.

⧼⧽

Abby sat quietly in a booth at Pete's Tavern. Located on 129 East Eighteenth Street in Gramercy Park, Pete's Tavern opened its door in 1864. Although its most famous patron was O. Henry, who wrote the classic *Gift of the Magi* there at his favorite booth by the front doors in 1902, the tavern had roots in modern television history with features on CNN, *Seinfeld*, *Law and Order* and *Sex and the City*.

Abby chose the late afternoon to avoid the busiest part of the lunch rush. However she knew the restaurant would be just busy enough so it wouldn't seem like she and Sam were secluded.

Abby was nervously stirring her seltzer with a straw when she noticed Sam heading toward the booth.

"Hi," He smiled warmly as he sat down.

"Hi."

"I hope I didn't keep you waiting long."

"No."

"I'm so glad you called me. I've been thinking about you."

"I've been doing a lot of thinking, too, and that's why I called you here to meet me face to face."

"I don't know if I like the sound of that." He said cautiously.

Abby steadied her nerves with a deep breath. "I'm sure you had reasons for ending your engagement, and that's your business. However, I want to make it clear that there won't be anything happening between us beyond working together."

"Why?"

"Do you really have to ask?"

"I know I just broke off my engagement. People break up all the time. It's nothing new."

"You are not most people. You are Sam Best. There is no way this is going to go soft."

"Why should I care what people think?"

"You have a lot at stake here. Not the least of which is your image."

"My image might be important, but it's not more important than my heart." He reached across the table and took her hand in his. "My heart is telling me that there's something between us. I feel it and I know you do, too."

Abby let her hand linger in his for a moment before she pulled it away. "I don't let my impulses lead me around." She reached into her bag, pulled out a business card and placed it on the table. "Here's my email address. I think it's best we work this way." She stood up and began to walk away when Sam grabbed her hand.

"Look me in the eyes and tell me you don't feel anything and I'll leave you alone."

"Please let go," she said, avoiding his eyes.

"See, you can't do it."

"Let go, Sam." She insisted.

When he released her hand, Abby placed a twenty-dollar bill on the table. "That should cover my beverage and tip. Email me, Sam." She grabbed her coat and walked away as quickly as she could.

I need some air fast. She thought as she put her coat on. As soon as she stepped outside, the cold air rushed around her. *I should have had a hot chocolate.* She thought as she bundled up and flagged a cab.

"Thanks." She said shivering.

"Where to, ma'am?"

Just as Abby was about the close the door, Sam rushed in next to her.

Sam closed the door and leaned forward. "Here's one hundred dollars. Drive." He told the cabbie.

"Yes, sir," he responded enthusiastically.

He started driving.

"What are you doing?" Abby asked. "Stop this," she began.

Before she could utter another syllable, Sam pulled her into a long, deep kiss. Abby resisted initially but the soft, gentle way his lips caressed hers wore her down and she slowly relented until she was enveloped in his arms.

Though he wanted more, Sam pulled away. "I thought so." He turned to the cabbie. "Stop the car."

"Yes, sir," he pulled over to the side of the road.

"I'm not giving up on you, Abby." He said as he opened the car door and stepped out. "Carry on," he smiled as he tapped the cab and walked away.

"Where to, miss?"

Abby was dazed.

"Are you all right, ma'am?"

Abby snapped out of it. "Oh, I'm sorry. 2145 Thompson Street between Broome and Prince."

Abby sat back in the seat. *Why did I let him kiss me like that? My intention was to be firm and keep things on a business level. Now it's all screwed up.*

❧

Feeling smug and satisfied, Sam strutted into his room. Reggie was already there.

"Hey, Reggie. I was going to call you."

"I thought I'd save you the quarter." Though it was an amusing answer, Reggie didn't look amused.

"You're awfully stone faced. What's up?"

"I don't know. You tell me." He handed Sam a newspaper. "This is the late afternoon edition of the paper."

"What's this?" Sam looked perplexed.

"Read it."

The headline read *Sam Best dumps longtime fiancée.*

"What?" Sam was astonished.

"Keep reading." Reggie said.

Maria Carrangelo, Sam Best's longtime girlfriend and fiancée, says she was blindsided by the former quarterback when she was unceremoniously dumped just four months before their June nuptials. "Going through that traumatic time of being heartbroken and then realizing there are other parties involved has turned my whole world inside out," Carrangelo tells columnist Cindy Harper.

"I thought Sam and I had the perfect relationship. I was ready to walk down the aisle and start a family with this man,'" the 36-year-old said. "I'm a traditional girl, and I believe in marriage, fidelity and commitment. I thought Sam shared those beliefs. I was wrong."

Carrangelo's family has hired famed attorney Antonia Redstone to represent their daughter's interests. Redstone, an attorney noted for taking on celebrity and high-profile cases, most recently represented Amber Henderson, a former cocktail waitress who was named a party in the divorce of NASCAR star Franco Cavaleri from his wife of eleven years, Elena.

"What the hell is this?" Sam threw the paper on the floor.

"A PR nightmare," Reggie answered bluntly. "I'm not going to ask how they got this in the paper so quickly. I know we have Toni Redstone to thank for that. I just want to know how they managed to get her. I know Big Bill has money, but I wouldn't have imagined even he'd be able to hire her."

"Toni and Maria's mom were sorority sisters."

"Now you tell me." He shook his head. "I knew I should have just gone ahead and released a statement the minute you told me."

Sam sat on the bed. "I'm sorry, man. I know this is my fault. I was the one who told you that I wanted to have another talk with Maria first."

"What happened with that?"

"I don't really have to tell you, do I? You read the paper."

"Saying it didn't go well is an understatement."

"Yes."

"But what the hell is this stuff about other parties involved in the break up?"

"She went through my papers and found some old bank statements."

"So?"

"When Maria saw the large check withdrawals, she assumed that I was keeping a mistress or two and the money proved it."

"Why didn't you just tell her they were charitable donations for retired NFL players?"

"Because I want to keep it anonymous," Sam said insistently.

"Well your little anonymous donations are about to cost you big time."

"I know I could have told her. I was so angry at the time. You should have seen what she did to the stuff in my office."

"I can imagine but you could have avoided this." He said pointing to the paper.

"I know you're right. I should have handled it better."

Reggie patted him on the back. "Don't beat yourself up about it now. We have to look ahead."

"In other words, damage control."

"That's precisely what we need."

"What's my next step? Do I have a press conference?"

"I'm not sure. I have to check with our PR crisis management team to see what your options are. They're working on that now. They'll be in touch soon. I should have something within the next couple of hours."

"What do I do in the meantime?"

"You need to lay low for the time being."

"So you want me to stay in my hotel room."

"You don't have to stay in here. However you can't bring too much attention to yourself. I already have a decoy here in the hotel for you." He took out a card and handed it to Sam. "When you want to go out, call him and he'll lure the paparazzi to follow him while you leave unnoticed."

Sam looked at the card. "Thanks. Who knew my life would become a B-list spy movie?"

Reggie laughed. "Remember to keep your clothes basic. Wear jeans, sunglasses, boots and a baseball cap to cover your eyes."

"So my decoy has an identical wardrobe?"

"It's one of the perks of being a decoy. When you call let him know what you're wearing and he'll do the rest. He's a professional." Reggie looked at his watch. "I've got to get to the office to meet with the team." He picked up his coat. "I'll be in touch soon."

"Okay." Sam stood up and walked him to the door. "Thanks for everything." He opened the door.

"Not a problem. Talk to you soon."

Reggie walked out.

Sam picked up the newspaper from the floor. "How's this for timing? Just when I made a little headway with Abby, this happens."

Back from lunch and still thinking about the cab ride Abby walked past a plethora of publicists and account executives as they worked the phones for Fashion Week.

She met Lauren as she walked out of Shana's office.

"Hi, Abby," she smiled warmly.

"Hi, Lauren. Is she busy?"

"No. Go right in."

"Thanks." Abby poked her head in. "I'm back."

"Oh, thank God! Come in." She motioned.

"What's the matter? Do you need me to strong arm another client?"

"No. Close the door."

Abby stepped in and closed the door. "Now you're worrying me. Has something happened?"

"Yes. It's not business-related, though."

"Whew!" Abby quickly swiped her forehead. "That's a relief. So what are you all worked up about?"

"You haven't seen the late edition of *The Post*, have you?"

"No. I was at lunch."

Shana tossed the paper on her desk.

Abby's eyes nearly bugged out when she picked it up. "What in the world?" She paused to read the article. "I don't believe this."

"Does she know?"

"Does who know?"

"Sam's fiancée. Did she find out about you?"

"There's nothing to find out."

"You and Sam have kissed a few times."

A picture of her and Sam kissing in the car flashed in Abby's mind before she caught herself. "Yes. We've kissed but that's all. She's saying there are other parties, plural, involved. Frankly it sounds like she's taking a stab in the dark."

233

"A stab in the dark or not, it's in Cindy Harper's column."

"Who calls the press for suspicions?"

"Toni Redstone."

"True." Abby tapped her fingers on the desk. "Well there is only one way to find out what's going on for sure."

"You're going to call Sam?"

"No. I'm calling Reggie."

"He's going to ask why you want to know."

"I have a legitimate reason. I am working with Sam. These kinds of things will affect his work." Abby said as she opened the door.

"That makes sense. Don't forget to give me the 411 once you know."

"I won't. I'll see you later." Abby waved.

Abby dialed Reggie on her way to the staircase.

"Hello?"

"Hi, Reggie."

"Thank goodness. Finally a friendly voice."

"It's nice to be appreciated." She paused. "You sound frazzled."

"I'm in the middle of spin central right now. I'm sure you heard about the breakup."

"Yes. I read Cindy's column."

Reggie groaned. "Remember when breakups were private?"

"Breakups have never been private for celebrities. It's us plain folks that get to lick our wounds without cameras. Remember how I found out about J.J.'s cheating?"

"Yes, but it seems like celebrity gossip is on steroids now."

"It is on steroids. We have the internet, tabloid magazines, Page Six, entertainment news channels and celebrity bloggers. Shall I go on?"

"Don't forget Toni Redstone."

"Who could forget her? I'm telling you if a D.A. indicted a ham sandwich at 10 a.m. you can be sure Toni would be representing the ham by lunch time."

Reggie laughed. "Thanks. I needed that."

"Anytime," she replied. "So what's really happening?"

"Maria's upset and angry about the breakup. She thinks Sam has other women."

"Why would she think that?"

"Don't repeat this, but she found out about some unaccounted for expenses."

"And she thinks it means he has a mistress?"

"Yes."

"Why doesn't Sam just tell her the expenses are anonymous donations for disabled and retired NFL players? That would solve everything."

"How did you know about that? Did Sam tell you?"

"No." She paused. "A couple of checks fell out of his portfolio. I just put two and two together. I'm not even sure he realizes that I know. He never said anything when I returned the checks."

"That sounds like Sam."

"So why doesn't he just save himself and you some grief and come clean?"

"He won't do it. He wants to remain anonymous."

"But that's crazy. It's not like he was spending money on hookers. It would clear everything right up."

"I know, but he's the client. I have to do what he wants."

"I guess you do." Abby said as she reached the top of the staircase.

"Listen, Abby, I've got to run. It looks like we have a press release."

"Okay. Good luck."

"Thanks." He hung up.

Abby felt a twinge of guilt for fishing for information from Reggie. She knew with this latest development that the press was tracking Sam's every move and she couldn't afford for them to be seen together. Whether Sam liked it or not, they were going to have to work via email.

∞

Sam lay on the bed and stared at the ceiling. His cell phone rang.

"Hello?"

"It seems all hell is breaking loose, son," his father said, half laughing.

"Hi, Dad," he sat up. "I guess you read the papers. I'm a lousy cheater with a harem of women."

"I didn't have to read the paper. I got an earful from Big Bill."

"I can only imagine how that conversation went."

"Oh yes. He wanted your mother and me to work with him and Kitty to help get you kids back on track. I told him I didn't interfere in my adult children's lives."

"I bet he didn't like that."

"That was his tough luck. How are you holding up?"

"I'm none the worse for wear, but it's still early. I'm sure there is more to come."

"The Carrangelo family is on the warpath. You can bet on it."

"I am the one who set this whole thing in motion."

"Well, son, it's better that you ended it now than after the wedding."

"I know."

"How about we change the subject? What's happening with Abby?"

Sam smiled. "I managed to make a little headway with her. Although I am sure it's shot to hell now."

"Remember when I used to take you and your brothers fishing for Largemouth Bass at Lake Houston?"

"Sure."

"We had to be real quiet to coax them to our spot, but every now and then some boat would go by and scare the fish away."

"God, I hated that."

"I did, too. But do you remember what I used to do to get the fish to come back?"

"We'd row out to another spot and change bait."

"Then we'd come home with more fish than we could carry, didn't we?"

"Yes. Momma hated that." Sam laughed.

"Don't remind me." His dad chuckled. "The point is, son, if you want Abby you're going to have to row a little further out and coax her to the surface. If you get what I mean."

"I get it. Thanks, Dad."

"You're welcome. Well I will let your momma know that you're okay. I have to help her gather some things for the church rummage sale."

"Oh that's nice of you, Dad."

"You're not the only one trying to avoid waves." He laughed.

"You do what you have to, right, Dad?"

"Right. I'll talk to you later, Sam."

"Okay, Dad, and thanks again."

Sam lay back down on the bed. "Row a little further out? I wonder how I can do that. I have to give it some thought." He closed his eyes.

Chapter 16

Dressed in a pair of black slacks and a sweater, Abby sat on the bed and made a phone call. Her suitcase was packed and ready to go.

"Good morning, High Meadow Inn." The voice answered.

"Good morning, Nanette. It's Abby Carey. How are you?"

Innkeepers, Brad and Nanette Charles, had run the High Meadow Inn for more than thirteen years. A lovely middle aged couple with grown children, they enjoyed interacting with the parents who came to visit Choate. They became fast friends with Abby when Justin began Choate in ninth grade.

"I'm fine, Abby. How are you?"

"I'm good. I apologize for calling so early, but I need to ask you for a favor."

"Sure."

"I wondered if it would be okay if I came up a day early. I'll pay extra for any inconvenience."

"Don't be silly." She said. "I don't see why not. It's no trouble at all."

"Thanks." Abby breathed a sigh of relief.

"If you don't mind me asking, is everything all right?"

"Yes. Everything is fine. I just want to get away from the city a little early. You know, give myself a chance to relax before another busy parent's weekend."

"I understand. What time do you think you'll be here?"

"I should get there around noon or maybe a little earlier. I have to wrap a few things up here first and then I'll be on my way."

"We're looking forward to seeing you."

"I'm looking forward to it too. I'll see you later."

"Okay, dear. Bye-bye." Nanette almost sounded like she was singing.

"Okay, bye." Abby got up and zipped her suitcase.

"All right, you asked me to come up here this morning," Shana said as she looked over at Abby's suitcase. "Why are you packed? It's not Friday."

"I decided to leave a day early."

"Did something happen to Justin?"

"No. Justin's fine. I'm just getting away early that's all."

Shana sat down on the bed. "You're fleeing."

"I'm not fleeing. What do I have to flee from?"

"It's not what you're fleeing from, it's who. Sam."

"Don't start, Shana."

"It's true and you know it."

"The man's life is complicated, and with this press thing it's only going to get more complicated. I don't need that in my life. I can't do that to Justin."

"You can't do what to Justin? Have a life of your own?"

"I know I can have a life of my own, but I don't want to do it at the expense of my son. I can't cause any more upheaval in his life. It's bad enough his father's love life is splashed across the tabloids."

"Who says you'll wind up in the papers?"

"Did you not see yesterday's paper, Pollyanna? I can promise you that's only the beginning." Abby said as she went over to check her hair in the mirror.

"You can't be sure of that."

"Shana, if anyone finds out about Sam and me, I might as well paint myself green, get a black witch's hat and audition for *Wicked*. There is no way to spin this."

Shana couldn't help chuckling. "Okay. At least give the guy a chance to sort it out before you head for the hills."

"I'm not heading for the hills," Abby replied. "Listen, Shana, I didn't ask you to come up here so we could debate this into oblivion. I need you to do something for me."

"Okay. Go ahead."

"There are three folders on the coffee table. I need you to give them to Kelly. She'll know what to do."

"Okay. I still can't believe you're going to leave your staff unattended for two whole days."

"I trust that they'll do their jobs. Besides, I won't be hovering over them next week, either."

"That's right you're our enforcer for Fashion Week. I'm telling you Abby, you really could have had a career as a Secret Service agent with the way you can spot a poser a mile away."

Abby chuckled, and then grunted as she lifted the suitcase off the bed.

"That looks heavy. Can you even carry that downstairs?"

"Don't worry. It has wheels." Abby pulled the handle and rolled it out of her bedroom. Shana followed.

"Do you have everything?"

"Yes. I think so." Abby stopped to put her coat and hat on. "I think I'm good." The doors opened the moment she pressed the elevator call button. "Okay, dear I'm off." She hugged Shana.

"Call me when you get there and give Justin a hug for me."

"I will." Abby stepped in. "I'll see you Sunday evening." She waved as the doors closed.

❧

Sam awoke to the sound of knocking.

"I'm coming." He called out as he slowly slid out of bed. "Hold your horses!" He slipped his robe on and headed for the door. "What time is it?" He mumbled. "Who is it?"

"It's Bo."

He opened the door. Bo was carrying a handful of papers and magazines. "Good morning, sunshine." He said as he walked in.

"Good morning." Sam hadn't quite cleared the frog in his throat.

"You look like hell."

"Thanks." Sam said sarcastically as he sat down on the bed. "I know you didn't come here to give me grooming advice. What's going on?"

"You are the lead story today." He said as he dropped all but one of the papers on the floor. "They've got you pegged as everything from a sex addict to a plain old everyday heel."

"I thought Reggie said we would have a statement by today."

"Oh, you do have a statement." Bo opened the paper. " 'Representatives for former New York Giants quarterback, Sam Best have confirmed the split with real estate heiress, Maria Carrangelo, a rep for Best said in a statement on Wednesday.' " Bo paused. "It reads, and I quote, *'We ask for your respect and consideration of their privacy during this difficult time. No further comments will be made.'* "

Sam grabbed the paper from him. "That's all it says?"

"Yes."

Sam went through the rest of the paper. "I guess Big Bill and Kitty are here." He held up the page with the photo of them entering Trump Tower.

"The reinforcements have arrived."

"I have a headache." He rubbed his forehead.

"In more ways than one," Bo added. "There are a swarm of photographers outside waiting for the first shot of you with your *kept women*."

"Oh this is ridiculous. There are no women." He shook his head. "It never ceases to amaze me the conclusions people will jump to when you spend a little money."

"Are you talking about Maria?"

"Yes. She found some old statements and wanted me to account for the large withdrawals. I don't know what she was so interested in. It wasn't her money."

"Okay so she found your donations. Why didn't you just tell her that?"

"I didn't see why she needed to know."

"I've got two words for you. Dennis Shanahan."

Dennis Shanahan, a former Patriots player and color commentator for the NFL got caught up in a paid escort scandal in the early nineties. A married man and father of four, Dennis reportedly spent nearly one hundred thousand dollars for the girl's company. Once the truth came out he lost his family, his television gig, lucrative sponsorships and his good name.

Though the scandal was more than a decade in the past, Dennis had sunk to doing payday loan commercials on late night basic cable.

"I'm not Dennis. He was named in that little black book."

"That might be true, but unless you come out and let people know about your donations, they will jump to that conclusion. It's not that big of a leap."

"Forget it."

"I understand why you wanted to remain anonymous. But this thing is spinning out of control. All you have to do is tell people and the whole thing will go away."

"No." Sam was firm.

"Why?"

"When I look at guys like Norm Green and I see what he's and others like him are going through. I see my dad. My father would have played in the NFL if the accident hadn't happened. I think in a lot of ways that accident saved my father's life in the long run. He was able to teach and earn a good pension for his retirement. Now he and my mother are enjoying their golden years. Did you know that Norm Green and my father are the same age?"

"No." Bo looked surprised.

"I didn't, either. The years of hard playing have taken their toll on Norm and when I think about it that could have just as easily been my dad. That's why I give."

"This is what the public needs to hear. Why don't you let me call someone at the network?"

"No. I don't do it so I can be a feature on ESPN. That might be okay for some guys, but not me. I don't need the accolades or the fanfare."

"I admire your conviction."

"Thanks."

"Although you don't have any kept women, you are interested in one woman in particular. How's that going? Have you spoken to Abby since the story broke?"

"I did see her yesterday, but that was before all hell broke loose. I was going to go over to her office today."

"How are you going to do that? I told you the barbarians are poised at the gate."

"I know." He picked up the card on the night stand. "I have a plan and you are going to help me."

"How am I going to help you?"

"You'll see." Sam smiled.

An hour later, Sam's decoy, Bernard, was in his room dressed just like him.

Bernard Sykes was a thirty-seven-year-old actor and model. He was a dead ringer for Sam down to the color of his eyes.

"How do I look?" Bernard asked.

"If I didn't know better I would say you were me." Sam laughed.

"That's the idea." Bo laughed, too.

"So we're clear on the plan, right?" Sam asked.

"I've got it." Bernard said as he put the baseball cap and sunglasses on.

"What about you, 007?"

"I'm ready."

Sam put on his cap and sunglasses. "Let's go."

The three men left Sam's room. A few moments later they were in the lobby of the W Hotel. Sam waited while Bo and Bernard left through the front door. Almost immediately the photographers swarmed around them as they walked away from the hotel towards Bo's car, which was parked three blocks away.

Sam waited a few minutes for the coast to be clear and then walked out to an empty sidewalk. *Good*, he sighed with relief. *I have someplace I have to be.*

Shana and Kelly were in Abby's apartment.

"I can't believe I left one of the folders up here." Shana said as she grabbed it from the coffee table.

"That's not a problem."

"Here you go." Shana handed it to her.

Kelly glanced at it. "Thanks." She paused. "Abby will be back in time for next week, right?"

"She'll be home by Sunday evening."

"Okay. Great."

Just as Kelly and Shana walked to the elevator the intercom buzzed.

"I wonder who that could be." Shana said aloud.

The elevator doors were open.

"Do you want me to wait for you?"

"No. You go ahead. I can take the stairs."

"Okay."

The doors closed. Shana went over to the intercom. "Yes?"

"Hi, it's Sam. Can I come up, Abby?"

"Sure." Shana pressed the buzzer. "Isn't this an interesting development?" She said aloud.

A few moments later the elevator doors opened.

Sam looked surprised to see Shana. "Hi, Shana," he looked around. "Did I press the button for the wrong floor?"

"No. You're in the right place. I just happened to be here."

"Oh, is Abby here?"

"No."

"Is she in her office?"

"No."

"Well, um, you know we're working on my book together and I needed to talk to her about something. It's book-related," he quickly added.

Shana stared at him with a blank look.

"You don't believe me for a minute, do you?"

"Not even for a second." She smirked.

"I suppose you know about the kissing."

"Yes. I also know about the break-up."

"You and millions of other people. Do you mind if I sit down?"

"Go right ahead."

Sam looked like there was a million pounds on his feet when he sat down. "Is Abby at a meeting? I can wait."

"No. She went away for a few days."

"She didn't say anything about leaving at lunch yesterday."

"Oh you saw each other yesterday?"

"Yes." He paused. "All right, I know I've got a lot happening around me at the moment, but it won't always be like this."

"I should hope not."

"I know. The timing is bad."

"Bad isn't the word I'd use."

"The timing is horrible. But since when does love follow a schedule?"

"Love," Shana repeated.

"Yes. This isn't a fling for me. I'm not a fling kind of guy. I want to pursue a relationship with her. Can you help me out? Where is she?"

Shana was touched by his sincerity and thought for a moment. "What the heck? It is Valentine's Day tomorrow." She took a breath. "Abby is visiting her son at Choate. She usually stays at the High Meadow Inn in Wallingford, Connecticut. You know she's probably going to kill me for this."

Sam leaped to his feet. "Thanks, Shana." He kissed her on the cheek and rushed towards the staircase.

"The elevator is over there."

"The elevator would take too long. I've got some ground to cover," Sam said as he disappeared down the staircase.

"Good thing he's a quarterback. We're both going to need a few Hail Mary passes once Abby finds out."

Chapter 17

When Abby pulled up to the inn, she felt a sense of calm come over her. Though she loved the beat of the city, Abby relished the idea of a little peace and quiet away from the all the white noise in her life. As she got out of her Land Rover, she was approached by Brad and Nanette Charles.

"Hello, Abby." Brad called out.

A retired engineer, Brad Charles was a tall, blond with ice-blue eyes. His wife, Nanette, was a petite, plump brunette with green eyes.

"Hi, Brad. Hi, Nanette." Abby smiled as she got her bag from the backseat.

"Let me take that." Brad said.

Nanette hugged her. "It's good to see you, Abby. You look good."

"Thanks. So do you." Abby pulled her coat closer to her body. "I forgot how cold it gets up here."

"Then let's get you over to the cottage. Brad has the fireplace going for you."

"Oh, that sounds nice and warm."

The three of them walked the property until they came to Brae House. It looked like it belonged on a winter postcard. The pond was frozen over and there was smoke coming from the chimney.

"Here we go." Brad unlocked the door.

The feeling of heat immediately surrounded Abby as she stepped in. "It feels nice in here."

"Would you like me to put your bag in the bedroom?"

"Yes. Thank you."

"Okay." He rolled the suitcase towards the master bedroom.

"The fridge is fully stocked with everything you asked for."

"Good. Thank you."

"You can join us at the main house for breakfast tomorrow if you like. There's no need to make your own eggs if we can do it for you."

"I'll keep that in mind, Nanette." Abby smiled.

"Okay. I think you're all set." Brad said when he returned. "Let's leave her alone to unpack, Nanette. Abby knows how to reach us if she needs anything."

"We're only a phone call away."

"I know." Abby hugged Nanette.

Brad put his arm around Nanette. "Enjoy." He waved as they walked out of the cottage.

Abby looked around for a moment before she headed back to the bedroom. "Do I feel like unpacking right this minute?" She eyed her bag. "It can wait." She kicked her boots off and lay on the queen-size bed.

"Maybe I'll watch a little television." She said as she flipped the television on and turned to *Headline News*.

"*In entertainment news, famed attorney Toni Redstone, who is currently representing New York Giant Sam Best's former fiancée, Maria Carrangelo, announced today that they are pondering a breach of contract case against the famed former quarterback.*

There is precedent for this case as Ms. Redstone represented, Delia Duncan a woman who took a $40,000-a-year pay cut to move from Atlanta to Kentucky to be with her fiancé, Lance Banfield. Redstone argued that her client's fiancé's promise of marital bliss amounted to a binding contract and Ms. Duncan suffered financial losses as a result of their breakup. A jury in Clark County, KY, agreed and handed down a verdict that gave Ms. Duncan an award of $300,000.

"*We have our own legal expert, Alan Weinstein, here to weigh in. Thanks for joining us, Alan.*"

"*Thanks for having me, Georgiana.*"

"*In 2008, there were 2.1 million plus weddings in the United States. So I imagine that for every couple that gets married there are more than a few that didn't make it down the aisle. What does this case mean for the injured party?*"

"*Well it depends on the circumstances. In the case of Toni Redstone's client in Kentucky, she uprooted her life in good faith and took a significant pay cut. Her financial damages were easily proven."*

"What about Maria Carrangelo?"

"It's my understanding that Ms. Carrangelo comes from a wealthy family and she didn't work during her relationship with Sam Best. I'm sure there is some emotional damage as a result of the broken engagement, but it doesn't look like she's sustained any financial damage."

"Some attorneys have argued that Redstone's case opened the door for frivolous lawsuits. What do you think?"

"I think that every case is different. I'm sure some cases are legitimate. However it might have set a precedent that every time a couple has a dispute and one party believes the other to be a cheat or miscreant, all you have to do is hire a lawyer and hope to hear sounds of a cash register emanating from the jury room."

"She's filing a breach of contract case? He broke off an engagement. He didn't climb into a bell tower with an AK-47," Abby said as she turned the television off. She could see that the matter was getting messier by the minute and was glad not to be involved.

With the coast still clear at the hotel, Sam went to his room, packed a small bag and managed to get downstairs to his Mercedes unnoticed.

As he pulled into traffic, he dialed Bo on his Blue-
tooth.

"Hello?"

"Hey. How is everything going? Are they still following you?"

"Yes. They're all perched outside of the building.
We even fooled a few people here at ESPN. They
thought I brought you in for an exclusive."

Sam laughed. "Good. I'll need you to bring Bernard back to the hotel tonight. He has to stay hun-
kered down there until I get back."

"Until you get back," he asked. "Where are you going?"

"It's better that you don't know. Trust me. I'll be
fine."

"Does Reggie know about this yet?"

"I'll let him know once I get to my destination. If I
call him before that, he'll try to talk me out of it."

"He'd be right."

"Well right now I have to do what feels right. I'll
call you once I arrive. Okay?"

"Okay."

"Thanks, buddy. I owe you one."

"You owe me more than one." Bo laughed and
then hung up.

Sam programmed the name of the inn into his GPS. "Ready or not, Abby here I come."

❦

Abby was awakened by the sound of someone at the door. "Just a minute," she called as she made her way from the bedroom to the front door.

"Yes?" She opened the door.

"You're a hard woman to find, Abigail Carey."

"Sam?" She was wide awake now. "What are you doing here? How did you know I was here?"

"I know you have a lot of questions, but I'd rather answer them later than sooner." He closed the door and kissed Abby passionately. Soon they were pressed up against the wall. Sam overtook Abby's senses as she melted with each kiss. Urgently his hands lifted her sweater and he began kissing and caressing her breasts.

"Sam," she whispered struggling to find her voice.

"No more talking," Sam said, pulling her sweater over her head. He swiftly unhooked her bra and continued kissing and gently sucking all around them.

"Oh," she moaned softly.

He continued kissing her neck. "Where's the bedroom?" He whispered.

"Down the hall," she answered softly.

He picked her up and carried her to the bedroom. Gently, Sam laid her on the bed. Abby's body quivered when Sam took his sweater off and she saw his well-defined chest and washboard abs. He lowered himself on top of her.

As their passion rose, Abby let her hands explore Sam's chiseled body. He was hard in all the right places. His grip was firm yet gentle. Sam was everything she'd ever wanted in a man. When his hands dropped to her zipper, Abby's body tensed up.

"What's wrong? Am I going to fast?"

"No. It's just that, she stammered slightly. "I haven't been with anyone in this way in a while now. I know it's silly but I'm nervous."

"That's not silly at all." He caressed her face.

"That's not all. I have a stomach, and it's more than a little pooch."

"So?"

"I've seen Maria and she's flat as a washboard. Between the pooch and the map of the Appalachians my stretch marks have formed over the years, it's not a pretty sight."

"Why? You did have a baby."

"It's nearly been sixteen years since I had a baby. What's my excuse now?"

"You know one of the things that attracted me to you was your confidence. When you walked into your office that morning you looked so sexy in that dress. It just hugged you in all the right ways. Then when you ate a muffin at our breakfast without breaking out a carbohydrate calculator and you didn't obsess over the calories, I thought to myself, this is my kind of woman. She's unafraid to be who she is."

"You got all of that from a few meetings?"

"Yes. So to hear you talk about how imperfect you think your body is really puzzles me."

"It is a little crazy to be overcome by neuroticism at this moment."

"I tell you what. We'll go as slowly as you need to." He kissed her neck. "You're beautiful." He kissed her neck again. "You're very sexy." He planted another kiss just above her cleavage. "And though I want you badly, I can wait."

With that reassurance, Abby looked into his eyes and slowly unzipped her pants. At the moment she was about to pull them down, Sam stopped her and took them the rest of the way down. His eyes turned to saucers when he saw the rest of her hourglass shape covered by a sexy black lace thong. He kneeled down and pulled them off slowly before he tossed them on the floor. He stopped to behold the body before him but only for a moment. He couldn't contain his excitement and took his pants and boxer briefs off in one fell swoop.

Abby's body shook as she felt Sam's skin next to hers. In mere moments she didn't know where he ended and she began as their bodies intertwined and rocked together in sweet ecstasy.

Chapter 18

When Abby opened her eyes, Sam smiled at her.

"I guess it wasn't a dream."

"Oh, it was the best kind of dream. The kind that really happened." He grinned.

Abby chuckled. "How long did I doze off for?"

"I don't know. It could have been a minute or an hour. I loved watching you sleep so much I lost track of time. I couldn't help it. You looked so beautiful."

"You already got me in bed. You don't have to over-do it."

"Who says I'm overdoing it?"

"Okay." She said a little embarrassed. "Thank you."

"You're welcome." He leaned over and kissed her.

"When I think about it, you never did answer my question from earlier."

"I was a little preoccupied."

"Uh, huh," she continued. "How did you know where to find me?"

"A little bee told me."

"Remind me to get fly paper."

"Don't be hard on Shana. It's almost Valentine's Day and she took pity on a love-struck boy."

"Love-struck?" she echoed.

"Yes. I told you that I couldn't get you out of my head before and when we kissed in the cab, I knew I had to be with you."

"But Sam."

He put his finger up to her lips. "No more talking." He leaned in and fervently kissed her.

In a flash they explored each other's bodies once more. The heat between them burned hotter by the moment. Abby rolled on top of Sam. Her long hair covered his face as she kissed him and worked her way from his neck down to his stomach. Abby loved the way his body tightened with excitement as she softly blew on his skin and peppered every inch with long light kisses.

Unable to contain himself, Sam turned the tables back on Abby. With one smooth stroke, she felt his passion throughout her body. She grabbed the covers as they rocked back and forth, her body pulsating so hard, she dug her nails into the comforter to steady herself. His eyes locked with hers as they reached the moment of sweet, satisfying release.

"Oh, my God," Abby said as she collapsed, breathless.

"That was incredible. You're incredible." He kissed her.

"You're something else, too." She wiped her brow. "How do you top that?"

"Easy," Sam said.

"Is that so?"

"Yes. We just have to do it again," he said as he pulled her to him again.

❧

It was late afternoon by the time Sam grabbed a shower while Abby made a couple of sandwiches.

I feel like he can eat both of these by himself. Abby thought as she looked at the plate. *I should make another one for me.*

Her phone rang. She wiped her hands and checked the caller ID. It was J.J. "Hello, J.J." She picked up.

"Hi, Abby. I called your office and they told me that you'd already left for Choate."

"Yes. I decided I'd come up early and get a little rest before all the activities." When she looked up, she could see Sam shower through the partially opened bathroom door. *Mmm, all the delicious activities*, she thought.

"So there's nothing wrong with Justin?"

"No. He's fine. But I'm meeting with the headmaster tomorrow to get a full report."

"If the boy says he's fine then he's fine."

"That's the difference between us. You're willing to accept something at face value. I want to look deeper and get an objective view." She paused. "Wait a second. Why did you call me at the office? What's going on?"

She could hear J.J. hesitate.

"Spit it out, J.J."

"You might hear reports that I'm engaged."

"I might hear a report?"

"No. You will hear one or a dozen reports."

Abby rolled her eyes. "You're engaged?"

"What if I am?"

"Well for one thing, you're not divorced yet." She slapped her head. "What am I talking about? We hadn't even signed our divorce papers when Beebe got her ring."

"Are you going to bring that up again?"

"What do you mean bring it up again? I think this might be the third time I've mentioned it in ten years."

"I'm sorry. I stand corrected."

"Damn straight you do. Does Beebe know? Oh, God, J.J. She's already on the 'he did me wrong' tour and now you're going to throw gasoline on her fire." She shook her head. "Did you call Justin?"

"No. I was hoping that you would talk to him."

"It's late. I won't be able to get into the school." She looked at the clock. "Why didn't you call me earlier?"

"I did call you. Didn't you check your phone? I left you three voicemails."

She looked at her phone and saw the missed calls. I must have been out of range. You know how it is when you're in the country."

"That's one good shower." Sam smiled as he walked out of the bathroom.

Abby quickly motioned for him to be quiet.

"What was that? Do you have company?"

"No. I unmuted the television by mistake."

"Sorry." He mouthed and then pointed to the sandwiches. Abby gave him the thumbs up and he dug in.

"Are you going to call him?"

"Fine I'll see if I can get in to see him this evening."

"Thanks, Abby. You're the best."

"I'm not doing this for you. I don't want him to hear about this accidentally."

"Thanks."

"I'll talk to you later." She hung up.

"Sorry about before, but that shower felt great. I wish you could have joined me."

"Maybe next time." She smiled.

"Thanks for the sandwiches."

"You're welcome."

"I take it that was your ex on the phone. Is everything all right?"

"He called to tell me that he's engaged."

"I didn't know he was divorced."

"He isn't divorced yet. Apparently the story is set to break tomorrow, and I've got to tell Justin before that happens."

"Why didn't he tell him? He is his father."

"I know, but J.J. hasn't been able to talk to Justin like a father since he was about five or six years old." She sighed. "I can't blame J.J. entirely though, he and his father have the same kind of non- relationship."

"That must be tough for Justin."

"I know it is though he will never tell me." She looked at the clock. "I'd better shower and then I'll call the school to get Justin out for dinner."

"I would come with you for support, but…" he began.

"I have enough explaining to do."

Sam eyed Abby's sandwich.

She looked down. "Go ahead and eat it."

"Thanks." He said hungrily.

Just as Abby walked by, he grabbed her hand and pulled her to him. "Make sure you fuel up. I think I have a fourth quarter in me."

They kissed.

"I suggest you make some calls beforehand. In case you haven't seen the latest from Toni Redstone, it looks like she wants to file a breach of contract case against you on Maria's behalf."

"What breach of contract?"

"She's essentially arguing that your proposal amounted to a binding contract."

"This is crazy."

"I know. You'd better call Reggie and find out what's going on. I'm sure he's called the National Guard by now."

"I will, but first I'm going to finish this sandwich."

"Okay. She gave him another quick peck before she headed to the bathroom.

"Breach of contract," he muttered aloud. "The whole thing is a circus." He took a bite of his sandwich and wiped his mouth. *I don't know why I didn't realize the circus theme would continue. The wedding was going to be a circus, so now the break up is one, too.*

⟋⟍

Over an hour later, Abby was seated across from Justin at Archie Moore's Bar & Restaurant on North Main Street. Opened in 1898 by Archibald Moore it became a popular eatery in town, known for its hot and spicy chicken wings. However Justin indulged in a double order of Archie's bar burgers topped with grilled onions, crisp bacon, barbecue sauce and melted cheddar cheese. Abby settled for a grilled turkey burger topped with Swiss cheese and a side of French fries.

Awed, she watched Justin polish off both burgers in record time. "I don't know where you put it."

"It burns off quickly." He shrugged.

"You're a teenage boy. When food goes in, your metabolism acts like the Earth's atmosphere. It causes it to disintegrate so it's a pebble before it hits the surface."

"So you're saying I'm eating pebbles?"

"Essentially." She laughed.

He laughed. "I'm glad you came up early, Mom."

"Me, too."

"You should come by lacrosse practice tomorrow afternoon."

"Are you sure you want me to come?"

"Yes."

"Then I'll be there."

"Great." Justin sipped his chocolate shake. "Okay, Mom. I know you didn't come all the way up here early so we could talk about lacrosse and my metabolism. What's going on?"

Abby put her burger down. "I suppose I'm pretty transparent, huh?"

"Yes."

"The best way to say it is to come out and get it over with." She took a deep breath. "Your father's engaged, and it's probably going to be common knowledge by tomorrow."

"Wow, that was fast. He's only been dating Lindy for five months that we know of."

"Yeah. You know your father. When it comes to this kind of stuff he moves fast, quick and in a hurry. How do you feel about that?"

"It's not really a question of how I feel. It's his life and he can do what he wants."

"Yes he can do what he wants. That doesn't mean it doesn't affect you. Please tell me how you really feel. You can trust me."

"I know, Mom. Still what is there to say? It's not like I haven't been through this before."

"It's one thing to be five years old when it happens. It's another to be nearly sixteen."

"You have to stop worrying, Mom. I'm fine. I'm not going to jump off a bridge. If dad wants to get married again more power to him," he paused. "How do you feel about it?"

"I'm not the issue here. Your father and I are divorced. I only care how his actions affect you."

"I love you for that, Mom but you're not going to get a Dr. Phil moment out of me. I've got a tough hide."

"That's what worries me. I think it's a little too tough for someone your age."

"What do I have to do to convince you that I'm okay?"

"Why don't you scream? Or curse him out? Do something."

"You never did anything like that, and I am my mother's son."

"Checkmate, son. Nicely played," Abby sensed that she wasn't going to make any headway. "I don't suppose I can interest you in the chocolate mousse cake?"

He waved the waitress over. "You don't have to ask me twice."

⌘

Sam stared out of the window into the darkness. *It's so peaceful.* He sighed. Despite the idyllic scenery, Sam knew he should bite the bullet and call Reggie. He picked his phone up and saw that his voicemail was full and he had seventy text messages from Reggie. Duty called, but…

He closed his eyes and speed-dialed.

"Hello?"

"Hello, Momma. I'm sure you know what's going on. I'm just calling you to see if you've had any trouble with the press down there."

"No. Reporters and the paparazzi know better than to come down here. This is gun country. I cannot believe the nerve of those Carrangelos trying to sue you over breach of contract. Don't the courts have enough real cases to deal with? Now they want to add scorned lovers to the docket? This stuff might fly on *Judge Judy*, but it burns my biscuits."

"It singes my biscuits, too." Sam was tickled by his mother's indignation.

"Hold on a second, honey. Your dad wants to speak with you."

"Okay, Momma. Love you."

"I love you, too, honey."

"Hey, Sam," his father said jovially.

"Hi, Dad."

"You don't sound any the worse for wear."

"In spite of everything, I feel pretty good."

"I guess you took my advice."

"Yes. I did. I know it happened fast, but I'm crazy about her, Dad. I don't think I've ever felt this way before."

"It sounds like you've been hit by the thunderbolt."

"I suppose I have. I know the real world is waiting for me back home, but I really don't want to deal with it. Reggie has sent me a truckload of text messages and voicemails."

"He called here, too."

"What did you tell him?"

"I told him that you probably went fishing and that you'd be in touch when you were on dry land. Have you rowed to shore yet, son?"

"No."

"Then Reggie can wait a little longer."

Sam laughed. "Please wish Momma a happy Valentine's Day for me. She should get some flowers from me tomorrow morning."

"I'm sure she'll love that. Good night, son."

"Good night." Sam hung up and went back to the window. He decided things were already a mess, so he'd wait one more day to call Reggie. Besides, he had Valentine's evening activities to set up, and he was anxious to get to it.

❧

It was after eleven when Abby came back to the cottage kitchen with groceries from Stop and Shop.

"Let me take those." Sam said as he took the bags from Abby's hands.

"Thanks. I thought I would stop in the store and pick up a few things. Nanette and Brad stocked the fridge for me but there's only enough for one person."

"That was sweet of you. Thanks." Sam started putting the groceries away while Abby took her coat off. "How was dinner with Justin?"

"It was good. I took him to Archie Moore's in town." She reached into her bag and took a container out. "I brought a slice of the chocolate mousse cake back for you. It's pretty good." She put it on the table.

"Thanks." He looked at it. "It looks good too." He paused. "So how did Justin take the news?"

"He was fine. He didn't even flinch."

"And that's not good?"

"On the surface it's a great reaction, but I just don't buy it."

"Maybe you're just making more of it than you have to."

271

"You might be right." She sat down at the kitchen table. "I could be worrying for nothing."

"Exactly," he said as he put the last container away. "I'm all done here."

"Good."

"Now," he put his hand out. "I have something for you in the bedroom."

"You do? Are you sure you that something isn't out here already?"

"Of course it's out here." He winked. "However I have something else waiting for you in the bedroom."

"Hmm, you've piqued my interest."

"That was the point." He held out his hand.

Abby took his hand and he led her to the bedroom. When they entered, she saw the red Cartier box in the center of the bed.

"What's this?"

"Open it and see."

Abby hurriedly grabbed the box. When she opened it a smile washed over her face.

"It's the—" he started to explain.

"It's the Cartier Diablo pen in Bordeaux," she interrupted.

"You know what kind of pen it is with one glance?"

"Gunslingers know their guns, and we editors know our writing instruments. Every warrior is familiar with his or her weapon of choice."

"Do you like it?"

"I love it." She said enthusiastically as she kissed his cheek. "Thank you."

"You're welcome."

"Now I feel bad because I don't have anything for you."

"Don't worry." He said as he pulled her to him. "I'm sure we can think of something."

"You're ready for a fourth quarter?"

"I'm a quarterback. I'm always ready for all four quarters." He playfully pulled Abby onto the bed.

Chapter 19

Dressed for her meeting at Choate, Abby whisked the Hollandaise sauce for the Eggs Benedict into submission. Her phone rang. She continued to whisk with one hand while she picked up the phone with the other. "Hello?"

"Are you still speaking to me?" Shana asked.

"I haven't decided yet."

"Come on, it's Valentine's Day. It's a day for love and forgiveness."

"I buy the love part, but I'm not so sure about the forgiveness part. I thought that's what Christmas, Easter and Yom Kippur was for."

"Well I'm making a case for Valentine's Day."

"I see."

"You sound like you're in a good mood. I take it the early weekend is going well, right?"

"Yes."

Shana giggled. "He's there, isn't he?"

"You already know he's here. You're the one who told him where to find me."

"You can thank me later."

"Is Raymond there yet?"

"No. We're meeting for dinner later."

"Don't forget your toothbrush."

"I won't." She paused. "Did you see Justin?"

"Yes. I had dinner with him last night. I had to tell him that J.J. got engaged."

"What?"

"You heard me. He's engaged. It will probably be in the news today."

"I can't believe he's marrying that child. I have shoes older than this girl. What did Justin say?"

"He said he was fine. It didn't bother him."

"Wait a second. Why were you the one telling him? You're not the engaged one. Unless you have something else you want to tell me."

"Bite your tongue. I'm sure you've seen the news about Sam." Abby checked the sauces consistency.

"I couldn't believe it. The woman is playing hard-ball."

"I know." She put the whisk down and checked on the poached eggs and Canadian bacon.

"Good morning." Sam smiled as he walked into the kitchen.

"Good morning."

He came over and planted a big kiss on Abby. "Now it's a really good morning."

"Ahem." Shana cleared her throat. "Tell Sam I said good morning, too. It sounds like he had an awfully good night."

Abby turned to Sam. "Shana says good morning."

"Good morning, Shana," he said as he sat down at the table.

"I'm sure you heard that."

"Yes. But you didn't tell him what else I said."

"I don't plan to. Listen, I'll call you later. I have that appointment this morning."

"Is that what they're calling it now?"

"Goodbye Shana. Have a happy Valentine's Day."

"You, too." Shana giggled.

Abby hung up. "Are you ready for classic eggs Benedict?"

"Yes."

Once the English muffins popped up in the toaster, Abby assembled the plate. She layered the Canadian bacon on the muffins, followed by two poached eggs and a generous portion of sauce.

She placed the plate in front of Sam. "Here you go."

"Oh, my God, this looks so good."

"Dig in," she said as she made her plate. "Don't wait for me."

Sam started eating. A few moments later, Abby joined him at the table.

"This is one of the most incredible breakfasts I've ever had."

"Thanks. Are you sure the sauce isn't too thick?"

"It's perfect."

She smiled then looked at her watch. "I have to get ready to leave soon."

"You have an appointment this morning. Sorry, but I overheard you talking to Shana. Does parents' weekend start today?"

"No. I'm going to meet with the headmaster and then I'm going to watch Justin's lacrosse practice."

"That part sounds like fun."

"I'm looking forward to it." She paused to wipe her mouth. "What about you? Are you going to call Reggie?"

"What makes you think I haven't called him?"

"Your phone vibrated off the night table this morning. I'd say that was a clue."

"I'm going to call him this morning. It's just that everything has been so nice and I don't want to ruin it."

"Eventually both of us are going to have to face the real world." She said as she stood up and picked her plate up.

"I know."

Abby put her dishes in the sink. Sam grabbed her as she began to walk by the table. "How about I buy this bed and breakfast? Then you can retire from your firm. I'll leave all my endorsements and everything behind and we can live here for the rest of our lives. No one will bother us." He planted a big kiss on her.

"That's a nice dream. If only it were that simple." She stroked his cheek for a moment before she stood up. "I've really got to get going. Call Reggie now. Once you find out what's happening, then we can talk about our re-entry plan."

"Okay. I'll see you later."

"You can bet on it."

⁓

In ten minutes, Abby pulled onto Choate's grounds. Founded by Mary Atwater Choate and Judge William Choate, the school began as a school for girls named Rosemary Hall in 1896 followed by a second school for boys in 1896. Choate's Rosemary hall sits on 400 acres with buildings that combined three architectural styles, from Colonial, Georgian and Modern.

Once she parked, Abby got out of the car, looked around and took a deep breath. *It's so beautiful here*, she thought. Five minutes later she sat in the reception area of the headmaster's office.

"I'm sure he'll be with you in a few minutes." The secretary reassured her.

"That's no problem. I'm early. I can wait." She sat back and opened the newspaper to the people section. There were dueling stories about Sam's breakup and J.J.'s engagement and divorce. *You just can't get away from it, can you?* She thought as she turned the page.

Just then Lloyd Baines, a tall, slim, elegant man with silver hair and a beard to match, entered the reception area. "I'm sorry to have kept you waiting, Ms. Carey." He held out his hand for a handshake.

"No trouble at all." She shook his hand.

"Please come in." He motioned to his office.

Abby walked in and took a seat in front of his desk. Mr. Baines sat down as well.

"Thanks for making time in your schedule to see me."

"That's not a problem. My door is always open for students and parents."

"Great." She leaned forward. "I'm here to get an idea of how Justin's doing. I know he's a good student. His last progress report was stellar. However, there has been quite a bit of upheaval around him lately and I'm a little more concerned about his social interaction."

"I understand your concerns." He took out a folder. "I checked with his teachers and the residential life advisors and they all say that Justin's been a model student."

Abby was relieved but she felt a transition coming.

"However, there have been a couple of incidents where Justin has been a bit more aggressive during intramural sports and lacrosse practice."

"There have been incidents?"

"Yes. A few weeks ago Justin got a little rough with another student during wrestling when he pinned him."

"Was the other student hurt?"

"No. He was just a little bruised. Justin apologized, but we felt it best that he didn't participate in intramural wrestling and switched him to racquetball."

"He didn't say a word to me. What were the other incidents?"

"They were minor things. It was pretty much boys roughhousing. Justin is a big boy, and it could very well be that he doesn't realize his own strength. "

"Maybe." Abby nodded.

"Perhaps since his father was a professional athlete, he can talk to Justin and help him get a handle on it."

"That's a good idea." *If he would do it,* she thought as she smiled through clenched teeth.

"Overall Ms. Carey, I'd say your son is a fine young man." He stood up.

Abby rose and shook his hand. "Thank you again for your time."

He smiled as he escorted her to the door. "I guess I'll be seeing you from time to time over the weekend."

"You can bet on it. Have a good day, Mr. Baines."

"You, too." He smiled.

Abby waved to the receptionist as she left. "Thank you." Then as quickly as her feet would take her she dashed out of the building, took out her cell phone and dialed.

"Hello?"

"J.J. It's Abby."

"Hi, Abby. Why do you sound so strange?"

"Perhaps it's because I'm trying not to look like a stark raving lunatic while I walk over to the school's practice arena."

"Hold up. What's going on?"

"The headmaster just told me that Justin has been a bit more aggressive lately. He even had an incident during wrestling."

"What happened?"

"Apparently he pinned another kid down so hard he left bruises."

"Well, they were wrestling."

"What kind of insane answer is that? You're supposed to pin your opponent down not pretend like it's the WWE."

"Naturally this is my fault, right?"

"I'm not saying that it's your fault but the timing of this increased aggression should be examined. You really need to have a one-to-one talk with Justin."

"I will."

"When?"

"I have a bunch of club openings coming up and then I'm going to Chicago to meet Lindy's parents."

"I can't believe this. You're penciling your son in."

"He's coming home for a break in less than two weeks anyway. I'll talk to him them. I promise. Everything will be fine."

"Sure it will. Forget it, J.J. Just forget I said anything."

"Oh, no, I'm not going to let you play the martyr role. Just because you put your social life on the shelf doesn't mean I have to."

"What are you talking about? What martyr role?"

"Nothing," he said sheepishly. "Forget I said anything."

"I'm sorry, but the horse has left the stable. Get it off your chest."

"You always do the right thing when it comes to Justin. How can I live up to that?"

"This isn't a competition and I am hardly a perfect mother. This is about you taking an active role in our son's life. I'm his mother, and as much as I want to understand everything he goes through, I've never been a teenage boy, you have."

"Maybe you've set the bar so high that I don't even bother to try to measure up."

"That is such a cop out. All I want you to do is take more of an active role in Justin's life. I didn't ask you to split the atom."

"I'm doing the best I can."

"I don't know why I even try," she muttered as she got closer to the building.

"What did you say?"

"I didn't say anything. I'll talk to you later, J.J. I'm heading into lacrosse practice." She angrily pressed the end call button. Abby stopped and took a couple of deep breaths. *I've got to pull it together.*

⚬⚬⚬

After a long, hot shower and a shave, Sam emerged from the bathroom.

"Let's see what's happening with *Sports Center*," he said as he turned on the television.

"And that's the latest from the spring training news as pitchers and catchers report to begin the drive toward the new season.

"Two-time Super Bowl champion, Super Bowl MVP and pitchman, former New York Giant quarterback Sam Best has had many titles. Now he can add another title: defendant. They say that breaking up is hard to do, but in this case it's also expensive. According to sources close to the case, Sam's former fiancée Maria Carrangelo is seeking a sum of $1.5 million and ownership of the apartment they shared in Trump Tower."

"What?" Sam quickly turned the television off and picked up his phone.

"Hello?"

"Hi, Reggie. It's Sam"

"Sam," he exclaimed. "Where the hell have you been?"

"I'll get to that in a minute. I just saw a report on ESPN that said Maria is suing me for over a million dollars and she wants the apartment. I paid for that apartment and only my name is on the deed."

"That's why I've been trying to reach you around the clock. I know someone in Redstone's office and they gave me a heads-up so I could warn you, but you didn't call me."

"It's my fault. I know you called. I just needed a little time to clear my head."

"And you wanted a head start before I could talk you out of it," he added. "That was a clever little ruse you and Bo pulled off the other day."

"It had to be done if I wanted to get any peace."

"I understand that you wanted to get away, but you chose a bad time to bolt. We're behind the story now. Maria and Toni Redstone are setting the narrative for this story and you're the big bad wolf to her Little Red Riding Hood. Where are you, anyway? Your father seemed to think you'd gone fishing."

Sam stifled a chuckle. "I'm in the country."

"When are you planning to come back to the city?"

"I'll be back by Sunday evening."

"Is it that you can't or you don't want to come back sooner?"

"What do you think?"

"Okay. Take the time you need to decompress, but you have to be ready to hit the ground running come Monday morning. A lot of companies have paid you a lot of money to endorse their products and they want to make sure your good image stays intact."

"I'll be a good soldier."

"Terrific. Are you at least getting some work done on your book?"

An image of he and Abby in bed popped into his head. "Yes."

"Good. That will make Abby happy."

"I bet it will." He looked in the mirror with a sly grin.

"Do me a favor though, don't ignore my calls. I don't call just for the sake of hearing my own voice."

"You call for the sake of hearing my voice." Sam joked.

"You've got jokes. The country air must do wonders."

"Yes, it does. In fact, I'm going to go for a walk. I'll talk to you soon, and I promise to answer my phone."

"Okay. Talk to you later."

Sam hung up and finished getting dressed. Once he was done he sat down with his iPhone to see if he could find a floral shop that still had flowers on Valentine's Day. He called the first shop listed.

"Hello, Barnes House of Flowers."

"Hi. I know this is a long shot, but I was hoping I could get a delivery of flowers today."

"This is our busiest day of the year, sir. We have a full day of scheduled deliveries."

"I understand. Do you have any flowers available for purchase in the store?"

"Yes, we do."

"Great. Would it be crazy to ask if you have roses?"

"We do have roses."

"Good." He sighed with relief. "What's your address?"

"We're at 866 North Colony Road."

Sam jotted it down. "I'd like an arrangement of two dozen red roses. What's your name?"

"Debbie."

"Thank you, Debbie. I'll be right down."

"Not a problem."

Sam hung up, threw his coat on and dashed out to the car. After he turned the ignition, he programmed the floral shop's address into his GPS. "This isn't far from here at all. I'll make it there in no time." He put his baseball cap and dark sunglasses on and then pulled away.

When he walked into Barnes House of Flowers ten minutes later the store had an arrangements lined up for delivery. A young blonde woman walked up to him.

"May I help you?"

"Yes. Are you Debbie?"

"Yes."

"I'm Sam. We spoke on the phone about fifteen or twenty minutes ago."

"Yes. They are just putting the finishing touches on your arrangement. It should be out here any minute. If you'd follow me over there," she pointed to the cash register. "I'll ring you up."

"Okay."

Sam followed Debbie to the register and looked around while she rang him up.

"With tax it comes to $151.33."

Sam reached for his wallet and pulled out $300. "Here you go, along with a little something extra for your help. You can keep the change."

"Thanks." Debbie stared at Sam for a moment. "I'm sorry, but you look so familiar. Do you have family here?"

"No. This is my first visit to your lovely town."

Just then a brunette walked out with a gorgeous vase of flowers topped off by a big red bow. "Are you Sam?"

"Yes."

"Here you go." She handed it to him.

Sam stared at the arrangement for a second. "This is perfect. Thanks again ladies. Have a Happy Valentine's Day."

"You, too," they echoed as he walked out of the store.

"Do you know who that was, Debbie?"

"He said his name was Sam, but he's not from around here."

"I'd say he isn't. That was Sam Best. He's the football player who dumped his fiancée and now she's suing him."

"Oh, my God," Debbie said with her mouth agape. "So that's why he looked so familiar. I wonder who he was buying flowers for."

"That's a good question."

The two women watched through the window as Sam got into the car with the flowers. Meanwhile, Sam was on his iPhone searching for stores stocking the other things he needed. After locating a wine store, he put the car into gear.

Chapter 20

"How about this?" Abby said as she held up a red Oxford shirt. "I think this is a gorgeous color on you and it goes with the Valentine's theme."

"I like it, too, Mom." Justin sat on his bed in his practice clothes.

"Are you going to wear a tie? I'm pretty sure I packed the new ties in your bag when you were home for the holidays. Are they in the back of the closet?"

"I can pick my own tie, Mom."

"I know. I'm just trying to help."

Justin got up and went over to the closet where Abby was. "And I love you for it, Mom," he said as he hugged her. "But you're killing me. I have to shower and get ready."

"Oh? Is that a not-so-subtle hint?"

"It's just that after three practice games I stink and I want to get out of these clothes."

"Okay. Are you sure it's not because you don't want me to meet the young lady you're going with?"

"I'm not taking anyone to the dance. I'm going stag."

"It's good to keep your options open." She laughed. "Before I leave I want you to know that you'll be having dinner with me at the cottage tomorrow evening."

"What are we having?"

"How does seafood bisque, French bread and chocolate chip cookies for dessert sound?"

"It sounds like what time is dinner."

"That's my boy." She kissed him on the cheek. "I'll let you get ready now. Have a good time and take at least one picture for me."

"I will and Happy Valentine's Day, Mom."

"Happy Valentine's Day, Justin. I'll see you tomorrow."

Five minutes later, Abby was in her car. She reflected on the day she'd spent with Justin. She hadn't seen any of the overt aggressive behavior Mr. Baines referred to. Never one to be naïve, she knew Justin was on his best behavior with her there. She turned the car's ignition on and pulled away. She needed to make a stop before she went back to the cottage.

⟡

Card in hand, Abby walked into the dimly lit cottage.

"Sam?" She called.

"I'm in here." He answered.

Abby followed the sound of his voice to the living room. There on the floor Sam had laid out a romantic picnic spread of oysters, strawberries, whipped cream and champagne. The roses were placed in the center of the aphrodisiacs along with a few votive candles to complete the atmosphere.

"I see you kept yourself busy while I was out."

"Yes I did. Happy Valentine's Day." He smiled and went over to kiss her. "May I take your coat?"

"Yes." She said as he helped her slip out of it. "This is wonderful. Are you saying you managed to slip through town unnoticed?"

"I wore my cap and dark sunglasses so I wouldn't be recognized."

"In that case, Happy Valentine's Day to you," she said as she handed him a card. "It's not two dozen roses or a Cartier pen, but it is from my heart."

"What more could I ask for?" He kissed her. "Shall we sit down to our little indoor picnic?"

"Yes."

Sam and Abby sat down.

"Look at all these goodies." Abby grinned. "The flowers are gorgeous. How did you manage to get roses on Valentine's Day?"

"I had a little help from cupid." He winked. "Would you like some champagne?"

"Yes."

When Sam pulled the bottle out of the ice bucket, Abby's eyes widened.

"You bought a bottle of Cristal?"

"Actually I bought two bottles. The other one is still in the fridge." He said as he poured two glasses of champagne. "Here you go."

Abby took the glass. "Thanks."

"Here's to the beginning of what I hope will be many more Valentine's Days together." He raised his glass.

"I'll drink to that."

They locked arms and took a few sips.

"Oh this is heavenly." Abby closed her eyes.

Sam put his glass down. "Would you like a strawberry?"

"Sure."

Sam took a strawberry and dipped it in the whipped cream. Just as he put it to her lips the whipped cream dripped near her cleavage. "Oops, let me get that." Sam leaned in and licked the cream off. "Mmm, I think this is sweeter than the berry." He continued to lick.

"I'm pretty sure you should have gotten it all by now."

"I'm just being thorough."

As Sam continued to kiss her, he unbuttoned her shirt and pulled it off. The picnic forgotten and their clothes quickly thrown aside, Abby and Sam explored the depths of passion once more. Her shyness a distant memory, Abby's skin tingled as Sam kissed her stomach and every inch of her curves. Her soft, supple skin was as smooth as ice cream, and, though Sam intended to move to the bedroom, he was ready for a double scoop right then and there.

As the intensity continued to rise, they held on to each other tightly as their bodies rocked to the point of sweet satisfaction.

∽

Later on Sam and Abby moved their picnic to the bedroom.

Abby watched as Sam slurped down an oyster. "The oysters are good, aren't they?"

"Yes. I didn't know you could get good seafood in a supermarket. I learned something new today."

"You're never too old." She smiled.

"Speaking of learning, how was your appointment?"

"Overall I'd say it was pretty good."

"I hear a 'but' coming," Sam leaned back.

"I don't want to talk about it. We're having a lovely evening and I'd like to keep it that way."

"We'll have many more lovely evening. Go ahead and tell me what's on your mind."

Abby put her champagne glass down. "The headmaster told me that Justin has been a little more aggressive during P.E. and lacrosse practice."

"How aggressive?"

"He left a few marks on a fellow student during intramural wrestling."

"Oh, boy," he sighed. "You think this has something to do with his father, don't you?"

"Yes. This incident happened about the same time J.J. and Beebe's divorce took a very acrimonious and public turn, but J.J. won't accept that he played a part in this."

"You called J.J.?"

"Yes. I dialed him the minute I left the headmaster's office. I told him that he needed to have a father son talk with Justin. The problem is when it comes to communicating with Justin he'd rather buy him something instead. To him that solves everything."

Sam was troubled by the look of worry on Abby's face. "I don't know if you think it would help, but I could talk to him. I'm not his father, but maybe he'll open up to another guy."

"You would do that?"

"Sure."

"He's coming here tomorrow for dinner." She paused. "We'd have to hide your stuff so he won't see it."

"I can throw my bag under the bed."

"Listen to me, if I'm not the pot calling the kettle black. I chastised J.J. for not talking to Justin and I'm just as bad."

"I don't have any objection to you telling your son about us."

"There really is an 'us'? This isn't just a fluke? A lost weekend?"

"This isn't a fluke. There is an 'us.' I'll shout it from the top of the Empire State Building. I'll even call a press conference and announce it to the world. It doesn't matter to me who knows."

"I love the sentiment, but you can't do that."

"Why? I wasn't married to Maria. I'm free to move on to another relationship."

"That might be true, but she is suing you over a broken engagement. If you announce that you've moved on with me you will be playing right into her and her lawyer's hands. You have to time this carefully."

"The fact is she's going to be upset whether I wait three weeks or three months. So why not do it?"

"You don't want to detonate your life. And then there's the fact that it would kill Reggie. She paused when a thought hit her. "That reminds me, did you call him?"

"Yes I did." He took another sip from his glass.

"What did he say?"

"The gist of it was that he's waiting for me to come back on Sunday to work on a plan to handle everything that's exploded in the last week."

"Oh boy," she sighed. "Reggie's another person I have to talk to."

"Why?"

"We've been friends for thirty-five years. I think I owe it to him to tell him the truth just like Justin."

"We can tell Reggie together."

"Okay." She still looked worried.

"Now that's enough of that. This is supposed to be a romantic night."

"You're right."

"Good, so you'll bring Justin here for dinner. I will meet him and you can decide if you want to tell him or not. Either way I'll have someone to toss a ball around with for a little while."

Abby laughed.

He reached over and dipped a strawberry in whipped cream. "Now open wide."

"Are you sure you're going to get in it my mouth this time?"

"Of course." He smiled.

Abby opened her mouth and as soon as the berry entered her mouth she felt a dollop of whipped cream land on her breast, again.

Sam smiled. "Looks like I've got a clean up on aisle B."

"That's aisle triple D to you." Abby laughed.

"Lucky me," Sam said as he leaned in for the clean up.

Chapter 21

Abby smiled as she watched Justin load the groceries into the car. Her day had begun early and was filled with classroom tours, parents' meetings and even more campus tours, so she was grateful that she didn't have to lug bags around.

"That's the last of it." Justin said as he closed the car door.

"Great." Abby said as she climbed into the driver's seat.

Justin climbed in and closed his door. "Can I drive? I have my permit."

"Maybe next time," Abby turned the ignition and pulled out of the space.

Justin stared at Abby while she drove.

"What? Do I have something on my face?" She asked as she blindly wiped the corners of her mouth. "I know I tried those turnovers in the store. Are there crumbs on my face?"

"No. You're fine."

"Then what is it?"

"You're wearing your hair down and you've got jeans and boots on."

"The theme for today was casual and comfortable. There was no way I was going to put on a pair of Jimmy Choos to walk around campus. My feet and my back would revolt. You don't like it?"

"Actually I think it's great."

"Good," she smiled wide.

"So what's this surprise you have for me?"

"Patience never was your strong point. We'll be at the cottage in just a few minutes."

"Mom…"

"You'll live," she quipped.

A few minutes later, Abby turned into the driveway for the cottage. Sam stood in the driveway.

"There's your surprise," Abby said and pointed.

"Who's that?"

As the car got closer, Justin's mouth dropped. "Mom, is that Sam Best?"

"Surprise," she grinned as she parked next to Sam's Mercedes and turned the car off.

Suddenly Justin kissed her on the cheek and burst out of the car.

Wow he's a strapping young man and he has the same warm grin as his mom. Sam thought as he walked over with his hand extended. "Hello, Justin. I'm Sam. It's nice to meet you."

"You're Sam Best." Justin fawned.

"Yes I am. At least I was the last time I checked." He smiled.

"This is so cool, Mom."

"I know. Sam is joining us for dinner. So if you'd be kind enough to bring the groceries in the kitchen for me I'll get dinner started and the two of you can hang out."

"You don't have to ask me twice." Justin turned and opened the back door to unload.

"I'll give you a hand." Sam added.

Sam and Justin unloaded and unpacked the groceries while Abby changed clothes and put her hair up in a loose bun.

"Wow that was fast." She said as she entered the room.

"We aim to please." Sam gave her a sly wink. "Do you want to head out now?"

"Sure." Justin said enthusiastically.

"Have fun." Abby said then watched as they left the kitchen. *He looks happy. Maybe he'll open up to Sam.* She put her apron on.

Once they were outside, Sam went to his car. "I think I have a ball in here." He rummaged around his trunk. "Here we go." He tossed the ball to Justin.

"Cool."

Sam closed the trunk and Justin tossed the ball back to him.

"Okay. Go long." Sam assumed the passing stance he was known for and threw the ball.

Justin ran and made the catch. "Got it!"

"Touchdown!" He yelled.

Sam and Justin continued to play catch and talk for a while before Sam stopped.

"Time," he called. "How about we take a walk?"

"Sure."

They started down the path to the pond.

"You've got a pretty good arm."

"Thanks." Justin smiled.

"You really have a nice spin on the ball. Who taught you to throw? I know your mom is a smart woman and can probably do anything, but somehow I don't see her with a football in her hands."

"You've got that right." Justin laughed. "As kids my uncles used to play every weekend, so they taught me the finer points of football."

"They did a good job."

"I think so, too." Justin was quiet for a moment. "Who taught you to throw?"

"My dad taught me. I think I must have been about four years old when he first put a football in my hands."

"Are you going to write about that in your book?"

"Yes. In fact it was your mom who helped me see that my football story really began long before I ever stepped onto a field. It's started with a boy and his dad."

"That's great that you have a lot of good memories with your dad."

"I think so, too, and I know there are more good ones to come." He paused. "What about you and your dad?"

"My father wasn't into tossing a ball around."

"He'd take you to play hoops instead."

"He took me a few times that I can remember." He looked down at his feet. "But I'm not really into basketball."

"Your mom says you play lacrosse and baseball. What positions do you play, respectively?"

"I'm a defenseman for lacrosse and I'm the left fielder for the baseball team."

"Nice. You're mom says you're pretty good at both."

"Of course she'd say that, she's my mother. There's some kind of unwritten law about that in the mom code."

Sam laughed. "But you do enjoy it, don't you?"

"Yeah I like it a lot. All the practice can get to be a pain, but it's fun."

"My father always said if you play for fun every game is a win, even if you didn't win."

Justin nodded.

"But winning is awful nice though." Sam's said in a Texas drawl.

"I hear that," Justin laughed. "So you and your dad are close?"

"Yes. He has a good relationship with my brothers and me. What about you and your dad? Are you close?"

"I love my dad and I know he loves me, but I can't say that we're close."

They stopped in front of the pond.

"Does that bother you?"

"No."

Sam looked at him.

"Okay. It bothers me, but not as much as it used to." He exhaled. "It seems like he's more interested in everything else but me."

"I'm sure he's very interested in you. Maybe he doesn't know how to show you."

"Yeah, maybe," he picked up a twig.

"I don't have any children, but I know that being a parent is a hard job and there's no manual or game plan. Every parent has to figure it out."

"I know that my dad is a great guy. He raises money for sick kids and donates money to build playgrounds and after-school programs for low-income neighborhoods. Then he goes and cheats on my mother with Beebe, and then he marries her and cheats on her with another woman. I mean it's crazy. He's his own news cycle."

"He's flawed, like all of us. Except his flaws make for good copy," Sam shook his head. "Take it from me, I know."

"Oh, I'm sorry. I totally forgot."

"Don't worry about it. In fact I wish more people would forget. This way I could just get on with my life. I'm sure your dad feels that way, too."

"Maybe," he shrugged.

"Have you tried talking to him man to man? You are old enough to do that."

"My dad would rather buy me crap than talk."

"Then tell him that you want the most priceless gift he can give, his time."

"You have a point. Maybe he'd stop treating me like a little kid who can be silenced with a trip to the ice cream shop. Or better yet, he'd stop making my mom be the bearer of all news."

"I bet that's frustrating."

"Yes. I can't tell my mom that. She worries enough."

"I hate to tell you this, but I think she's going to worry no matter what. It's her job."

"I know."

Sam looked at his watch. "It's getting late and I'm cold. What do you say we head back?"

"Yes." Justin shivered. "I bet soups on by now."

They started to walk back up the path.

"Race you," Justin shouted and took off.

"Oh, that's not fair. I'm coming!" Sam took off after him.

Abby had just placed the last table setting when Justin and Sam burst into the cottage then into the kitchen.

"What good timing. I hope you're hungry."

"I'm famished." Justin rubbed his stomach.

"Okay. Go wash up and then dinner is served."

"Okay, Mom."

"I'm going to wash up, too. By the way, it smells great in here."

Abby smiled and went back to the stove. Once Sam and Justin came back they sat down to a nice dinner filled with talk of sports, movies, music and college. Abby excused herself to put the chocolate chip cookies into the oven. When she walked back in she stopped to look at how Justin seemed to hang on Sam's every word as he discussed sports and academics. *This is such a nice picture. I wish I could frame it.* She smiled.

⋯⋯

After they'd devoured one full pan of cookies and watched a little junk television, it was time to get Justin back to campus.

The three of them stood outside by the cars.

"Thanks for coming over, Sam. It's been great."

"Believe me it was my pleasure."

"Why don't you drive with Mom and me back to the school?"

"I'd love to, but I've got to keep a low profile, even in the dark."

"I understand."

"I'm glad one of us does." Sam joked. "God knows I still can't figure it out."

All three laughed.

"Why don't you stick around for coffee? We can do a little work on your book."

"Are you sure you want to do that?"

"Sure." She looked at her watch. "I'd better get him back."

Sam went to shake Justin's hand when he hugged him. "I hope I can see you again soon."

"Me, too," Sam was touched.

Abby and Justin got in the car and drove off while Sam watched.

Justin stared at Abby with a goofy grin.

"Now what?"

"You and Sam like each other don't you?"

"Yes. We like each other."

"You really like each other. I mean like boyfriend and girlfriend."

"I guess the answer to that would be yes. Do you think that's terrible?"

"No. Why would I think that? My mom and Sam Best," he said excitedly. "That's totally cool."

"He was just engaged."

"People break up all the time."

"Aren't you a little young to be so cavalier?"

"I didn't mean it that way, Mom."

"There are other people involved and they have feelings, too. I want to take it slow and easy otherwise who knows what will happen."

"Okay. Well it must be something because he came all the way up here to spend the day with you."

Abby's smile belied her nervousness at lying to her child about the extent of her relationship with Sam. *All in due time,* she thought. *At least he knows about us and is okay with the idea.*

Just as Abby drove through the heart of town, she noticed a number of news vans parked on both sides of the road.

"What's going on here?" Abby asked.

"I don't know. I don't think I've ever seen so many cars on this street at one time before." Justin said as he looked out of the window.

"Whatever it is you can bet that we'll find out soon enough," Abby made the turn to head to Choate.

A few minutes later they were parked in front of Justin's dorm.

"Here we are." Abby got out of the car.

"You don't have to walk me to my dorm, Mom. I can go alone." Justin shut the car door.

"I know. You don't want your old mom tagging along and getting all mushy in front of your classmates."

"You're not old, Mom."

"Thanks." She started to choke up. "I've been doing this with you for the last three years and it still isn't any easier to leave you."

"Come on, Mom please don't start crying." He put his arms around her.

"I'm sorry. I can't help it." She hugged him tightly.

"Mom, I can't breathe."

Abby playfully hit him. "I don't exactly have a death grip on you."

"I know, Mom." He laughed. "I had to lighten it up."

"Okay." She stood on her tippy toes to kiss his cheek. "If you get any taller, I'm going to have to travel with my stepping stool."

"Now who's the comedienne?"

Abby and Justin hugged again. "You know you can call me in the morning if you need anything. I'm not leaving until one."

"Okay." He paused. "You know I'm going to be home in a couple of weeks anyway."

"Yes. I'm looking forward to it."

"I am, too." He took a step toward the building. "I'd better get in before they call curfew."

"Okay. I love you."

"I love you, too, Mom."

Abby watched as Justin dashed into the dorm. Although he was a teenager, she could still picture him as a five-year-old on his first day of school. *He's so grown up now*, she thought.

With a couple of chocolate chip cookies in one hand and a cold glass of milk in the other, Sam sat down on the sofa in the living room.

"It doesn't get any better than this." He said as he dipped a cookie into the milk and took an enthusiastic bite. "So good," he said aloud.

The sound of his cell phone broke up his little cookie party. Sam looked at the caller ID and picked up. "Hey, Reggie," he said jovially.

"Hi. Don't you sound good?"

"I feel pretty good. What's up?"

"I have a question for you."

"Shoot," he finished his cookie.

"You said you were in the country, right?"

"Yes."

"Are you in Wallingford, Connecticut by chance?"

"Yes. How did you know?" He asked dumbfounded.

"Do you have a television there?"

"Yes."

"Turn on EEN and see for yourself."

EEN, *Everything Entertainment News*, started as a celebrity news web site in the new millennium that eventually expanded to include a daily television which reports on all celebrities from reality show personalities to athletes. EEN went far beyond the Hollywood sign.

Although the show claimed not to pay for stories or interviews, they were known to occasionally pay sources for leads on stories.

Sam turned on the television and searched the channels until he found the station.

A reporter was standing in front of the floral shop. *"We received a report that Sam Best who is in the midst of a messy breakup with longtime fiancée, Maria Car-rangelo, was here at this floral shop behind me in Wall-ingford, Connecticut buying two dozen roses on Valen-tine's Day.*

"Sources in the store say he came and personally picked up the arrangement. Apparently he didn't write out a card, but when we checked with Ms. Carrangelo's representatives, they stated that she hadn't received flowers. Sam Best's representatives had no comment. Leaving us to wonder what mystery lady received the posies?"

Sam shut the television. "What the hell?"

"My sentiments exactly," Reggie agreed. "What's going on, Sam? You told me that you needed time to think and now I find out that you were seen buying roses on Valentine's Day. Is there something you want to tell me?"

"Listen, Reggie I can't talk to you about it now. But trust me I will talk to you about it when I get back."

"Please don't tell me that you've had a girlfriend this whole time."

"I never cheated on Maria when we were together."

"I know that should make me feel better, but some-how it doesn't."

"Do you trust me, Reggie?"

"Yes." He sighed. "You have always been a straight shooter."

"Good. We'll talk about this when I get back. I'll tell you everything."

"Okay. In the meantime we'll continue to fend off the vultures. Wherever you are up there must be secluded because I'm sure there's an army of media up there by now."

"I'm going to keep it that way."

He heard the car door. "Okay, Reggie. I've got to go. I'll talk to you sometime tomorrow."

"Okay. Good night."

"Good night."

Abby walked into the living room. "Hey." She said as she took her coat off.

"Hey. You got Justin back to the dorm okay?"

"Yes. I was hanging tough until I saw the dorm and I realized that he was leaving me."

"Aww, that's sweet. You miss your baby."

"I know it's crazy. He's sixteen and he's going to be home in a couple of weeks. I don't know why I get so weepy." She sat on the sofa next to him. "You two got along like a house afire though."

"He's a great kid."

"If I may ask, what did you two talk about?"

"We talked about a lot of different things."

"Did his father come up?"

"Yes. He knows that his father loves him but he's also acutely aware of the fact that he doesn't know how to express it."

"That's the truth."

"I told him to talk to J.J. man-to-man to let him know how he feels. I know he would really like a real relationship with him."

"It sounds easy when you say it."

"I told Justin to tell his father that what he wants from him doesn't come in a box. It's his time and his love, that's something you can't put a price tag on."

"You are awfully good at this father relationship thing."

"I got lucky. I have a good relationship with my father and I really think it's made all the difference in my life. I'd like to see the same for Justin. He's already got a great mom, he just needs the other part of the equation and he'll be unstoppable. He's a great kid."

"I know."

"It makes me wonder why you and J.J. only had Justin. Was it a tough pregnancy?"

"No. It was a breeze. I didn't have morning sickness. I was only in labor for two hours, and, to top it off, Justin was an early baby."

"So what stopped you from having another? You didn't want to tempt the fates?"

Abby laughed. "No. I wasn't afraid of the fates. With J.J. on the road so much, I was basically a married single parent."

"Even in the off season?"

"Yes." She thought for a moment. "That's not exactly true. J.J. would take Justin to the park or out for ice cream, but those times were few and far between."

"I'm sorry. That must have been hard on you as a mother."

"When Justin was about two years old, I asked him what his father's name was. He said New York Knicks forward J.J. Stokes, just like the announcer at Madison Square Garden."

"You're kidding," Sam said, astonished.

"I wish I were kidding. That's when I knew one was enough."

"You shouldn't beat yourself up about Justin's relationship with J.J. He's a great kid."

"Thanks. What about you? You want children?"

"Yes," he said without hesitation. "Is that a dealbreaker for you?"

"I don't think so, but it has been sixteen years. I'm not a spring chicken."

"But it's something that's up for discussion, right?"

"Let's just say I'm willing to keep an open mind."

"That's all I need to know." Sam smiled.

She looked over at the cookies. "I see you're all set for an evening in front of the television." She paused.

"Speaking of television, there were a bunch of news vans when I drove through town. It looks like they're here for some big story."

"I know. I'm the big story."

"What?"

"Reggie just called me. EEN just ran a story about me buying roses in the flower shop here on Valentine's Day."

"What?"

"I don't know how they found out. I had on dark sunglasses, a baseball cap and I paid cash."

"Someone in the shop must have recognized you. It was probably someone who worked there."

"But l left a pretty big tip."

"I'm sure you were generous, but EEN pays for story leads and, the last time I checked, they probably pay more than a floral shop clerk would earn in a month or more."

"There's no florist customer privilege?"

"I'm afraid not." She sighed. "I was hoping we'd have a few more hours in the bubble, but that's out of the window."

"Why? We still have tonight." Sam pulled Abby into a long kiss.

Abby and Sam undressed each other slowly to make every second count. Once they were nude, Sam carried Abby to the bedroom and laid her on the bed.

He stopped to take in the beauty of her silky mocha skin before he joined her.

Sam kissed the length of Abby's body from the nape of her neck to the tip of her toes. Abby's senses buzzed and by the time they kissed, she was ready to return the favor and then some.

With deliberateness, she kissed and lightly ran her tongue over his chest. As she headed further down, she turned up the intensity with light strokes on his inner thigh. With every kiss she slowly inched her hand upward ever so slightly until his body quaked with expectation. Sam's breathe increased and his heart raced as the suspense built to the point of no return.

"I have to have you now." He whispered as he rolled on top of Abby.

In an instant, they were moving as one. Abby's hands frantically searched for the post to hold on to, but Sam took both of her hands into his. He wanted to be her only stay. As their bodies seized with pleasure, Abby and Sam's eyes locked.

"I love you," Sam said.

"I love you," Abby responded breathless.

"Marry me," Sam called out as pleasure pulsated through them.

Chapter 22

Very early the next morning, Abby got dressed and made breakfast while Sam showered and got ready to leave. *He didn't mean what he said last night.* She flipped a pancake on the griddle. *It was the heat of the moment. Every woman knows declarations of love and marriage proposals uttered en flagrante don't count.* She ladled more batter on the griddle. *Is that my excuse, too? What made me say I love you? Everything that I know is telling me that it's too soon for the L-word.*

Dressed with his bag in hand, Sam walked into the kitchen. He put his bag down and went over and kissed Abby. "Good morning again, my love," he smiled.

"Good morning."

He slid his arms around her. "You're making blueberry pancakes. I love blueberry pancakes."

"Good." *See how easily he uses the word love? He'll probably propose to the pancakes in a few minutes.* "Sit down and I'll get the rest of the pancakes from the oven."

"No. I can do it." He looked around. "Where's the oven mitt?"

She pointed to the baker's rack.

He got the mitt, took the pancakes out of the oven and placed it on the table. "They look so good." He smiled.

"Thanks. Go ahead and dig in. There's maple syrup on the table."

"No. I can wait until you're ready to eat."

"Okay." Abby turned the last two pancakes onto the plate, grabbed the carafe and joined Sam at the table.

"The coffee will be ready in a minute."

"Okay."

The timer on the coffee maker went off. Abby was about to get up when Sam stopped her.

"Sit. I'll get it." He got up and brought the carafe back to the table.

"Thanks."

She reached into her apron pocket. "Here are the directions you'll need to avoid the media crush in the center of town." She put the directions on the table.

He picked it up. "You know the back way out of here?"

"Yes. Brad and Nanette told me about it a couple of years back. Take it from me, you haven't seen anything until you see the mass exodus of parents headed for I-91 on their way to I-95."

"Thanks." He took a few more bites. "This is so good."

"Thanks."

"What's on your agenda for work this week?"

"We have several clients showing at Fashion Week, so I'll be at Lincoln Center helping Shana keep the madness somewhat in check."

"I get invites for Fashion Week every year. Maybe I'll go this time. Who's your first show?"

"It's Mr. Cedi out of Detroit."

"Cedi? I don't think I've heard of him before."

"He designs for full-figured women. In fact, he's the first designer to show an entire full-figured line at Fashion Week."

"You'll be a part of history." *Maybe I'll call Mindy and see if I can get into the show to witness history in the making and see Shana.*

"Yes, and we're really excited about it."

Sam finished his pancakes. "Speaking of excitement, I have to get back so I can talk to Reggie and bring him up to speed, but I'm going to need an answer from you." He put his napkin down.

"An answer from me?" She asked.

"Yes. I know I didn't ask in the traditional way but I did ask you to marry me."

Abby dropped her fork. "What?"

"I know we were in the middle of something at the time, but I did ask you to marry me right after I said that I loved you."

Abby felt her head spin. "I didn't think you were serious. I thought it was the heat of the moment."

"It wasn't." His facial expression turned serious. "I love you, Abby. I know it doesn't make sense because we haven't known each other long, but I know how I feel and can't spend another day without you in my life. I won't." He reached over and took her hand. "You said you loved me too. Do you?"

Abby took a breath. "As crazy as it sounds, I do."

"Will you at least think about marrying me?"

"I promise I will give it some real thought."

He kissed her hand. "That's all I need to know."

"Wait a minute. What are you planning to do?"

"I'm going to handle this thing with Maria and then I'll be able to concentrate on a formal proposal."

"That's great, but there are a lot of peripheral factors going on here besides Maria. There's my son, my family, your career, your fans, the media, and don't get me started about my ex-husband. It's not going to be easy to ride off into the sunset together. There will be repercussions."

"I know. I'm not going to make any move before discussing it with you."

"I appreciate that. But you saw what happened when you bought flowers in town. It's going to be much worse once we get back to the city."

"We'll deal with it."

"That's easier said than done, Sam. You may have hit it off with Justin, but I can assure you that my ex-husband won't be a picnic."

"Why should he have a problem with me? I'm not trying to take his place as Justin's father."

"He won't see it that way. J.J. is used to having his cake and eating it, too. He knows that the simple fact that I'm in a relationship means that another man will be around Justin."

"So this is some kind of territorial thing for him?"

"Yes."

"Again, we'll deal with the issues as they come. There's no point in getting worked up about them now."

"I take it you weren't in the Boy Scouts."

"As a matter of fact, I was in the Boy Scouts. We'll be prepared, okay?"

"Okay. As long as you know what we're getting into here."

"I do." He got up and kissed her. "I really want to peel out of my clothes and take you back to the bedroom." He started to kiss her neck.

"This is going to get you in trouble."

"I like this kind of trouble." Sam took Abby's hand and quickly pressed her against the kitchen wall. He feverishly lifted her skirt and with a few well timed strokes, Abby and Sam had dessert before breakfast was over.

∞

With Abby's directions, Sam was able to leave town undetected. Within two hours, he was back in the city, which gave him a bit of a head start on the media. However he didn't head back to the W Hotel. Instead he drove to Reggie's place on the Upper East Side. After he circled the block three times, he finally found a space to park three blocks away.

As he walked to Reggie's street, he dialed his phone.

"Hello?"

"Hey, Bo."

"Well if it isn't the man of the latest news cycle." He joked. "Are you still in Connecticut?"

"No. I'm back. I'm heading to Reggie's place now."

"I know he'll be glad to see you. It couldn't have been easy to be him for the last twenty-four hours with you M.I.A."

"I'm sure he's going to tell me all about it."

"So what, or should I say who, was of interest in Wallingford?"

"Abby."

"You spent the weekend with Abby? So that explains why Reggie couldn't get you on the phone."

"Yes. I had a great weekend with her. I met her son. We had a good time. Everything was perfect and we didn't have any distractions until…" he began.

"You didn't have any distractions until you bought her flowers in person."

"I played it low key. I was incognito."

"I guess your disguise didn't work. Someone recognized you and called EEN's story tip line."

"I know and now I've got to get a handle on the situation. That's why I'm heading to Reggie's place."

"So the media scandal aside, what's the story with you and Abby?"

"I love her, Bo."

"What?"

"I know it doesn't make any sense, but I'm in love with her and I want to marry her."

"Oh, boy," Bo sighed. "You don't want to make life easier for yourself, do you?"

"What I don't want to do is live another moment of my life without her in it."

"I do believe you're serious."

"I'm very serious."

"Then I suggest you put all your cards on the table with Reggie. That means you're going to have to tell him the woman in question is Abby."

"I know." He arrived at Reggie's building. "Well I'm here."

"Good luck, buddy."

"Thanks." He hung up and took a deep breath.

Reggie wasn't crazy about high-rise buildings. He and his family lived in one of those quaint little apartment buildings in a relatively quiet enclave not far from Gracie Mansion.

Sam pressed the buzzer.

"Hello?" A female voice answered.

"Hi, Danielle. It's Sam. Can I come up?"

"Sure."

The buzzer sounded.

While Sam did like the warm comforts of Reggie's building, he couldn't help but flash back to football training camp as he hiked the five flights to get to the apartment. Once on his floor, Reggie had the door open.

Danielle and Reggie's apartment was sumptuous, inviting and cozy and it often served as Sam's home away from home. The apartment was a mere 1,200 square feet, but Danielle and Reggie knew the trick to living well in Manhattan was the ability to make a small space appear larger. Their less-is-more approach to décor worked.

"It's nice to see you, Sam."

"It's nice to see you, too, Reggie."

Reggie's wife Danielle walked in. Danielle was a beautiful chocolate skinned woman, with skin so smooth it looked like velvet. Long and lean, her shape gave no indication that she had two children.

"Hi, Sam." She kissed his cheek.

"Danielle, you are as lovely as ever."

"Thank you." She smiled. "Can I get you any-thing?"

"I'll take a bottle of water if that's not too much trouble."

"No trouble at all. I'll be right back."

"Have a seat, Sam. We have a lot to discuss."

"I know."

Danielle returned with two bottles of Pellegrino. "Here you go, gentlemen. I'll leave you to your business."

"Thanks, honey," Reggie said.

Sam opened the bottle and took a sip. "Are the girls at home?"

"No. They're with my parents this weekend. They'll be back later."

"Oh." Sam paused. "I guess you're waiting to hear the story."

"Yes. After spending the last few hours fielding calls and fending off vultures, I think I deserve to hear the whole truth and nothing but the truth so help you God."

"I don't know where to start."

"Then tell me, is there another woman in the picture now?"

"Yes."

Reggie's face fell. "I was afraid of that."

"You wanted to know the truth."

"But like Jack said, sometimes you can't handle the truth." He sighed. "Was it just a fling? If it was, then we can downplay it."

"It's not a fling. I'm in love with her."

"Who is she?"

"Does it matter?"

"Yes. I need to know if she can be discreet until we figure out how to handle this. Antonia and her people have been waiting for something they can use as a salvo to fire your way."

Sam paused for a moment.

"Well?"

"It's Abby."

"Abby who? What's her last name?"

"It's Abigail Carey."

Reggie looked dumbfounded. "I'm sorry. Did you say Abigail Carey?"

"Yes."

"You're talking about the same Abigail Carey that I called in to edit your book?" he asked, incredulous.

"Yes."

"I don't believe this." Reggie looked like he'd been punched.

"Are you all right?"

"You and Abby? I know you said you thought she was attractive, but I would have never guessed this in a million years."

"Why? She doesn't seem like the type of woman I'd go for?"

"No, it's not that. You're an athlete, and after J.J. I thought she'd sworn off athletes."

"Technically I'm a former athlete," Sam said, trying to inject a bit of levity.

"Any other time I would laugh, but this is serious. I don't understand how she went from your editor to your new girlfriend. Is she the real reason you broke up with Maria?"

"No. As much as I tried to ignore it Maria and I had grown apart. We weren't the same people we were when we first met, and getting married wasn't going to make it better."

"I get it."

"I didn't cheat on Maria. I wasn't sneaking around with Abby. We didn't set out to fall in love. It just happened. And though I'll admit I did the chasing. I didn't do it until after we'd broken up."

"In this media world that's just splitting hairs. Don't forget Maria's alleging that you've been supporting a mistress. It won't take them much to jump to Abby as being the woman you're supporting."

"That's crazy. The bank statements Maria found were from more than a year ago. I just met Abby a few weeks ago."

"Since when does the truth matter in an entertainment news cycle."

"You're right."

Reggie sighed heavily. "You realize that you're going to have to keep your involvement under the radar for a while."

"We are still working on my book together."

"So when paparazzi show up, you'll just say it's a work session?"

"You know Abby, if she says we're working on the book. We're working on the book."

"I can't say that there's ever been a dull moment working with you. Although right now I'd kill for something perfectly boring."

"What fun is that?" Sam joked.

"All kidding aside, you have to be ready for the questions once this comes out. I love Abby like a sister, but they're going to say some not so nice things about her."

"What kind of negative things can they say? She's sexy, smart and successful."

"She's also older than you, African-American and full-figured."

"So?"

"Maria fit the profile most athletes go for: tall and thin."

"What does that have to do with anything?"

"In a perfect world, nothing," he said, hands clasped. "However, this world is very concerned with appearances, so there will be comments."

"Let them say whatever they want to. I love her and that's what matters."

"Okay. In the meantime I have a lawyer I want you to meet with." Reggie went into his wallet and pulled out a business card. "Her name is Blake Campion." He handed the card to Sam.

"Is she any good?"

"She specializes in family law. She's smart, focused and she's the only attorney Toni Redstone has ever lost to."

"I'm impressed. How did you manage to get her?"

"Abby and I went to college with her. She was a Political Science major."

"And you've stayed in touch?"

"Yes. She's a good friend and a Yale-educated attorney. I know you'll be in good hands, but she's a busy woman. She's going to call me when she has an opening in her schedule. Once she does, you're going to have to be ready to meet with her right then and there."

"If she's as good as you say she is, that's not a problem."

"Good. Remember no communication with the other side, that's what the lawyers are for. They will do all the talking and negotiating. Are we clear?"

"We're crystal clear." Sam looked at his watch. "It's getting late. I'd better get going." He stood up.

Danielle entered the living room. "You're going already, Sam? I thought maybe you'd like to stay for dinner."

"That sounds tempting, but I'm a little beat. I'm going to head back to my hotel. But thank you for the offer. Can I get a rain check?"

"Sure." She kissed him on the cheek. "It was good seeing you. Hang in there."

"I will."

"Dinner will be ready soon, Reggie." She said as she went back to the kitchen.

"Okay, baby."

"I'll let you two enjoy the rest of your alone time." Sam winked.

Reggie walked him to the door. "Remember to keep it low key." He opened the door.

"I got you. I'll see you later." Sam stepped out into the hall.

"Take care, man."

"You too, Reggie," Sam said as he made his way down the stairs.

Sam made it to the lobby in record time. *Not bad for a guy that just retired. Then again, coming down is a whole lot easier than climbing up. I guess that's true for more than just stairs.*

⁂

Once she said her goodbyes to Brad and Nannette, Abby took to the back roads of Wallingford to make her way out of town. She was back in Manhattan in a little over two hours.

Happy but exhausted, Abby parked her Land Rover, grabbed her roses and suitcase and went through the back to the elevator.

When the doors opened to her apartment, she stepped out. "Home sweet home," she walked into her living room and saw Shana on the sofa.

"Hello, Shana."

"Welcome back, Miss Parents' Weekend." She got up. "How was it?"

"Good."

"Girl, don't try to pretend. I heard Sam was in Wallingford. I mean, what are the chances?"

"I need to unpack." Abby tried to head to her room.

"Unpacking can wait. Did you spend the weekend with Sam?"

Abby looked away.

"Oh, no you don't." Shana stood in Abby's path. "Look at me." Shana studied her. "Oh, my God, you're in love."

"What?"

"It's written all over your face."

"Don't be ridiculous." Abby continued to head for her bedroom.

Shana followed her.

When she got to the bedroom, Shana stood in the doorway. "Abigail Carey I've known you for a long time, and, though it was a lifetime ago, I remember how you looked when you loved J.J. You have that same look on your face now, and you're carrying quite a bouquet of roses to boot."

Abby put her suitcase down and placed the flowers on her night table. "But it doesn't make sense. How can I be in love with a man I essentially just met?"

"Ever hear of a little thing called love at first sight?"

"I'm forty-one years old. That doesn't apply to me."

"What has age got to do with love? Obviously there was something about him that made you run from him in the first place. Lucky for you, he ran after you."

"Oh, God," Abby sighed as she flopped onto her bed. "What's going on with my life? A couple of weeks ago I was a happy publicist."

"And now you're a happy woman who is living her life for a change."

"As much as I hate to admit, I've lived more in the past four days than I have in years."

"Not to mention you had great sex too."

"Shana," Abby groaned.

"Please don't deny it. I don't think ET's finger glowed as brightly as you are right now."

Shana and Abby laughed.

Shana sat down on the bed and nudged Abby. "So how was it?

"You know I never talked about this before, and I'm not going to start now."

"Okay. On a scale of one to ten, where did he fall?"

Abby thought for a moment. "I'd say he was a twenty."

"Woo-hoo! Or as the girls in the office say, the man can ball."

"Yes he can. Whatever that means."

"Did Justin meet him?"

"Yes. They spent an afternoon together and became fast friends."

"That's good. Did Justin realize there was something between you two?"

"Yes. I think he did. Though I am pretty sure he hasn't figured out the extent of the relationship yet."

"It's the new millennium, Abby. You're nuts if you think he doesn't know you and Sam have had sex."

"You think so?" Abby sounded mortified.

"Kids these days are really perceptive when it comes to these things."

"He didn't say a word to me about it. I would have thought he would have asked me."

"Seriously, Abby, what kid wants to ask their parent about their sex life? I'm forty-three and I'd rather subscribe to the 'don't ask, don't tell' policy when it comes to my parent's sex life." Shana shuddered as she made a face.

Abby made a face in kind. "When you put it like that, I see what you mean."

"So everything was cool."

"It was cool until this weekend when the news got out about that." She pointed to the flowers.

"I heard. It's been all over the internet sites and the entertainment networks."

"It seems they flooded Wallingford last night. It was like some warped version of Paul Revere's midnight ride. 'Sam's mistress is coming!' "

"Speaking of cameras, how did Sam get out of town unseen?"

"I gave him the directions to leave the back way to avoid the camera crews."

"That was good."

"Yes." Abby looked around. "I guess it's time to get back to the grind."

"I should hope so." Shana winked.

"You're terrible." She got up and unzipped her suitcase. "Now that we've talked about me to death, how was your Valentine's Day weekend?"

Shana lay back on Abby's bed. "It was really nice. We had room service at The Plaza for two days. It was heavenly. He gave me this." She held her wrist out to show her diamond tennis bracelet.

"It's gorgeous." Abby said as she looked at it closely. "Where is Raymond? Is he downstairs at your place?"

"No. He had to leave this morning. There was an emergency with a client. He'll be back sometime to-morrow."

"Good. I'm looking forward to seeing him. Speaking of tomorrow are we all set for Fashion Week in its new location?"

"Yes. Lincoln Center here we come. All systems are go, captain." Shana got up. "I'm going to take advantage of the quiet before the storm and get some rest. I suggest you do the same."

"I'm going to rest my eyes after I unpack."

"That young man wore you out. You go, girl," she joked.

Abby shook her head. "Whatever you say."

"I'll see you later."

"Okay."

Abby continued to unpack as she watched Shana leave her room. She had everything unpacked and in its place within ten minutes.

"That's enough for now." She looked around the room then climbed onto her bed. "Time to rest for a few minutes. " She closed her eyes and drifted off.

⊗∾

A while later Abby felt someone nudge her. She slowly opened her eyes.

"Abby?" Shana said.

"Hmm?"

"Abby. Wake up." Shana nudged her.

"What's up, Shana?"

"Reggie's here to see you."

"What?" she said groggily. "What time is it?"

"It's seven-fifteen."

"Good grief. I thought I closed my eyes for a minute." She sat up.

"You were tired."

Abby got out of bed and went over to the mirror to check her reflection. "I don't look too drunk tired." She rubbed her eyes. "He's in the living room?"

"Yep."

Still in her jeans and sweater, Abby smoothed out her hair before she and Shana walked out of the bedroom to the living room.

"Here she is." Shana pointed to Abby.

"Hi, Reggie."

"Hi."

"I'll see you guys later."

"Thanks, Shana."

"Not a problem." She said as she walked to the door for the staircase and disappeared.

"From the look on your face, I can tell that you've talked to Sam."

"Yes. I have."

"Am I allowed a drink or a cigarette before I face the firing squad?"

"You don't smoke."

"Then I guess I should have a drink instead." She walked over to her wine rack and bar. "Here's a good one." She picked out a bottle. "Terlato pinot noir

2007," she said as she placed it on the bar. "Shall I get two glasses?"

"Sure."

Abby uncorked the wine and poured it into two glasses. She walked over to Reggie. "Here you go." She handed him the glass.

"Thanks." He took a whiff. "It smells good."

Abby sat down. She took a whiff. "It smells like raspberries and strawberries. It's practically dessert in a glass. Cheers." She lifted her glass.

Reggie did the same.

"Now that we have our drinks we can talk turkey, right?" Reggie asked.

"Yes. So fire away."

"You and Sam," He shook his head. "That's one thing I wouldn't have seen coming."

"That makes two of us. I didn't see it coming, either. Once I did, I tried to get away from it, but Sam…" she started.

"I know. He's very persistent. Once he gets something in his head, he keeps driving until he reaches his goal. It's what made him such a successful quarterback."

"I noticed." She sipped her wine.

"Abby, I'm not here to chastise you or make any judgment. I know love is something that's a precious and unexpected gift. And if anyone deserves to be happy, it's you."

"Thanks but you're concerned because of what happened with J.J."

"Yes. I remember how hard that was on you."

"It was a tough time for me."

"Even though it was a big thing back then, I don't think Sam knows."

"Why would he? Ten years ago he was a twenty-six-year-old quarterback with the world as his oyster. Sam was reading the sports page and watching *NFL Primetime* and *Sunday NFL Countdown* with Chris Berman on ESPN. He had no reason to pay attention to tabloid headlines like *NBA Player's Wife Too Fat to Keep Husband*. He had better things to do." She took a deep breath. "God, it is amazing how quickly those feelings can come back." She sipped her wine.

"Are you okay?"

"I'm fine. I know I'm not the same person I was back then. I've gotten a lot stronger."

"I know you're a strong woman, Abby. However, Toni Redstone is out for blood and headlines. And Maria's father, Big Bill is out for his pound of Sam's flesh. This isn't going to be pretty."

"I saw all the news vans in Wallingford. Believe me I know this isn't going to be a cakewalk."

"Are you going to be able to handle it if your relationship somehow comes to light? The news vans in Connecticut are going to seem like a school of goldfish compared with to the piranhas Redstone's camp will unleash."

"It tested my metal once before, and I'm still here. If it comes down to it again, I'll handle it."

"I told Sam that he's going to have to keep things low key with you for a while until we address this issue and get it off Page 6, EEN and every other media outlet."

"I understand."

"I'm glad you do. Sam is another story. Since you're his editor, he thinks that's his in to see you without raising any red flags."

"Does he?"

"He doesn't know that if he says he's coming to work on his book that's exactly what's going to happen, isn't it?"

"Yes. He does need to work on the manuscript. The wedding might be off the calendar but his submission deadline isn't."

Reggie laughed. "You're still the Carey's daughter, aren't you?" He finished his glass of wine.

"Good or bad, I am."

Reggie looked at his watch. "I've got to get back, but, before I do, I have one more question."

"Do I love him?"

"Yes. Do you?"

"Yes."

"Good." He stood up. "You know when I saw Sam today there was something different about him. Then it hit me, he's in love. Sam is really in love."

Abby got up. She and Reggie hugged. "Thanks for telling me that."

"No need to thank me. It's the truth."

"You know I thought you were going to be upset with me about this. Sam is your best client."

"Yes, he's my best client, but I'm not one of those managers who needs to control every aspect of my client's life. He can make his own choices and I adapt to them. It's that simple."

Abby kissed him on the cheek. "You're a good man, Reggie Dawes."

Abby walked Reggie to the elevator and the two embraced before he stepped in. "I'll talk to you soon." She waved as the doors closed.

Abby walked over to the coffee table and picked up her wine. As she sipped, she walked over to the window. *I guess this will really be the test I need to see if I've truly managed to make my psyche bulletproof.*

⋙⋘

With his head held low, Sam made it through the lobby and upstairs to his room. As he approached his room he took out his key card.

"Sam," a voice called out from behind him.

Startled, he turned around and saw Big Bill. At six feet, six inches, Bill Carrangelo lived up to his nickname. A big, imposing man, his people style was reminiscent of President Lyndon Johnson, another Texan who was skilled in the fine art of glad-handing and arm-twisting to get what he wanted.

"Mr. Carrangelo. What are you doing here?"

"I thought I'd come by and talk some sense into you man to man."

"I don't think this is a good idea. We both have lawyers, and I'd rather they do the talking." Sam turned, swiped his card and opened the door.

"Okay. What's your price?"

"Excuse me?" Sam couldn't believe his ears.

"What's the magic number to get this wedding back on track?"

"There is no magic number. I can't be bought, and I'm sure Maria would be horrified if she knew you were willing to buy me off just so I'd go through with the wedding."

"My daughter knows that I would do anything to make her happy. For me her happiness is the bottom line."

"Then why don't you concentrate on helping her get on with her life instead of conjuring up lawsuits?"

"The Lord only knows why, but she wants you."

"And she thinks the way to get me back is to sue me?"

"We're making a point. She's not going to slink off in the background while you go off with another woman."

"I'll always love Maria and she will hold a special place in my heart. But I'm not in love with her. I'm sorry."

"You don't know what sorry is yet."

"Is that a threat?" Sam snarled.

"Son, I can make this go real hard for you. Are you ready for that?"

"Bring your best, old man. I'll bring mine. Now if you'll excuse me, I'm calling it a night." Sam went into his room and closed the door.

"That man has a set of brass ones," he said as he tossed his bag on the bed. Sam took his phone out and dialed his parents. The machine answered. "Damn. They're out." He waited for the tone to leave a message. "Hey, Momma and Dad. It's me. I called to let you know that I'm back in the city. I'll call you later. Love you."

Just as Sam was about to hang up another call came in. It was his brother, Zeke.

"Hey, Zeke. What's up?"

"I could ask you the same question. How are you?"

Zeke Best, Sam's middle brother lived a comfortable life in Texas. He and his wife of twelve years commuted between Houston and Dallas for business. A successful restaurateur, he owned two Best's Barbeque locations in Houston and Dallas. He also owned The Rose Room, a Michelin-rated upscale restaurant in Dallas.

"I'm hanging in there."

"You sound a little pissed to me."

"It's that obvious?"

"Of course it does to me, I'm your brother. What's eating you?"

"I just had a run in with Big Bill. He was lurking outside my hotel room."

"What did he want?"

"I'll tell you what he wanted. He wanted to buy me."

"Come again," Zeke asked.

"He offered to pay me to marry Maria. I knew Bill played dirty, but I didn't know he could go this far in the mud."

"You better believe that he'd roll around with hogs in the mud when it comes to his daughters. I know you turned him down."

"Without flinching," Sam responded.

"I admire your resolve, Sam but you should know that you haven't heard the last of him. He's going to get to you one way or another."

"He told me as much."

"The restaurant business has its share of questionable and scary characters, but not even the toughest of

the bunch could hold a candle to Big Bill. Watch your
back, little brother."

"I will." Sam paused. "Let's change the subject.
How's Jane?"

"She's good. Thanks. She's at Best's Barbeque location here in Houston overseeing things tonight."

"And you're not working?"

"I'm here dealing with the books. I have a meeting
with my accountant tomorrow morning."

"Better you than me."

"Thanks," he said sarcastically. "I've got to get back
to this, but next time you're going to have fill me in
about the girl."

"Who told you?"

"You know Momma."

"Yes, and we love her."

"Ain't that the truth?" He laughed. "All right, little
brother, remember what I said."

"I'll remember."

"Call me if you need me."

"I will. Love you, bro."

"Love you, too."

Sam hung up, took his coat off and sat down on the
bed. *Indeed there is a girl, and I miss her already.* Then
he remembered that she was doing Fashion Week and
decided for the first time he'd use the invitation he got
every year.

Chapter 23

The minute his feet hit the floor Monday morning, Sam glanced at the clock. "I bet she's in by now." He picked up his cell phone and dialed.

"Good morning. This is Mindy."

"Hi, Mindy." He said cheerfully.

Mindy Feldman was one the best publicists in Reggie's office. Always the first one in and the last one out, she had a way of making any request a reality as if by magic, and Sam needed her to wave her wand once more.

"Sam. Okay. What do you need?"

"Mindy. I'm wounded."

"And I need you to get to the point."

"Okay. I need to get on the list for New York's Fashion Week."

"You're kidding, right? You get invitations every year and you never go."

"I know. A man is entitled to change his mind, isn't he?"

"Of course you can change your mind. But please tell me that you're talking about the September shows. This week is fully booked by now."

"Mindy, I know that if anyone can get me on the list today, it's you."

"I'm glad you know that. It's the other people I'm worried about."

"Please," he said sweetly.

"All right. What show are you interested in?"

"I think the designer's name is Cedi."

"He's doing the first full-figured runway show at Fashion Week. That's going to be a tough ticket."

"You like a challenge."

"This isn't just a challenge. I'm climbing Mount Everest in my shorts. Cedi's show is a hot ticket. Nevertheless, I'll make some calls and give you a ring in a little bit. Okay?"

"Thanks, Mindy. You're the greatest."

"We'll see." She hung up.

Confident Mindy would deliver, Sam headed for the shower.

The environment was electric as Shana and Abby worked the room before the House of Cedi debut. Interns checked the list as the line for the guests got longer. Dressed in a fitted tweed suit that accentuated her curves, Abby walked guests in and seated them for the show after she double-checked her master list.

As she escorted Kiana German, a writer for *Detroit Fashion Pages* and a longtime supporter of Cedi's work, Lauren came over.

"Excuse me, Abby."

"Yes."

"Can I speak with you for a moment?"

"Sure." She turned to Ms. German. "If you'd excuse me for a moment, I'll be right back."

"No problem."

She and Lauren stepped out of earshot.

"What's going on, Lauren?"

"That's Kiana German you're escorting, right?"

"Yes."

"Then who's that in her seat?" She turned toward a woman with long dark hair and a somewhat pale complexion seated in the front row.

"I don't know. Tell her to get up."

"I tried. She doesn't speak English."

"What does she speak?"

"I'm not sure. It sounds Russian but I don't think it's Russian."

"Excuse me." Abby walked over to the woman. "Pardon me."

"Yes."

"That's not your seat."

"Ja ne razumijem engleski," she responded in Croatian.

"Of course you don't speak English." Abby put her hand in her hip. *"To nije svoje mjesto. Morat ete do i gore,"* Abby responded. "In case you do understand English that means this is not your place. You have to get up."

The woman looked shocked.

"Razumjeti?" Abby asked again. "Understand?"

She quickly got up.

"Evelyn! Can you make sure security escorts her out?"

"Sure thing, Abby," she answered.

Abby walked back over to Kiana German. "Sorry for the delay. Please take your seat."

"Thank you." She smiled.

Lauren walked over to her. "Thanks, Abby."

"No problem."

"Can I ask what language was she speaking?"

"It was Croatian."

"I didn't know you spoke Croatian."

"I had a friend in college who was from Croatia. She tutored me in the language. I knew it would come in handy someday."

Abby walked back over to the front of the room. An excited Shana met her there.

"Can you believe we have a full house?"

"Yes. We even had some crashers."

"Now I know Cedi is going to be big." Shana said excitedly. "It looks like everyone is in their seats and we even have standing room only."

"I know you live for this."

"Oh, you've got that right." She grinned. "I'm going to head back to see if we're ready to go."

"Okay. I'll be right here."

Abby scanned the crowd and then looked at her watch, hoping the show would start on time. She went backstage and found Cedi pacing like an expectant father.

"Are you okay, Cedi?"

A tall, distinguished man with skin so brown he looked like he'd been dipped in bronzer, Mr. Cedric Johnson began his fashion career in the shadow of the stacks of General Motors. He worked the assembly line by day and the pattern board by night before he retired from GM after twenty years of service. Able to devote more time to his passion, he created the House of Cedi and designed pieces for local celebrities before he branched out.

"I don't mind telling you I'm nervous."

"You have nothing to be nervous about. The clothes will speak for you."

Shana walked over. "All the wranglers are in place and the girls are lined up to go. We're ready to start."

"I know you're excited, Miss Thing in your one-of-a-kind asymmetrical Cedi dress," Abby teased.

"I know. Are you watching from back here or are you going out front."

"I'm going out front."

"Good luck." She kissed Cedi on the cheek before she ducked out to watch the show from the front.

The house lights went down and Cedi walked out to thunderous applause.

Abby took a spot in the back near the security team.

"Good morning. I'm Cedi and thank you for coming. This line is for the every woman. Women want something that's both functional and beautiful. That's why I created the Fall into Romance collection. I hope you enjoy." He walked offstage.

The models began the show as the high-energy music played.

Abby swayed in the back to the beat of Earth Wind and Fire's "Shining Star." Suddenly she felt a hand tug her. "What?"

"Hey, beautiful."

"What are you doing here?" she asked, shocked.

"I wasn't coming. I asked my publicist to make a few calls so I could make today's show."

"You know Reggie said we have to keep a low profile."

"It's dark and this is the back of the room. Who's going to notice us with all those great clothes and sexy models on the runway?" He asked as he slid his arms around her waist and kissed her cheek.

"We don't want to take anything away from the show."

"Okay. You're right." He stood next to her and grooved to the music until all the models walked down the runway with Cedi behind them.

Abby clapped furiously. "I think he's a hit."

Sam looked at Abby with her curly hair pulled up into a loose bun, a sexy fitted suit that was just short enough to show off her legs. *Mmm*, he thought. "I want you so much right now," he whispered in her ear.

Abby's body tingled at the thought. "That's not fair. I'm working."

"Can we get together to work later?"

"You do realize that if you say we're going to work on your book, that's what we're going to do."

"That's fine with me. As long as I get to work on you later, it's all good." He said with a sly grin.

Shana walked over. "Sam. I didn't know you were coming. Abby didn't say a word." He gave him the international fashion greeting of a kiss on each cheek.

"She didn't know."

"Oh. How did you enjoy the show?"

"I thought it was great."

"I think it was well received," Abby added.

Lauren rushed over with pad. "Ladies, they love Cedi. I've already taken down the names of at least five A-list stylists who want to pull from the collection."

Shana and Abby high-fived each other.

"I'm going backstage to tell Cedi and congratulate him for a successful show." Shana smiled. "It was nice to see you, Sam. Thanks for coming."

Just as Shana turned to leave, Evelyn walked over. "There is a line of reporters who want to interview Cedi. Should I send them back?"

"Where are they?" Shana asked.

"Over there," she pointed.

"I'll take care of this."

"I'm going to find our photographer and take a peek at the photos he snapped for the look-book. I have a feeling we're going to need it ASAP," Abby said.

"Cool. I'll catch up with you later. We've got three more runway shows today."

"I know."

Shana walked away with Evelyn.

Abby turned to Sam. "I'm so glad you came but I've got to work now. I'm sorry."

"That's okay. I know you're working." He leaned close to her ear. "Your place tonight at 7:00," he whispered.

"Okay. Bring your manuscript."

"I will." He leaned in again. "Love you."

"You, too." Abby winked at him.

The moment she turned her back, she heard people call out Sam's name.

Here we go. She thought as she walked away.

Chapter 24

Although Sam enjoyed the freedom of being behind the wheel, he was happy to surrender the driving duties to Bryan, his regular driver.

Sam felt his phone vibrate. "I forgot I changed the setting," he muttered as he picked up. "Hello?"

"Sam?"

"Hi, Reggie."

"Would it be possible for you to meet Blake at her office in say a half hour or so?"

"Okay."

"Good. I'll let her know you're on the way."

Sam hung up and took the business card out of his wallet. He leaned forward and handed the card to Bryan. "We need to get to this address."

Bryan glanced at the address. "You've got it."

Given that New York City's traffic is often a nightmare at best, Sam managed to arrive at Blake Campion's office in just slightly more than a half hour. When he arrived at her suite her secretary seated him in the waiting area. Sam looked around at all the photos of dignitaries, politicians and even a celebrity or two that hung on her personal wall of fame.

"Ms. Campion will see you now." Her secretary announced. "You can go right in."

"Thank you," Sam said as he got up and walked into her inner office.

When Sam entered he expected a stately old mahogany desk and Colonial-style furnishings. Instead he found a very modern office with an executive desk with a shiny black veneer and a contemporary black sofa set. There were a few more personal photos displayed in a black executive cabinet set in the corner.

This is the first time I've ever been in a lawyer's office that didn't make me feel like I was in the principal's office at school. Sam thought as he sat down.

A tall, elegant, African-American woman in a tailored navy pant suit walked in.

"Hello, Sam. I'm Blake Campion. It's a pleasure to meet you."

"Likewise, Ms. Campion," he said as he rose to shake her hand.

"Please call me Blake."

"Okay, Blake." He remained standing.

"Please have a seat." She said as she sat down. "Reggie tells me you're in a bit of a pickle after a broken engagement."

"I think that's putting it mildly. As you probably know, she's suing me."

"I heard. Have you been served yet?"

"No."

"Sam, do you have a dollar?"

"I think so." He went into his wallet, took out a dollar and handed it to her.

"You've got yourself a lawyer now. From what I understand, she's saying she gave up a potentially lucrative career to be by your side."

"That's crazy. I never said I didn't want her to work. In fact, I encouraged her to use her degree."

"Unfortunately, that's your version of events. The truth usually lies somewhere in the middle."

"I'm telling you the truth."

"I don't doubt you. What about the apartment? Who bought it?"

"I did. The deed and the mortgage are in my name."

"Good." She made a note on a yellow sheet of paper. "So she really has no legal claim to the property. You and she just lived there together."

"Right."

"Okay. I'll let Redstone's office know that you're represented by council so you can be served. Once you're served you can either bring the papers to me or I'll meet with you at Reggie's office. Is that all right with you?"

"It's fine with me." He sighed. "I feel better already."

"I'm glad to hear it." She paused. "That's all we need to cover for now. We'll go into more detail later." Blake got up and walked around her desk.

"Okay." He rose and they shook hands again before she walked him to the door.

"I'll be in touch." She patted him on the back as he walked out.

Sam left her office and went down the hall to the elevator. He pressed the call button, feeling he was ready to fight fire with fire. *If Big Bill wants a fight, he's got one now.* He stepped onto the elevator.

❧

With day one of Fashion Week behind them, Abby and Shana shuffled through their building's lobby, shoes in hand.

"I never realized how long this hallway was before." Shana groaned as she walked.

"Neither did I," Abby agreed.

After what seemed like an eternity, they reached the elevator. When Shana pressed the button the doors opened.

"Thank God," they chorused.

"Oh, my feet are barking." Shana winced.

"Be grateful your feet are just barking. My feet are biting me." Abby groaned. "I can't manage twelve hours in heels like I used to."

"Tell me about it. But sometimes we have to suffer for fashion."

"Speak for yourself. I'm bringing my Aerosoles tomorrow."

When the doors opened for Shana's apartment there stood Raymond with a bottle of wine in one hand and a pair of fuzzy slippers in the other. "I thought that you could use these after your day."

"Baby," Shana's face lit up at the sight of her light chocolate honey. Raymond was tall, broad shouldered and always looked sharp as a tack. "You are a sight for sore eyes and feet." She said as she practically fell into his arms.

"I told you that I'd be back."

"And here you are."

The two of them kissed.

Abby cleared her throat. "Hi, Raymond."

"Hey, Abby," he said as he wiped his lips of lipstick. "How are you?" He leaned into the elevator and gave her a kiss on the cheek.

"I'm tired but I'm good. It looks like you've got the right stuff for our girl here."

"I figured she could use a little TLC." He pulled Shana closer to him.

"That sounds like a plan. I'll leave you two alone. Enjoy!" Abby waved as the doors closed.

Once she reached her apartment, Abby dragged herself to the bathroom, ready for a relaxing hot bath.

She turned the water on and poured in her favorite bath oil.

While the tub filled, she undressed, put on her favorite robe and re-pinned her hair. A few minutes later a happy Abby was submerged in the sunken tub while the jets worked her aches out.

Abby sighed as she closed her eyes.

"Now there's a picture."

Abby jumped. "Sam? How did you get in here?"

"I had a little help from my friends." He smiled as he held up his portfolio. "I brought the manuscript."

"Good."

He started to walk toward the tub.

"Is your portfolio waterproof?"

"I don't think so."

"Then you'd better stay over there."

"But you know," he put the portfolio on the bathroom counter, "I think I'm waterproof."

"Sam," she warned.

"I'm not climbing in there with you though it's quite tempting." He knelt down next to the tub and rolled up his sleeves. "Give me one of those tired little tootsies."

Abby lifted her foot onto the side of the tub. Sam began to massage it, pressing gently on all the pressure points.

"Oh, that feels so good."

"I saw the shoes you wore today. They were gorgeous, but I know they had to hurt."

"By the end of the day I sounded like Gunnery Sergeant Hartman from *Full Metal Jacket*."

Sam laughed. "Now that's saying a lot."

"I know. I'm going to have to make up for it with a nice breakfast spread tomorrow."

"I'm sure everyone understood." He stopped. "Now give me the other foot, please."

Abby lifted her other foot and closed her eyes while Sam massaged it.

"You know I met with a lawyer today. I think you know her."

"Oh yeah?"

"Yes. Her name is Blake Campion."

"Yes. I know Blake. She roomed across the hall from me at U of Penn. She was a Political Science major. She's a smart woman and an excellent lawyer."

"That makes me feel better."

"Ah, this makes me feel better." She pointed to her feet.

"It doesn't have to stop there. I know of some other sensitive pressure points further north."

"Naturally you're talking about my temples, right."

"It's a temple, all right." He got up, grabbed a towel and put his hand out to take Abby's.

"What if I want to stay in the tub?"

"Then I'm either coming in or you're getting out, it's your choice."

"I don't have a maid to clean up my bathroom. So I guess I'm getting out." Abby took his hand and got out of the tub.

"Allow me." He began to towel Abby off.

"You're getting all wet, Sam."

"I can easily rectify that." He said as he took off his shirt.

Sam toweled and kissed every inch of Abby's body slowly and deliberately from the bottom up. Once he reached the top, he unpinned her hair as he kissed her neck and shoulders. Abby let her hand fall to his waist where she unhooked and unzipped his pants. Sam quickly stepped out of them and kicked them to the side. The next article to fall was his boxers, which quickly joined his pants in a pile.

Their bodies pressed together, they moved into the bedroom where they collapsed into a lover's heap on the bed. The steam continued to rise as Abby wrapped her legs around Sam's muscular back. Her toes curled as she felt Sam's passion fill her once more. Sam moaned as her softness enveloped him. Caught up in the rapture of love, their bodies rocked as a heavenly sense of ecstasy washed over them.

Early the next morning, Sam rolled over to an empty pillow. He opened his eyes.

"Abby? Baby? Where are you?"

Abby walked out of the bathroom in a black slinky, body-conscious matte jersey Zelma dress by Ralph Lauren it had a dropped waist, three-quarter sleeves and a ballet neckline she dressed up with a long gold necklace. "Good morning." She said as she put her earrings in.

"Look at you."

"Do you like it?"

"Come back to bed. I'll show you how much I like it."

Abby giggled. "I would love to take you up on that, but I've got to get over to Lincoln Center. I have four shows today."

"What time is it?"

"It's almost six."

"It's too early. Come back to bed." He patted the bed.

"You're making it hard for me."

"I was thinking the same thing."

"You are so bad. But seriously, sweetheart, I have to leave and I've got to make up for turning into Captain Ahab yesterday." She went over to the mirror and checked her hair.

"Why don't you wear it down for a change?"

"The upsweep is more in keeping with my image. I let my hair down for you." She turned and winked at him.

"I feel special."

She walked over to her closet and pulled out her shoe rack. "As chic as they are, I don't think my feet will survive another day in Jimmy Choos."

"I could come back and massage them for you again tonight."

"That would be lovely." She pulled out a pair of boots. "I think I'll stay with my Ralph Lauren theme. I'll wear the Sahara Vachetta riding boots over there and then change into my Cala Snakeskin Heels for the shows." She tapped her foot. "Oh yes, I'm bringing my black Amarissa satin ballet flats for backup." She took both pairs of shoes out.

"You're certainly making sure that you're prepared today."

"Yesterday, I could barely walk at the end of the day. I don't want to go through that again. Although I won't turn a foot massage down."

"That's good to hear."

Abby sat down in a chair and put her boots on. "Okay. I am about ready to go. You can stay here as long as you like."

"What if I want to stay here all day and wait for you?"

"Be my guest." She got up, walked over to the bed and kissed him.

"Come on, you really can't play hooky?"

"I'm afraid not. Our clients pay us to be there."

"Okay. Can I at least get a better kiss than that?"

"All right." Just as Abby leaned over to kiss him, Sam grabbed her, pulled her on top of him and kissed her deeply. "What about a quickie? All you have to do is lift up that lovely dress and I promise I'll do the rest."

"I'm wearing Spanx, Sam. It's practically the modern day equivalent of a chastity belt." She kissed him and got up.

"I can't believe you're going to leave me hanging like this."

"I don't want to, Sam. I have to. I'll see you later." She blew him a kiss as she walked out. "Love you."

"Love you, too," he called back. "I guess the best thing I can do is go back to sleep." Sam closed his eyes and rolled over.

⚍

An hour later the sound of Sam's cell phone woke him.

He scrambled to get his phone and waited a moment for his vision to clear before he read the caller ID. "It's too early, Reggie. I'll call you back." He put the phone back on the nightstand and rolled over again.

A few minutes later the phone rang again. He reached over to the nightstand and checked the ID. It was Bo, apparently in conspiracy with Reggie to rob him of sleep. He didn't answer.

The phone remained quiet long enough for Sam to doze back off. When it rang again, he picked it up.

"Hello, Reggie."

"Turn the television on."

"What? To what channel?"

"It doesn't matter. You can put on any of the morning shows you want. The news will be the same. Call me back."

Sam hung up and turned on the television.

"*And in other news, the broken engagement between former New York Giants' quarterback Sam Best and real estate heiress Maria Carrangelo took another turn when photos of Sam and New York publicist, Abby Carey surfaced on the web and in* The Post."

"Oh, my God," Sam said aloud when several photos of him with his arms around Abby flashed across the screen.

"*The public canoodling took place at the Cedi fall fashion show. Onlookers said the couple was very affectionate. Representatives for Sam Best had no comment.*"

Sam shut the television off.

So much for keeping it low key. He sighed. *I'd better call Abby and warn her.*

Sam dialed and waited. "Please pick up, baby. Damn! It's her voice mail." He waited for the tone to record a message. "Abby, someone took pictures of us at Cedi's show yesterday and leaked them to the press. It's all over the news. Please call me. Love you."

He hung and called Reggie back. "I'm on my way to your office. I'll be there in about an hour."

"Good. I asked Blake to join us."

"Okay. See you shortly." Sam hung up. He looked around the bedroom before he went into the bathroom and returned with his portfolio. He took a piece of paper out and sat down on the bed and wrote a note. Once he was done, he got up and put it on Abby's dresser.

"I really wish I could stay but I don't have a choice now, baby." He let out a heavy sigh and went into the bathroom.

⁕

Abby walked through the staging area of the Mark Botelli show with her notepad. She waved two interns over.

"Sienna and Michelle, I need you to make sure the dresses on this rack are in order. The numbers correspond to how the models are going out onto the runway, and it looks like someone has scrambled them."

"Sure thing, Abby," Sienna said.

As Abby continued her walk through, she watched Mark make last-minute hair and makeup changes with his styling team.

Suddenly a panicked Lauren ran up to Abby. "I don't know what's going on out there." She said out of breath.

"Calm down Lauren. I've never seen you like this. What's the matter?"

"I just went outside and there are all these reporters and cameras everywhere. They're practically clawing to get in."

"What's wrong with that? We want them to be excited for the show."

"It's not the usual fashion and lifestyle reporters who are out there. There are general desk reporters, a few people from the gossip networks and more paparazzi than I've ever seen."

"I know we've got quite a number of A-list celebrities coming to the show, but this sounds like they're expecting someone notorious." Abby handed Lauren her notepad. "I'm going to check it out."

Abby walked over to the entrance and opened the door. The second she came into view, she was barraged by cameras and questions were hurled at her at lightning speed from all directions.

"How long have you been involved with Sam Best?"

"How old are you? Are you a cougar?" another reporter shouted.

"What's the status of your relationship with Sam?"

"What does it feel like now that you're the home-wrecker and the other woman?"

Abby quickly closed the door. "What the hell is going on?" She walked over to the corner and called Sam.

"Abby?"

"Sam."

"Thank God you called me."

"Of course I called you. There's a sea of reporters here and they seem to want to know about me and you. I don't understand."

"Someone snapped photos of us at Cedi's show yesterday and they sold them to the media. It's all over the morning news shows. I don't know how anyone got those shots."

"I do. You can make a lot more money selling photos to the tabloids than shooting a fashion show. It was a matter of economics."

"If I ever get my hands on who did it, they're going to wish they hadn't."

"That's a nice sentiment that can get you into trouble. People are going to try to make an extra dollar any way they can these days."

"You're right. Not to mention there's no paparazzi honor code."

Abby's heart leaped into her throat. "Oh, my God." She hung her head. "I can't stay here now. I'm a working mother. I'm here as part of my job, not to be a tabloid headline for my son to read."

"I know, baby. I'm on my way to Reggie's office to talk about how we're going to handle this."

"I bet he's thrilled."

"I can come by later once the meeting is over."

"No. I'm sure they're going to stake out my building, too." She shook her head. "This is my business and my career, Sam."

"I know, baby."

"I have to figure a way out of here. Call me later."

"I will. I love you."

"I love you, too." Abby hung up. "Lauren!" she called.

"Yes, Abby?"

"Do you know where Shana is?"

"I think she's in with the models in the back."

"Thanks."

Abby walked as quickly as she could to the model's dressing area.

"Desiree, I need you to get into hair and makeup now," Shana said.

"I'm going," Desiree answered.

"Shana, I need to speak to you for a minute."

"Sure. What's wrong? You look like you've seen a ghost."

"I should be so lucky. Someone sold photos of Sam and me at Cedi's show to the media."

"Oh, no," Shana said as she covered her mouth. "So it's all over the news now, right?"

"Yes and now there's a sea of reporters and cameras out there trying to get my photo and trying to get me to answer vile questions." Abby's emotions welled up. She stopped to take a deep breath. "I've got to get out of here. I'm a mother. What's Justin going to think? These shutterbugs can ruin my life."

"They're not going to ruin your life."

"You've seen what they've done to J.J."

"J.J. is completely different. He doesn't worry about how his actions affect Justin. You always put Justin first, and I'm sure Justin knows that."

"Thanks. But how am I going to get out of here? I did come here to work."

Shana looked at her. "The photographers saw you already, right?"

"Yes."

"Take your dress off."

"What?"

"You heard me. Take your dress off. We're going to switch."

Shana slipped out of her aubergine Michael Kors asymmetric drape dress. "Here, put this on." She handed Abby the dress.

"Okay." She handed Shana hers.

A group of models watched as the two women slipped into their new looks.

"That looks hot on you," a model said to Abby.

"Thanks." She looked at Shana. "That dress looks good on you."

"It does, doesn't it?" She smiled. "Okay enough of that, we need to change your hair." She looked around. "Oscar!"

"Yes, my darling," he said as he walked over.

Tall, slim, and cocoa-skinned Oscar Booth was one of the top hair stylists in the city. With four salons that bore his name, his client list read like a who's who of Hollywood, fashion and high society. Women waited months for his chair.

Shana pointed to Abby. "She needs you to work your magic on her."

He looked at her hair. "Darling you have beautiful hair. Why are you hiding it?"

"I just prefer to wear it in a bun or pinned up."

He looked her up and down. "With those curves, honey, you need to work it like a bombshell. Come with me."

Abby followed him to a chair where a model was already seated.

"Sweetie, I need you to get up for a minute please." The model obliged.

"Thank you. I'll get right back to you in a minute." He turned to Abby. "Have a seat."

Abby sat in the chair. Oscar pulled all the hair pins out and brushed her back length hair out. "Look at all

369

of this body. Do you know how many clients I have that would kill for your hair?"

Abby smiled.

Oscar demonstrated his finesse with a curling iron. He spiral curled her hair with a large barrel iron to give Abby loose curls, and then he ran his fingers through to give it a little definition.

"All we need is a little hair spray and you are good to go," he said as he spritzed her hair. "Voila!"

"You're a genius, Oscar." Shana grinned.

Abby looked in the mirror. "Wow, this looks great. Thank you." She got out of the chair.

"It was my pleasure. Call my salon anytime. I'll make time to get you in my chair."

"Thank you."

"Thanks, Oscar." Shana said as she and Abby walked away. "Now no one will be able to recognize you. Do you have your sunglasses?"

"Yes." Abby went over to the rack where she'd hung her coat.

"You don't want to switch coats?"

"I don't think anyone saw me in my coat. I should be okay. If I leave now you'll be able to open the doors and start the show on time."

"Okay."

"I'm sorry to have to do this to you."

"Don't worry about it. I can handle things, and I have everyone here to help me."

"I'll see you later," Abby said as she put her sunglasses on and dashed out the side door.

Chapter 25

Sam sat in the back of his Mercedes as it made its way through traffic. As the car approached Reggie's building, he saw the crush of media that awaited him.

"I could keep driving."

"That would be nice, Bryan, but I eventually have to face this one way or another. I appreciate the offer."

"Just thought I would ask," Bryan smiled in the rearview mirror.

When the car pulled up to the curb, two security men from Reggie's office opened the back door to let Sam out.

"Sam what do you have to say about the photos?" A reporter said as he tried to shove a microphone near him.

"Step back, sir." One security man warned.

"They're calling your new love the voluptuous vixen. Do you have any comment?" A female reporter shouted.

As the security guards flanked him, Sam covered his eyes from the flashbulbs as he continued to walk to the entrance. He didn't respond to any of the questions. The guards stayed with him on the ride up to the twenty-first floor.

Reggie was in the hallway when Sam arrived on the floor. "Thanks guys. I'll take it from here."

"No problem, Mr. Dawes."

The security men positioned themselves outside of the office while Reggie took Sam back to his office. Blake was already there.

"Hello, Sam."

"Hello, Blake."

"I would ask how you're doing, but it's written all over your face."

"I bet it is." Sam sighed as he sat down.

Reggie sat across from Sam with his arms folded.

"I know you're dying to say it, Reggie. Get it over with."

"I thought we agreed that you'd keep things with Abby low key until we sorted all the legal and PR stuff out."

"I know. I messed up."

"I haven't been able to get off the phone. I've heard from every company you're a spokesperson for. They want to know what's happened to their golden boy."

"He fell in love. That's what happened to him."

"I don't doubt that you're in love, but there's a scorned woman and an angry, rich father in the mix to make sure things don't go well."

"What do you want me to say, Reggie?"

Just then one of Reggie's assistants poked her head in. "Mr. Dawes?"

"Millie, we're in a meeting. I asked not to be disturbed.'

"Yes, Mr. Dawes but Edgar in PR asked me to come in here and tell you to put on Fox. There's something you should see."

"Thanks."

She closed the door.

Reggie reached over and used the remote to turn the television on. He switched to Fox.

"We're outside of Trump Tower where Bill Carrangelo just spoke to reporters with his daughter, Maria, by his side.

" 'Naturally my daughter's devastated, as any woman would be. She is shocked to learn that the man she was to marry this June isn't the man she thought he was. More will come out soon.' "

"Can you tell us more now?"

"No, that's all."

"Ask Sam about the money he spent on her," Maria screeched.

"What money?"

"I'm sorry. My daughter is upset," Bill responded as he took Maria by the hand and pulled her into the building.

The camera cut back to the anchor. *"That comment about money, were we able to get any more information?"*

"No. However Maria's allegation is reminiscent of former New England Patriot Dennis Shanahan, another famous quarterback who got in trouble with women and money. But for now Maria's statement is unsubstantiated."

"Now that wasn't on script." Blake commented.

"No. But it was the opening we needed. Maria did us a favor. You can talk about the money now."

"No Reggie."

"Sam."

"I said no."

"Will someone tell me what's going on?"

"Sam's been making anonymous donation to aid retired and disabled football players. However, when Maria found some statement she assumed Sam was supporting a mistress."

"I see. Reggie's right. You can easily counter her with the truth."

"I don't do it for publicity and I want to keep it that way. Let's move on."

Blake and Reggie looked at each other.

"All right, we'll move on. We can talk about this lawsuit. Have you been served yet?"

"No."

"That's strange. I wonder what's taking Toni so long. She's usually on top of this kind of thing."

"I'm sure it's coming."

"No. It should have come already. Something else is going on here." Blake picked up her briefcase. "I need to get back to my office to check a few things. I'll be in touch." She got up and shook Sam's hand. "Hang in there. Reggie, I'll talk to you later."

Blake left the office.

"I'm not going to change my mind, Reggie so don't bring it up again."

"Fine," he huffed. "The press is going to continue to cream you."

"Let them do their best. I can take it."

"I don't think you get it. This isn't just about you anymore."

∞

Abby flagged a cab three blocks away from Lincoln Center and the driver let her out two blocks from her building. She slipped in through the back alley and took the stairs to her apartment.

She hung her coat up and took her shades off, unable to believe that her life had been reduced to cloak and dagger stuff.

She exhaled deeply and rubbed her eyes. "What the hell are you doing here, J.J.?"

"I don't know why I thought I could sneak up on you. I keep forgetting you grew up with deaf grandparents and you're sensitive to footsteps."

"It's a good thing I am otherwise you would have scared the life out of me. So I will ask again, what are you doing here?"

He showed her the newspaper. "You're the voluptuous vixen who stole Sam Best from his poor, unsuspecting fiancée. Where else would I be?"

"I would think you'd be spending time with your new fiancée and not worrying about tabloid garbage."

"I don't know if I'd call it garbage. You and Sam look pretty cozy in those pictures." He sat down on the sofa. "When we were married you hated public displays of affection. It looks like times have changed."

"If the point of this visit is to aggravate me, congratulations you've accomplished your mission. Can you leave now?"

"You know it's funny for all your talk about my life, here you are in a quandary over a messy relationship. A relationship I didn't know anything about."

"We're not married. I'm not required to tell you about my relationships."

"You are where my son is involved."

"Oh, now you're concerned about your son. Where was that concern when you started dating a twenty-three-year-old while you were still married to Beebe? The papers had a field day with that."

"We're not talking about me and Beebe. I'm talking about the fact that you had that man around my son in Connecticut. You didn't think I would connect the dots? Sam Best was seen buying flowers in Wallingford, which just happens to be where Justin's school is, and it was the same weekend you were up there, too."

"I'm impressed, J.J. Considering the fact that you've only been there once in three years, I didn't think you even knew the school was in Connecticut, let alone Wallingford."

"You had another man around my son. A white man," he huffed.

"You're kidding me, right? Your fiancée is white. Hell, J.J., you're better than the E.E.O.C. You don't discriminate in your dating life. You're totally equal opportunity. Now you have the nerve to be upset that Sam is white?"

"You don't understand."

"You're right. At the moment I think it's a case of the pot calling the tea kettle white." She growled.

"We can go around in circles about this for hours." He stood up. "I came here to tell you that when Justin comes back home, I want him to stay with me."

"Why did you come by to tell me that? We always split the time for his break."

"I'm not talking about his winter break. I'm talking about the end of the school year and beyond."

"What?"

"I'm going for custody."

Abby leaped to her feet. "After ten years, now you want custody?"

"Yes. I think Justin needs to be with his father now."

"You son of a bitch," Abby yelled. "The only reason you're doing this is because you think some other man is going to take over the role of father in Justin's life. You know I wouldn't let that happen, but I'll be damned if I'm going to let you dictate who I can and cannot see."

"You're messing around with an unavailable man."

Abby's face grew hot as she leaped out of her chair. "I suggest you stop talking about something you know nothing about."

"I know enough. You'll be hearing from my attorney, Nancy Bloom." He started to walk away.

"Nancy Bloom? How in the hell did you get her? It's not like she's listed in the Yellow Pages."

Nancy Bloom was a matrimonial and family lawyer who represented only the biggest names in Hollywood. Whenever there was a split or custody issue in Hollywood or high society, she served as the on-air legal expert for major network television news organizations. She had a reputation for getting her clients what they wanted, and she had the claws to prove it.

Abby picked up a knick-knack from the table. "Walk faster, J.J. I may not have played basketball, but I'm a damn good shot."

J.J. headed for the elevator.

"Take the stairs. You'll get away faster." She warned.

Upon hearing the tone of her voice, J.J, quickly went to the staircase.

Abby placed the statue back on the table. "He wants to take my child from me." She sat back down. "Oh, God, what's happening with my life?" She dissolved into tears.

❦

The security men rode with Sam back to the W Hotel. Again they escorted him through the crush of media that clamored for any tidbit they could chew on. Once Sam arrived at his room, one security man remained near the elevator while the other stationed himself outside his door.

When he opened the door he saw his mother and father.

"Momma and Dad, what are you doing here?"

"Oh Sam we had to come." His mother hugged him.

"Don't get me wrong. I'm very glad to see you. How did you get up here?"

"We talked to the hotel manager. He remembered seeing us on that *60 Minutes* report with you," his mother answered.

He and his father embraced. "How are you holding up, son?"

"I'm hanging in there. I've been better, though."

"I know you have," his father said.

Sam sat on the bed. "I fell in love with someone else, and now it's being made out to be something ugly and shameful. As soon as I realized that I was just going through the motion and I wasn't in love with Maria anymore, I ended it. I won't say it was an easy thing for me to do, but…"

"You had to do it." His mother completed his sentence as she sat next to him.

"You want to tell him, Sara?"

"Tell me what?"

His mother and father glanced at each other knowingly.

"I was engaged to someone else when I met your father."

"What?"

"Yes." She nodded.

"I thought you and Dad were college sweethearts."

"We were, in some ways." His father paused. "At least for our senior year," he smiled.

"His name was Rich. We grew up together in Tyler. Rich and I started dating as high school sophomores and when it was time to head to college, we naturally went to the same school. The plan was that we would marry right after graduation."

"What happened?"

"I happened. Your mom took one look at me and it was over right there," he said jokingly.

"Stop being silly, Don." She laughed. "He's exaggerating, but not by much. We met in a required biology class we had to take in our senior year. The professor paired us for labs, and it didn't take long for me to realize that I belonged with your father." She looked at her husband lovingly.

"I knew right after she said, 'My name is Sara.' "

"So how I feel about Abby doesn't sound crazy to you?"

"No. If there's anything we've learned is that when it comes to love there's no rhyme or reason to what the heart feels. It just feels," his mother said as she took his hand.

"When I first saw Abby something in me just said 'I take this woman.' I didn't know anything about her. It was just a feeling."

"It's a pretty good feeling, isn't it?" His father asked.

"Yes. It felt better this morning before all this nonsense exploded." Sam paused. "I've got to call Abby and see how she is. The vultures had descended on her while she was working Fashion Week and I need to check in on her. Will you excuse me?"

"Sure." His mother said.

Sam got up and went into another part of the suite. He dialed Abby.

"Hello?" Abby's voice sounded hoarse.

"Abby?"

"Yes." She said weakly.

"Baby, are you all right?"

"No. J.J. was here. He's suing me for full custody of Justin."

"What?"

"You heard it correctly. He wants to take my baby away from me."

"I can't believe that."

"He's actually hired Nancy Bloom."

"What?"

Abby's voice caught. "I can't talk right now. Can I call you back?"

"Yes, of course. I love you."

"Love you, too. Bye."

Sam felt flush with anger. "I bet that son of a bitch is behind this." He dialed Big Bill.

"Hello?"

"Mr. Carrangelo?"

"Sam. I thought I'd be hearing from you. Have you come to your senses?"

"I was going to ask if you had taken leave of yours."

"I'm sure I don't know what you're talking about."

"I just got off the phone with Abby, and she told me that her ex-husband has hired Nancy Bloom to represent him in a custodial case against her."

"He is the father. He has rights."

"Yes, he has rights, but I know for a fact that there's no way he could have gotten access to a heavy hitter like Nancy Bloom without a little help."

"I just reached out to J.J. Stokes, father-to-father, to offer a little advice and help if he wanted it. He took me up on it."

"That was a low thing to do. Abby's a wonderful mother. Justin always comes first for her."

"You could have fooled me if she had time to steal another woman's fiancé."

"She didn't steal me. Maria and I were over a long time ago. I just put a period at the end of the sentence and closed the chapter. You need to get over it."

"I told you that I could make life hard. I didn't say it would be limited to you."

"You're problem is with me. Leave the people I care about out of it."

"You know what you have to do to make this go away."

"I can't be bought or threatened. You can go to hell, Bill."

When Sam turned around his father was there.

"How long have you been standing there, Dad?"

"Long enough to smell a rat named Bill Carrangelo."

Sam took a few moments to calm down. "He helped Abby's ex get Nancy Bloom so he can sue for full custody of their son, Justin." Sam began to pace. "I feel awful. This is my fault."

"No, this is Bill's fault. If he couldn't get to you, he's going through the people closest to you."

"Dad, you should have heard her on the phone. She sounds so bad, it's killing me."

"Then you have to make some decisions on how you're going to fight fire with fire."

∽

Still upset, Abby sat on her bed in the dark.

"Abby? Are you in here?" Shana asked as she turned on the light.

"Yes." Abby wiped her eyes. "How did the shows go?"

"The shows went fine." She sat down next to her. "I'm not here to talk about that. It's obvious that something else has happened. Did you have a fight with Sam or something?"

"J.J. was here."

"Oh, no," Shana groaned.

"He came here to tell me that he's suing me for custody of Justin."

"What?"

"He's questioning my commitment to being a parent."

"He's got some nerve. You're a great mother."

"That's not the way he sees it."

"He's upset that you have another man in your life. It's okay for him to parade women up and down the block, but he can't take the idea that another man will be around his son, especially a white man." Shana shook her head. "There's no way he's going to get custody. You don't have anything to worry about."

"I'm not so sure. He's hired Nancy Bloom."

"Get out of here!"

"I don't know how he managed to get her, but he did." Abby choked up. "This is what I get."

"What do you mean, this is what you get? You don't think you deserve this, do you?"

"Don't I? Am I not guilty of the same thing I said Beebe did to me?"

"No. You didn't go after Sam. What's more, Sam broke off his engagement. He didn't try to have his cake and eat it, too, like J.J. did. The only thing you're guilty of is falling in love."

"But now I could lose my son for it."

"I'm telling you that won't happen."

"Damn straight it isn't."

When Shana and Abby looked up, they saw Abby's brother Franklin Jr. Still long and lanky, the only hint of his age was a little grey hair around his temples, which was pretty good for the father of three teenage girls.

"Frankie!" Abby jumped up and the two embraced. "When did you get here?"

"I flew in a couple of hours ago. Naturally it took the cab forever to get here from the airport, but that's something I've grown to expect whenever I come to New York."

"You are a sight for sore eyes."

"When my big sister needs me, I'm here in a flash." He hugged her tightly and looked over at Shana. "How are you, Shana?"

"I'm good, Frankie." She got up and kissed him on the cheek. "I'm going to head back down to the office, Abby. I think you're in good hands now. Call me if you need anything."

"Thanks."

"I'll see you two later." Shana waved as she left the room.

"Where are your bags?"

"I put them in the spare bedroom."

"I forgot. You know the drill."

"Yes, I do."

"I haven't picked up my phone, but I'm sure Mom and Dad have called at least a dozen times."

"That would be a safe bet. They're worried about you."

"Are you sure they're not mortified?" Abby looked down at the floor.

"Hey." He lifted her chin. "They know you, Abby. They know you're not the kind of woman the media is trying to make you out to be. After all, they are the ones who raised you and the rest of us."

"That's good to hear." She sighed. "I guess I got worked up."

"You've been watching television haven't you?"

"Yes. It's not like I haven't been through this before, but I wasn't on this end of it with so many people assuming the absolute worst about me."

"Right now, it's a feeding frenzy. It will die down."

"I hope so. I need to focus on keeping my son."

"Don't worry, we'll deal with that. Wes is in the middle of a case, but, as soon as he can get a continuance, he'll be here. And Nick is working on getting some professors to cover for him so he can be here, too. Between the four of us, I think we can handle whatever J.J. throws our way."

Abby hugged him again. "You know I really love you guys."

"We love you, too, sis. Now how about I fix some tea for us and you fill me in about this Mr. Best. I mean, I know about him as a player but I want to know about him as the man my sister fell in love with. Does that sound like a good deal?"

"It's the best deal I've had all day."

Chapter 26

While Sam made arrangements for his parents' accommodations, his father Don made a phone call.

"Hello?"

"Hello, Norm. It's Don Best. How are you?"

Though Don didn't play in the NFL, he and Norm met at a fundraiser years earlier and had become good friends.

"I'm good, Don. How are you?"

"I'm all right, but I could be better. That's why I'm calling you."

"I think I know what this is about, and you can count me in."

"Thanks so much."

"No need to thank me. It's the least I can do."

"I'll be in touch with the details soon."

"I'll wait to hear back from you."

"Okay. Talk to you shortly." Don hung up.

"Don are you sure you want to do this? You know how Sam feels."

"Sometimes our son is a little too pigheaded for his own good."

"I wonder where he gets that from," she said facetiously.

Don laughed. "I'm aware that he comes by that trait naturally," he said as he dialed Bo.

"Hello?"

"Hello, Bo."

"Hello, Mr. Best. It's good to hear from you. Are you in town? What am I saying? Of course you're in town."

"We flew in this afternoon. We're at the W Hotel with Sam." He paused. "In fact he's the reason I'm calling. I wondered if I could prevail upon you to use your influence at ESPN to get some air time tomorrow."

"Sure. Whatever you need."

"Great. I think it's time for the world to meet the other side of Sam Best."

"I couldn't agree with you more. "I'll make some calls and get back to you."

"Thanks." Don hung up. "Now to call Reggie for the last piece of the puzzle," He said as he began to dial.

Just then Sam entered the room. "Okay. I have your key cards. You're in the suite across the hall."

"Thanks, son," his father answered.

"You know, Sam, I'd like to go down to that Olives restaurant. I've heard it's pretty good."

"It is good. But considering the madness going on, wouldn't you prefer if I order up room service?"

"We don't have anything to hide. Let's have dinner downstairs."

"Are you sure, Momma?"

"Yes. I'm sure they'll take us without a reservation." She picked up her purse. "Come on, you could use a change of scenery and a good meal."

"Okay, Momma. Are you coming, Dad?"

"Yes. Why don't you give me the key card and I'll put our stuff in the room and then I'll catch up to you."

"Are you sure? I can have the bellman do it."

"Nonsense, it's just a couple of bags."

"Okay," Sam said reluctantly.

"I heard the pan roasted cod is supposed to be good." His mother gently led him out of the room.

Don waited a moment then called Reggie.

"Hello, Reggie. I don't have much time to talk. I need you to listen and move as quickly as possible."

"I'm all ears," Reggie said.

❧

Unable to sleep, Abby turned on the television and scanned through the channels. Hesitantly, she turned to HLN.

She turned the volume up when she thought she caught a glimpse of Beebe.

"*Entertainment reporter Joanna Kelp caught up with J.J. Stokes's estranged wife Beebe outside of her apartment to get her reaction to the recent developments* with Abigail Carey. As many of you know, Beebe had an affair with J.J. while he was married to Ms. Carey."

"Ms. Stokes do you have any comment about Sam Best and Abigail Carey?"

"No. I wish Abby and Sam the best."

"Even under these circumstances?" Joanna inquired further.

"Who am I to pass judgment? Even in the midst of everything that happened between J.J. and me, Abby was never anything but nice to me, even though I didn't deserve it. I just wish everyone would leave it alone. Thanks. That's all I have to say."

"If I hadn't seen it for myself, I wouldn't have believed it," Abby said aloud as she turned the television off. "Now if everyone else would follow her lead, I'd be okay." She rolled over and tried to sleep.

❦

The next morning Frankie awoke to find his sister dressed and seated at the kitchen table with a stack of papers.

"Good morning. There's coffee if you want."

"Thanks." He went over to the cabinet and got a mug. "I didn't expect to see you up and dressed for work." He said as he poured his coffee.

"I didn't think I'd get out of bed either but then I decided that staying in bed wasn't an option."

"You need to keep your mind occupied, right?"

"Yes. I tried watching television last night."

"How did that work out for you?"

"The only things on in the wee hours are infomercials, home shopping, bad movies and the news."

"You watched the news, didn't you?"

"Of course I did and who did I see? Beebe."

"Please tell me you turned it off."

"I didn't. I wanted to hear what she had to say since the shoe is on the other foot and I'm the man-stealing hussy."

"Abby…" Franklin groaned.

"It turned out that I had nothing to worry about. She basically said she wished me the best and thought everyone should leave us alone."

"Wow that is shocking coming from her."

"It's awfully magnanimous of her, but it won't garner ratings or sell papers." She lifted the stack of newspapers on the table.

"You should toss all of them into the shredder."

"I will. Then I'm going to head down to my office. In the midst of all of this work, it's the only thing that I feel I have control over. Does that make sense to you?"

"It makes perfect sense. I think we're all wired that way." He chuckled. "When I find myself baffled by the whirlwind known as teenage girls, I head to the office."

Abby laughed. "I can empathize, having been a teenage girl."

"Yes, but you didn't have a cell phone, text messages, instant messages and video chats. I tell you Barbara and I don't know whether we're coming or going sometimes."

"I feel for you, little brother, but you should enjoy it while it lasts. They grow up so fast. I only have a couple of years before I send Justin off to college." Abby took a deep breath and stood up. "That's enough of that. I've got to head downstairs and face my staff. You can come down later if you want."

"Okay. I'm just going to have a couple of cups of java and hit the shower and then I'll be downstairs."

"Okay. I'll see you later."

Abby headed for the staircase instead of the elevator. She didn't want to allow herself even a moment to dwell on all that was going on around her. Once she got to the floor, she handed out her papers and headed into her office.

She tried to get through the stacks of messages on her desk.

"God, how many phone calls could I have missed?" She turned her chair around toward the window. She felt her emotions bubble up. *No more crying.* "Candy?" she said over her shoulder.

"Yes?"

Abby turned around and then checked her watch.

"I know. I'm early for once."

"I see. Is everything all right?"

"I was going to ask you the same thing." She had a stack of papers in her hand. "I went through every one of these and there isn't a red mark on any of them. I thought maybe you wanted to re-check them."

"No. There's no mistake. I didn't make any corrections because you didn't need any."

Candy looked shocked.

Abby laughed. "Thank you, Candy. I needed to laugh. Although I realize it was totally unintentional."

"You're welcome."

"You really are getting the hang of this. Keep up the good work."

"Thanks, Abby." She smiled. "I am sorry, though."

"What do you have to be sorry about?"

"First I'm sorry for everything that you're going through right now. You don't deserve it. You're a good person."

"Thanks. What's the second thing?"

"I'm sorry that I've ruined the 'Candy's late pool' today. I know Kelly had her eye on the Manolo Blahnik Napoleona boots."

"I'm sure she'll live." Abby smiled.

"Yes. I'll let her borrow mine sometime." Candy kicked up her leg to show off the boot.

"That's very gracious of you. I'm sure she'll take you up on it."

After Candy walked out of her office, Abby stared at her phone, remembering she had promised to call

Sam back. She sighed. "Maybe later." She looked at the clock. "I need to call Justin before his first class." She fed in the number.

"Hi, Mom," he answered cheerfully.

"Hi. How are you?" Abby was a little taken aback.

"I'm good. I'm getting ready to head to biology in a few minutes."

"Okay."

"Are you calling me about you and Sam?"

"Yes. It's in the papers and on the news now, and this is not the kind of thing you expect from me. So I wanted to see if you were okay."

"I'm fine, Mom. It's not like I didn't know there was something going on with you and Sam. I told you that when you were here."

"I didn't exactly tell you the extent of things between us."

"You didn't have to, Mom. No disrespect to Connecticut but he came all the way to Wallingford. This isn't exactly a resort town."

Abby chuckled in spite of herself. "No. Wallingford isn't a hot spot." She paused. "So all of this stuff in the paper and on the news doesn't bother you?"

"No. My friends got a kick out of the papers dubbing you a voluptuous vixen. But I am a little creeped out when they say you're hot."

"What?"

"You are my mother after all. Who wants to hear that?"

"I see your point." She laughed. "I'm relieved that you're not freaked out about this."

"It's okay, Mom. You can date. I'm fine with it."

"I wish the rest of the world shared your sentiment."

"They will. Don't worry, I'm pretty sure that Paris or one of the Kardashians will do something outrageous and they'll leave you and Sam alone." Justin laughed. "Listen, Mom I'm outside my classroom."

"Okay, honey. I'll talk to you later. Love you."

"You, too, Mom."

Abby hung up the phone. *I never thought that I'd wish for the day I could read about one of the Kardashians, but from your lips, Justin, to God's ears.*

Abby looked up. *I don't know what I did to get such a great kid, God. But thank you. Nancy Bloom or not, I'm going to fight to keep him.*

❧

Sam knocked on his parents' door with a bag full of pastries and a tray of coffee.

"Good morning, son," his mother said cheerfully as she opened the door.

"Good morning, Momma." He kissed her on the cheek. "I brought some goodies for you and Dad." He said as he put them down on the table. "Where is Dad?" He looked around.

397

"He had to run out." His mother opened the bag. "Do you have any bear claws in here?"

"Yes. Where did Dad have to run to?"

"He just had an errand to run. Did you get cream for my coffee? You know how I hate that low fat stuff. It tastes like you're adding flavored water."

"Yes. I know you like your coffee light with cream and two sugars."

"Thank you." She picked up the cup and sipped. "This is good."

"Okay, Momma. I know when you're avoiding something, and you're doing it right now."

"I don't know what you're talking about. Do you want the blueberry pastry or the cheese danish?"

"Momma," he said.

Her cell phone rang. "Hold that thought, Sam. I need to get this." She picked up. "Hello? Yes? It's on now? Okay. I'll turn it on now." She hung up and turned on the television. "What channel is ESPN here?"

"They have FIOS here, so its channel 570."

"Thank you." She turned the channel.

"Good morning. We have a special report brought to us by ESPN analyst Bo Clemson."

"Good morning. I'm here with NFL Hall of Famer Norman Green and co-chair of the Association of Retired Football Players Association. Thanks for being here Mr. Green."

"Thank you for having me."

"Mr. Green, would you like to tell our audience why you're here?"

"Yes. I'm here to set the record straight about Sam Best."

❧

Frankie rushed into Abby's office. "Abby?"

"Frankie. You scared me to death. What's the matter?"

"Turn on ESPN right now."

"Okay." She got her remote and turned the television on.

"For the last several years, Sam has been making donations to help retired and disabled players supplement their retirement benefits and take care of their medical costs. It's because of his generosity that a number of players have been able to receive the surgeries and rehabilitative services they need to live their lives with dignity. As you know, I am in a wheelchair now, and the cost of my medical care could have easily bankrupted my family and caused us to lose our home. However Sam's donations have made it possible to cover my medical bills so my family and I can stay in our home. Sam has done this anonymously because he didn't feel the need to trumpet his good deeds, but, now that his reputation is at risk, I felt that I needed to come forward

to let people know the truth about this wonderful young man."

❧

"Momma, did you know about this?"

"Yes. Your father got the ball rolling yesterday."

"I knew you were acting strange last night. I should have known. You know I didn't want this."

"We know, but we couldn't stand by idly and let Big Bill besmirch you."

Sam flopped down on the bed.

"Sometimes a parents got to do what they've got to do." She said as she bit into her bear claw.

❧

"I guess that knocks Maria's harem theory out of the water." Frankie said.

"I can't believe that Sam had anything to do with this interview. He was determined to keep his philanthropy a secret."

"Well, someone let the cat out of the bag, and it's a good thing they did."

"Yes. Now everyone knows that he's the real deal. Sam's truly a great guy."

"For an athlete," Frankie added, "as our mother would say." He winked.

❧

Back in his parents' suite the door opened.

"Don't shoot. We're not armed." Reggie said jokingly with his hands up.

"Don't tempt me. I know how to use a gun."

"That's the truth. I should know since I'm the one who taught him." Sam's father said as he entered the room.

"Dad…" Sam began.

"I know you're upset, son. But I had to do something before the speculation turned you into the second coming of Dennis Shanahan."

"I guess I should be grateful for that."

"You should be." Bo said as he walked in.

"What took you so long to come in here?" Sam asked.

"I wanted to make sure you were unarmed."

"I would have thought ESPN would have named you head of the network by now."

"Yes. They offered me a kingship, but I turned it down. I kind of like life behind the big desk." He smiled.

Reggie went over to the pastry bag. "Ooh do you have a blueberry danish?"

"Leave it to Reggie to focus on what's really important, pastry," Sam joked. "Yes, there are a couple of them in there."

"Nice," he said as he took one out.

"Have you heard from Abby?" his father asked.

"No. She was supposed to call me last night, but I guess she was too upset."

"Rightly so," his mother added.

Sam's cell phone rang. "Hello?"

"Hello, Sam. It's Blake."

"Hello, Blake. And before you ask I haven't been served."

"And you're not going to be served. I just heard through the grapevine that Maria fired Toni."

"What?"

"I know. I'm surprised, too. I guess the lawsuit isn't moving forward after all."

"That is good news."

"By the way, I saw the report on ESPN, so I'd say this was more good news. I've got to run. Give my best to Reggie. Bye."

"Thanks, Blake. Bye."

"What was that about?" Reggie asked.

"Maria fired Toni Redstone. There isn't going to be a lawsuit."

"That is good news." His father smiled.

"I wonder what changed her mind."

"Son, you know the old saying about gift horses," his mother said.

"You're right, Momma."

"You know what will really make this a celebration?" Bo asked.

"What?"

"If there's another bear claw in that bag," he grinned.

"Here you go." Reggie handed him the bag.

Sam's cell phone rang again. "Hello?"

"Hello, Sam? It's Maria."

Genuinely surprised, Sam got up and walked into the other room. "Hello, Maria."

"I know I'm the last phone call you expected to get."

"You'd be right about that."

"I fired Toni. I'm not pursuing a lawsuit."

"That's good news. Thank you."

"Can we meet to talk?"

"I don't have a problem with that, but at the moment I'm practically a prisoner in this hotel."

"I can come there. We can talk in the lobby or the restaurant."

"We can talk in the hotel's living room. It's public but it's quiet."

"Great. I'll be there in about an hour."

"Okay." He hung up.

"Who was that?" his mother asked.

"Maria."

"What did she want?"

"She wanted to tell me that she fired Toni. Now she wants to talk."

"Is she coming here? Or are you going there?"

"She's coming here. We're going to talk in the hotel's living room. It's a public space."

"Do you think that's wise?"

"I think we'll be fine. Now that the lawyers are gone, maybe we can talk like civilized people."

"I hope so too, son."

Chapter 27

Though she was still in her office, Abby wasn't concentrating on author's book tours or spring releases; she was researching family law attorneys. The lawyer she used for her divorce had long since retired and moved away, so she was at square one until her brother Wes could get out of court long enough to give her some direction.

Her cell phone rang. She checked the caller ID. "Hey, Shana."

"Hi. Did you hear the news?"

Abby's heart sunk. "What are they saying about us now?"

"No. I'm not talking about that. I just read on the news feed that Maria fired Toni Redstone."

"What?"

"Yes."

"Thank God. At least Sam's headache is over."

"Your headache will be over soon, too. You mark my words."

"You might be getting ahead of yourself. If I don't find a lawyer soon, I can be sure that my headache will grow."

"You've got to think positive."

"I plan on being positively prepared."

"Okay. I've got to run. I have another show starting in a few minutes."

"Okay. Knock 'em dead."

"You know we will."

Abby hung up and went back to her computer. "Yes, Leo?"

"There's someone here to see you."

"Who is it?"

Dazz stepped into the doorway. "Hello, Abby."

"What are you doing here, Dazz? Is J.J. with you?"

"No. I came alone. Can we talk?"

"Sure. It's fine, Leo."

"Okay."

Dazz walked in.

"Would you close the door behind you, Leo?"

"Sure thing." He closed the door.

"Have a seat, Dazz."

"Thanks." He sat down.

"So what brings you here? Are you here to serve me or something?"

"No. I'm here to tell you that there's not going to be a custody suit."

"What?"

"I know that I've never been your favorite person, and a lot of that has been my fault. I ran interference when he was cheating on you, and Beebe for that matter. I set up his appearances and I've been his yes man for years."

"You won't get any argument from me about that."

"Then a couple of days ago this Bill Carrangelo calls and sets up a meeting with J.J., but he didn't ask me to come with him. The next thing I know he's hired a lawyer and he's going for custody. The whole thing was out of left field to me."

"That makes two of us."

"I told J.J. that this Bill was using him to get back at Sam. I said as far as I'm concerned anyone who would use a mother's love for her child as a pawn in some kind of twisted revenge plot was a sick son of bitch. He wouldn't listen to me. So I quit."

"You what?" she said astonished.

"I quit." He leaned back in the chair. "Over the years I've made a lot of compromises for J.J. that I'm not proud of at all, but he's gone too far this time. I had to draw the line."

"I'm stunned."

"Believe it or not, I have a mother, too." He smiled.

Abby laughed. "And here I thought the stork brought you."

Dazz chuckled, but then his face turned serious. "You know, Abby, you were a good wife and you're a great mother. Justin is a lucky kid."

Abby could barely believe it when her eyes welled up. "Thank you for saying that, Dazz. The funny thing is that no matter how many years have gone by, I always had that nagging little feeling that there was something wrong with me that I couldn't make that marriage work."

"Abby, you had the patience of Mother Theresa. There was nothing wrong with you. I love J.J. like a brother, but he can be a real ass."

They laughed.

"What are you going to do?"

"I'm going to head back home and visit my mom in Detroit for a little while. Then I'll come back here and pursue a few job opportunities I've got lined up. I'll be okay."

"Now I feel bad that I spent so much time disliking you."

"Considering what my part was in J.J.'s follies, who could blame you? But that's water under the bridge now. Can we start fresh?"

"Yes. I'd like that."

"I want you to know that you can count on me if you need me for depositions, court or whatever."

"Thank you, Dazz. I really appreciate that."

"You're welcome." He looked at his watch. "I'd better get going if I'm going to make my flight." He stood up.

"You're leaving today?"

"Yes. Sometimes a boy just needs to see his mom."

Abby got up from behind her desk and walked to the door.

"You have a safe flight." She said as she opened the door.

"Thanks." Dazz went to shake her hand.

"I think we're past that now." Abby said as she and Dazz hugged. "Have a good trip."

"I will." He waved as he walked away.

Her brother Frankie stopped and watched Dazz leave and then went over to Abby. "Are my eyes playing tricks on me? Or was that you hugging Dazz?"

"Your eyes aren't playing tricks on you." She sighed. "Come on in and I'll fill you in on the latest."

"This I've got to hear."

A couple of hours later, with the office empty and Frankie off at Macy's, Abby picked up the phone.

"Hello?"

"Hello, Beebe. It's Abby."

"Abby?"

"I know you're surprised to hear from me."

"Yes. After our last conversation, I thought I'd be the last person you'd call voluntarily."

"If there's anything I've learned in the last few days, it's that things can change on a dime."

"You can say that again."

"I caught you on *Headline News* last night."

"You did? I didn't think anyone would even see it since I didn't give them what they wanted."

"That's why I'm calling. You could have said so much more if you wanted to. You could have blown me to bits."

"I didn't feel the need to do that. I meant what I said. You were good to me even when I know it must have hurt."

"I appreciate the acknowledgement. So thank you."

"You're welcome."

"Have a good night, Beebe."

"You, too." She hung up.

"Did you just say 'Beebe'?" Shana asked. "I know I've been under water with Fashion Week, but I thought I was still on the planet."

"Yes that was Beebe. You didn't just step into another time and space continuum."

"If you're speaking to her without a gun to your temple I want to hear this." Shana chuckled as she sat down.

"Let's just say we reached an understanding." Abby got up and went over to the bar in her office. "Can I interest you in a glass of cabernet sauvignon instead?"

"That sounds good to me." Shana kicked her shoes off.

She poured two glasses and handed one to Shana before she sat across from her. "Tell me if there's been any fallout from that photo fiasco for Cedi."

"It's been just the opposite. He has more requests for look-books than he has books to give. Major celebrity stylists are requesting looks for the red carpet and three fashion magazines have called about doing a designer profile piece on him. I'd say he's ahead of the game."

"That's a relief."

"The saying all publicity is good publicity held true."

Abby exhaled and sipped her wine. "At least it's working for someone."

"I've got more news for you."

"You do?" she said, interest piqued.

"I finally talked with Raymond about where our relationship is heading."

"Oh." Abby leaned forward.

"He's opening an office here in the city and his office manager is going to run the D.C. office."

"That's great news."

"I know. By April, he'll be here full time."

"Does that mean we'll be hearing wedding bells in the near future?"

"I think so." Shana smiled warmly. "Just do me a favor…"

"Don't worry. I'll point him in the direction of Tiffany."

"I knew you'd have a sister's back." Shana laughed. "Can you believe it? I'm getting engaged."

"Not only do I believe it, I couldn't be happier for you." Abby raised her glass. "Here's to your happiness, Shana. You deserve it."

Shana raised her glass. "Thanks. You deserve to be happy, too."

"With everything I have going on at the moment, I hope you're right."

"This too shall pass, my friend."

"I'll drink to that."

Sam waited in the W Hotel's plush living room area with its warm browns, comfortable chairs and sofas. Maria was so bundled up she was barely recognizable, but Sam spotted her Rachael Zoe sunglasses. He waved her over.

"How did you know it was me?" she asked as she sat across from him.

"It was the sunglasses."

"Oh, yeah." She placed them on the table.

"So, why are we here?" Sam asked.

"I came here to apologize. I let my family get me worked up and things got blown out of proportion."

"Wow, I've never heard you say anything negative about your family."

"I know my family loves me and they didn't want to see me hurt, but things turned into an all-out war with lawyers, the media and back-room deals. It was too much."

Sam nodded. "Why did you fire Toni? If you don't mind me asking," he added.

"Toni wanted me to say things that weren't exactly lies but it wasn't the truth, either. You never kept me from working. She wanted me to say that you were the reason I didn't take the docent position at MOMA when I was the one who didn't want to take the job because it interfered with wedding planning. In fact you were the only one that tried to encourage me to use my art history degree. I wasn't going to lie. So I fired her."

"I'm glad you stuck to your guns."

"Then there were the pictures of you and Abby. At first I was upset, but then I really took the time to look at them. You looked so happy, and I couldn't remember the last time we looked that happy together. Then it hit me, you were right, we were staying together because it was a part of the next step."

"I hope you know that I wasn't trying to make any less of the time we spent together. I still love you. You're always going to be a part of me."

"I know that now." She looked away.

"What's wrong?"

"There's something else. It's something my father did."

"Are you talking about Nancy Bloom?"

"So you know?"

"Yes."

"When I found out that not only had my father contacted Abby's ex-husband, he went so far as to retain Nancy Bloom to help him get custody of their son. I was sickened." She took a breath. "I told him to take Nancy off retainer or I would never speak to him again."

"You did?" Sam was shocked.

"Yes. I always knew my father played to win and he didn't always play by the rules, but this went too far. I refused to be a party to something like that."

"I'm impressed. I know it took a lot of guts to stand up to your father."

"Thanks. I had to do the right thing. Speaking of the right thing," she reached into her purse and took a ring box out. "This is yours." She put it on the table.

"Are you sure you want to give it back? I think that under the rules since I broke the engagement, you can keep the ring."

"I know." She pushed the box toward him. "I want you to have it."

Sam took the box and put it in his pocket. "Okay."

Maria looked around. "I know this is a nice hotel and all, but I'm sure you're ready to get back to your apartment." She put the keys on the table. "I've had all my stuff packed and it's getting shipped down to my sister's in Houston. I'm going to stay with her for a while until I find a place of my own in the city."

"You're not going to stay with your parents?"

"No."

"What are you going to do?"

"I was thinking about going back to the University of Texas to get my master's in interior design next year."

"That's great news."

"I'm looking forward to it. In the meantime, I'm going to hang out in Texas, meet people and maybe travel to Europe before classes begin next spring."

"I'm happy for you."

"Thanks. Whether you know it or not, I really want you to be happy. If Abby makes you happy, I wish you the best." She got up. "I have a plane to catch."

"You're traveling commercially?"

"Yes. My parents wanted me to fly with them on the jet but I took a pass. I'm ready for life on my own."

Sam rose and hugged her. "I'd say that you're well on your way."

"Thanks, Sam." She hesitated for a moment. "You take care."

"I will. You do the same."

Maria put her sunglasses on and quickly made her way downstairs and out of sight. A few minutes later, Sam's father walked over.

"Are you okay, son?"

"I'm fine, Dad." He showed him the ring and the keys. "It's over. Maria's heading back to Houston."

"I know you've moved on, but it's never easy when a love affair ends."

"No but I'm okay with it because I know that Maria's going to be okay."

"And so are you." He put his arm on his shoulder.

"Now I've got to let another very important person know that we're going to be fine, too."

Chapter 28

The day over, Abby sat in her living room with a glass of wine. Her phone rang. She checked the caller ID.

"Hello J.J. I'm sure you're attorney has warned you against talking to the other side without counsel present."

"I don't have an attorney."

"Pardon me?"

"I don't have an attorney anymore."

"You don't?"

"I got rid of her. I'm not going for full custody anymore."

"Good."

"Is that all you're going to say? I thought you would have been happier."

"I am happy, but I'm not stupid. Nancy Bloom issued a statement earlier saying that any reports of her representing you in a custody case were erroneous. So you can quit trying to sound like you did me a favor."

"I'm sorry. I was angry."

"I don't accept your apology."

"What?"

"I don't accept your apology right now. Maybe I'll feel differently later, but I'm angry that you would use Justin as a weapon against me when I never did that to you."

"I know. I'm ashamed of myself for going that far," he admitted quietly.

"Sam was never going to marginalize you in Justin's life. You've done a pretty damn good job of that all by yourself."

"Yes, but being a father isn't like playing basketball."

"You didn't come out of the womb with a basketball in your hand. You had to learn the game. You had to practice constantly until you got better. It's the same thing when it comes to being a parent. We didn't get a manual when we left the hospital. We had to figure it out, and that's what parenting is about. It's a constant state of learning."

"That's easy for you to say, you're a natural."

"Don't hand me that self-pity bag. I'm not buying it. You need to get it together."

"That's what Dazz said before he left. You know he quit."

"Yes. I think it's the best thing he could have done for himself and you."

"You never were one to mince words."

"What's the point?"

"Maybe I should head up to Choate on Saturday and spend the day with Justin."

"I bet he'd like that. What about your fiancée? What is she going to do?"

"That's been put on hold for a while. I just finished negotiating a settlement with Beebe, and she's not that happy with me at the moment."

"You reached an agreement with Beebe?"

"Yes. We decided to meet in the middle. I think she's happy with it."

"Good. Justin will be happy to know that both of his parents won't be headline news for a while."

"He couldn't be any more relieved than we are." He laughed.

"I'll drink to that."

"All right, I just wanted you to know that the legal stuff is over."

"Thanks."

"By the way, Abby I really do wish you the best. God knows you deserve to be happy."

"Thanks, J.J. Bye."

Abby walked over to the window and stared out at the city.

"Hello, Sam."

"How did you know I was here? I didn't use the elevator."

"Usually I can tell from footsteps, but this time I saw your reflection in the window."

He rushed over and lifted her off her feet. "Sam!"

"I'm just so happy to see you. " He put her down and the two kissed passionately.

"I've missed you, too. I've got so much to tell you," Abby said happily.

"I do, too. But ladies first."

"J.J. isn't going for full custody."

"Great. I know that's a relief."

"He's even going to make more of an effort to spend time with Justin."

"Now that is good news."

"So what's your news?"

"Maria and I talked. She's moved out of the apartment, and she gave back the engagement ring. She's going back to Texas and starting her life over."

"That's great."

"I have to say that I'm happy for her. She's striking out on her own without her parents, and I think she's going to make it."

"Good. Now maybe we can go back to living under the radar. Well at least *I* can go back. You are Sam Best."

"Well hold on a minute, little lady, you're the woman in my life, so wherever you are I'm going to be there, too." He kissed her.

"I almost forgot, my brother Frankie is here. He went out to buy presents for my nieces, but I'd love if you hang around to meet him."

"I'm looking forward to it. And maybe tomorrow we can have dinner with my parents. They're in town."

"I figured they were in town. How else did that ESPN exclusive happen?"

"True." He looked lovingly into Abby's eyes. "I love you."

"I love you, too."

"Well you know, your life in the spotlight isn't exactly over. There are the ESPY awards in the summer, and I want to make all the other athletes jealous when I escort my voluptuous vixen down the red carpet."

"You like saying voluptuous vixen, don't you?"

"Oh, yes. There is something very satisfying about it."

"There is?"

"Definitely," he grinned. Sam squeezed Abby tightly as he opened the window.

"What are you doing? It's not spring time. It's cold."

"I can brave a little cold." He said as he leaned closer to the window. "Hey New York I'm Sam Best and I take this woman, Abigail Carey to have and to hold from this day forward. So look out world, here we come."

Abby laughed. "Do you know where we're going right now?"

"The bedroom." Sam raised his eyebrows.

She walked over to the table and picked up her Cartier pen. "We have a deadline to meet." She waved the pen in the air.

"You're kidding me, right?"

"This is the reason we met in the first place. I think it's time we get to work. It's time the world met the Sam Best I know."

About the Author:

A native New Yorker by way of Amityville, Long Island, *Chamein Canton* is a freelance writer, author, and owner of a small literary agency in New York. She holds a degree in Business Management and continues to live on Long Island with her twin sons.

2011 Mass Market Titles

January

From This Moment
Sean Young
ISBN-13: 978-1-58571-383-7
ISBN-10: 1-58571-383-X
$6.99

Nihon Nights
Trisha/Monica Haddad
ISBN-13: 978-1-58571-382-0
ISBN-10: 1-58571-382-1
$6.99

February

The Davis Years
Nicole Green
ISBN-13: 978-1-58571-390-5
ISBN-10: 1-58571-390-2
$6.99

Allegro
Adora Bennett
ISBN-13: 978-158571-391-2
ISBN-10: 1-58571-391-0
$6.99

March

Lies in Disguise
Bernice Layton
ISBN-13: 978-1-58571-392-9
ISBN-10: 1-58571-392-9
$6.99

Steady
Ruthie Robinson
ISBN-13: 978-1-58571-393-6
ISBN-10: 1-58571-393-7
$6.99

April

The Right Maneuver
LaShell Stratton-Childers
ISBN-13: 978-1-58571-394-3
ISBN-10: 1-58571-394-5
$6.99

Riding the Corporate Ladder
Keith Walker
ISBN-13: 978-1-58571-395-0
ISBN-10: 1-58571-395-3
$6.99

May

Separate Dreams
Joan Early
ISBN-13: 978-1-58571-434-6
ISBN-10: 1-58571-434-8
$6.99

I Take This Woman
Chamein Canton
ISBN-13: 978-1-58571-435-3
ISBN-10: 1-58571-435-6
$6.99

June

Inside Out
Grayson Cole
ISBN-13: 978-1-58571-437-7
ISBN-10: 1-58571-437-2
$6.99

2011 Mass Market Titles (continued)
July

The Other Side of the
  Mountain
Janice Angelique
ISBN-13: 978-1-58571-442-1
ISBN-10: 1-58571-442-9
$6.99

Holding Her Breath
Nicole Green
ISBN-13: 978-1-58571-439-1
ISBN-10: 1-58571-439-9
$6.99

August

The Sea of Aaron
Kymberly Hunt
ISBN-13: 978-1-58571-440-7
ISBN-10: 1-58571-440-2
$6.99

The Finley Sisters' Oath of
  Romance
Keith Thomas Walker
ISBN-13: 978-1-58571-441-4
ISBN-10: 1-58571-441-0
$6.99

September

Except on Sunday
Regena Bryant
ISBN-13: 978-1-58571-443-8
ISBN-10: 1-58571-443-7
$6.99

Light's Out
Ruthie Robinson
ISBN-13: 978-1-58571-445-2
ISBN-10: 1-58571-445-3
$6.99

October

The Heart Knows
Renee Wynn
ISBN-13: 978-1-58571-444-5
ISBN-10: 1-58571-444-5
$6.99

Best Friends; Better Lovers
Celya Bowers
ISBN-13: 978-1-58571-455-1
ISBN-10: 1-58571-455-0
$6.99

November

Caress
Grayson Cole
ISBN-13: 978-1-58571-454-4
ISBN-10: 1-58571-454-2
$6.99

A Love Built to Last
L. S. Childers
ISBN-13: 978-1-58571-448-3
ISBN-10: 1-58571-448-8
$6.99

December

Fractured
Wendy Byrne
ISBN-13: 978-1-58571-449-0
ISBN-10: 1-58571-449-6
$6.99

Everything in Between
Crystal Hubbard
ISBN-13: 978-1-58571-396-7
ISBN-10: 1-58571-396-1
$6.99

Other Genesis Press, Inc. Titles

Other Genesis Press, Inc. Titles (continued)

Other Genesis Press, Inc. Titles (continued)

Do Over	Celya Bowers	$9.95
Dream Keeper	Gail McFarland	$6.99
Dream Runner	Gail McFarland	$6.99
Dreamtective	Liz Swados	$5.95
Ebony Angel	Deatri King-Bey	$9.95
Ebony Butterfly II	Delilah Dawson	$14.95
Echoes of Yesterday	Beverly Clark	$9.95
Eden's Garden	Elizabeth Rose	$8.95
Eve's Prescription	Edwina Martin Arnold	$8.95
Everlastin' Love	Gay G. Gunn	$8.95
Everlasting Moments	Dorothy Elizabeth Love	$8.95
Everything and More	Sinclair Lebeau	$8.95
Everything but Love	Natalie Dunbar	$8.95
Falling	Natalie Dunbar	$9.95
Fate	Pamela Leigh Starr	$8.95
Finding Isabella	A.J. Garrotto	$8.95
Fireflies	Joan Early	$6.99
Fixin' Tyrone	Keith Walker	$6.99
Forbidden Quest	Dar Tomlinson	$10.95
Forever Love	Wanda Y. Thomas	$8.95
Friends in Need	Joan Early	$6.99
From the Ashes	Kathleen Suzanne	$8.95
	Jeanne Sumerix	
Frost on My Window	Angela Weaver	$6.99
Gentle Yearning	Rochelle Alers	$10.95
Glory of Love	Sinclair LeBeau	$10.95
Go Gentle Into That Good Night	Malcom Boyd	$12.95
Goldengroove	Mary Beth Craft	$16.95
Groove, Bang, and Jive	Steve Cannon	$8.99
Hand in Glove	Andrea Jackson	$9.95
Hard to Love	Kimberley White	$9.95
Hart & Soul	Angie Daniels	$8.95
Heart of the Phoenix	A.C. Arthur	$9.95
Heartbeat	Stephanie Bedwell-Grime	$8.95
Hearts Remember	M. Loui Quezada	$8.95
Hidden Memories	Robin Allen	$10.95
Higher Ground	Leah Latimer	$19.95
Hitler, the War, and the Pope	Ronald Rychiak	$26.95
How to Kill Your Husband	Keith Walker	$6.99

Other Genesis Press, Inc. Titles (continued)

Other Genesis Press, Inc. Titles (continued)

Other Genesis Press, Inc. Titles (continued)

Path of Thorns	Annetta P. Lee	$9.95
Peace Be Still	Colette Haywood	$12.95
Picture Perfect	Reon Carter	$8.95
Playing for Keeps	Stephanie Salinas	$8.95
Pride & Joi	Gay G. Gunn	$8.95
Promises Made	Bernice Layton	$6.99
Promises of Forever	Celya Bowers	$6.99
Promises to Keep	Alicia Wiggins	$8.95
Quiet Storm	Donna Hill	$10.95
Reckless Surrender	Rochelle Alers	$6.95
Red Polka Dot in a World Full of Plaid	Varian Johnson	$12.95
Red Sky	Renee Alexis	$6.99
Reluctant Captive	Joyce Jackson	$8.95
Rendezvous With Fate	Jeanne Sumerix	$8.95
Revelations	Cheris F. Hodges	$8.95
Reye's Gold	Ruthie Robinson	$6.99
Rivers of the Soul	Leslie Esdaile	$8.95
Rocky Mountain Romance	Kathleen Suzanne	$8.95
Rooms of the Heart	Donna Hill	$8.95
Rough on Rats and Tough on Cats	Chris Parker	$12.95
Save Me	Africa Fine	$6.99
Secret Library Vol. 1	Nina Sheridan	$18.95
Secret Library Vol. 2	Cassandra Colt	$8.95
Secret Thunder	Annetta P. Lee	$9.95
Shades of Brown	Denise Becker	$8.95
Shades of Desire	Monica White	$8.95
Shadows in the Moonlight	Jeanne Sumerix	$8.95
Show Me the Sun	Miriam Shumba	$6.99
Sin	Crystal Rhodes	$8.95
Singing a Song...	Crystal Rhodes	$6.99
Six O'Clock	Katrina Spencer	$6.99
Small Sensations	Crystal V. Rhodes	$6.99
Small Whispers	Annetta P. Lee	$6.99
So Amazing	Sinclair LeBeau	$8.95
Somebody's Someone	Sinclair LeBeau	$8.95
Someone to Love	Alicia Wiggins	$8.95
Song in the Park	Martin Brant	$15.95
Soul Eyes	Wayne L. Wilson	$12.95

Other Genesis Press, Inc. Titles (continued)

Other Genesis Press, Inc. Titles (continued)

433

Order Form

Mail to: Genesis Press, Inc.
P.O. Box 101
Columbus, MS 39703

Name _____
Address _____
City/State _____ Zip _____
Telephone _____

Ship to (if different from above)
Name _____
Address _____
City/State _____ Zip _____
Telephone _____

Credit Card Information
Credit Card # _____ ☐ Visa   ☐ Mastercard
Expiration Date (mm/yy) _____ ☐ AmEx   ☐ Discover

Qty.	Author	Title	Price	Total

Use this order	Total for books	_____
form, or call	Shipping and handling: $5 first two books, $1 each additional book	_____
1-888-INDIGO-1	Total S & H	_____
	Total amount enclosed	_____

Mississippi residents add 7% sales tax